# Patricia Rice

# Notorious Atherton

## *The Rebellious Sons*

# Notorious Atherton

Patricia Rice

Copyright © 2013 Patricia Rice
First Publication:
Book View Cafe, July 2013

ISBN 978-1-49353-093-9

Cover design by Hot Damn Designs

ALSO IN THE REBELLIOUS SONS:
*Wicked Wyckerly*
*Devilish Montague*

# Prologue

*London, 1799*

TUCKING A KNIFE into his battered boot, Devil Nick leaned against the rail of his ship and studied the new warehouses of the West India Docks emerging through the soot-laden fog. After five long years of fighting his way back here, he approached London with more gut-wrenching trepidation than a merchantman sailing into pirate-infested Havana.

London. *Home.* Or was it?

He could sell his purloined barrels of sugar and coffee here, sail around to the export dock, and upload a legitimate cargo within day. He'd provided for his loyal crew as promised. The next twenty-four hours determined his fate.

"You goin' back to bein' a genmun, Dev?" his first mate asked in curiosity.

"Excellent question, Rog," Nick replied. "Guess that remains to be seen." He tucked his tarnished pistol into his trouser band where he'd carried it all these years. It had saved his life more than once.

After wiping his tattered shirt sleeve over his filthy beard to remove remnants of his breakfast, he slung his sack over his shoulder and swung down the ropes to the small rowboat waiting to take him ashore.

He made his first mistake in civilization by seeking a reputable hostelry. The innkeeper sneered at the dried bloodstain on his linen. Aware that he stank and that his hair hung on his shoulders in a dark mat, Nick flung a gold coin on the counter.

The proprietor tested its worth with his teeth, then held out a hand for the pistol and cutlass. "We're respectable. We don't like no trouble here."

Nick gritted his teeth, silently surrendered his visible weaponry, and scribbled a shortened version of his real name across the ledger.

A copper coin sent a boy scurrying into the busy streets with a note.

Half an hour later, Nick was up to his filthy neck in water, with a barber working on his straggling hair, when someone knocked at his door. Not expecting a reply so soon, he verified that he could reach his knife before answering. "Enter," he shouted.

Charles, Viscount Dabney slipped in warily, bearing a leather portmanteau.

In the last five years, Dabney had filled out a bit around the middle, but he remained the dandified young lord Nick remembered. The viscount was ten years Nick's elder. They'd never been close, but they'd never been at odds either. Yet. Nick's muscles tensed as he studied his brother's expression.

"The countess will expire of relief at your return," Dabney said in greeting. Crinkling up his nose in distaste, he studied the plain furnishings of the most palatial environs Nick had inhabited lately.

"It's our father who concerns me," Nick admitted now that Dabney hadn't tried to drown him. "Am I disowned?"

Dabney looked surprised. "For quitting the Navy? Our stepmother is the one far more likely to kill you for not sending better word of your whereabouts."

Which meant the earl hadn't received word of Nick's infamy—or hadn't told his family. Either way, he was on shaky ground should the story emerge.

With dry mouth, trying not to reveal his hopes or fears, he asked, "How is he? I'd got word that he was ill."

Dabney beat his beribboned walking stick against his Hoby boots. "The old man's not well, there's no denying. That doesn't stop him from trying to produce another heir in case you don't come home."

Nick snorted. "How many sisters do we have now?"

"Five. Georgiana was born after you left, and they lost two more." Dabney continued hitting his stick on his boots.

Nick recognized the nervous tic and asked sympathetically. "Is he still trying to talk you into marriage?"

Dabney exhaled noisily. "If you come home, he might accept that I'll not marry." He glanced at the barber and spoke more circumspectly. "I've found someone. I want to stay in Sussex. If you're home, you can be the proper son he wants."

And there it was. Nick sank deeper into the bathwater and washed off the layer of shorn hair on his neck. Home, everything he'd dreamed of for five long miserable years—if he played the role properly, if he was very, very circumspect, he could have his family back.

All he had to do was pretend he was who he wasn't anymore, and not a soul would connect the younger son of the Earl of Atherton with anything so sordid as mutiny and piracy. A life of comfort awaited—except for that marriage bit. He couldn't fool a wife for long.

"I'm scarcely one and twenty," Nick argued, setting his terms. "He can't expect me to marry until I'm past thirty."

Dabney brightened. "I'll tell him that's a condition of your returning. It might take his sights off me."

Surely ten years would give him time to unlearn bad habits and not terrify delicate misses into leaping off tall cliffs. It hadn't taken him an hour to appreciate the luxury of hot water.

"You brought clothes?" Nick asked.

Dabney opened the valise. "They might not fit, but my...friend...is close to your height. I'll take you to my tailor this afternoon."

An hour later, newly shaved, his golden locks barbered into a perfect Brutus, lace discreetly edging the wrists of his blue superfine, his knee boots polished into mirrors, the Honorable Nicholas Montcroft Atherton strolled downstairs into the lobby of the shabby waterfront inn. He nodded regally at his landlord, inhaled, and strode into the morning fog—without the weapons the innkeeper was holding for a dirty sailor.

# Chapter One

*London, April 1809*

"BELLISSIMA, YOUR BEAUTY is like the morning dawn, and I am but a cloud on your horizon. You will thank me for this one day." In the perfumed boudoir of his latest conquest, Nicholas Atherton checked the mirror, straightened his sadly wilted neckcloth, then produced a jeweler's box from his inner pocket as he turned to face the bedchamber's other occupant.

The nearly naked viscountess sitting upon the rumpled sheets gifted him with a look of scorn and tugged on a filmy robe, concealing her fair breasts in shadow. "Damn your feeble hide, Nicholas! I merely suggested we travel together to Brighton. I did not ask for your hand in holy matrimony."

Amused, he set the trinket on her dressing table and tugged his tailored coat to remove a wrinkle. "Given that I'd have to murder your husband to agree to matrimony, that is a relief, *cucciola mia*. I am but a passing fancy, after all. You are just learning to use your wiles. Use them well, and I shall admire from a distance." From a *safe* distance.

With the instinct born of experience, Nick bowed just as she flung her slipper at his head. It bounced harmlessly off the door.

"You are a jaded rake, Atherton! One of these days, you'll wake up old and wrinkled, and we'll all laugh."

"I can only hope that your wish comes true," he said wryly, topping his golden hair with his hat and picking up his walking stick. "But I've never expected to live to a ripe old age. *Auf Wierdersehen, Leibling*. Smile when you see me next."

Nick sauntered out, leaving the lady cursing like a fishwife. A footman waiting outside passed him a hastily scribbled message that caused his smile to fade. His next appointment would have to wait.

He slipped the messenger a coin and took to the street at a more rapid pace than was his wont.

Only one set of females commanded Nick's true obedience. No matter where he was or what he was doing, he always answered their summons.

Loping up the familiar marble steps a few streets down from his assignation, he swallowed the lump of fear in his throat and whacked the knocker as the church bells rang half past midnight. The butler opened the polished mahogany door as if he'd been waiting, as he most probably had. Before Nick could remove his hat, he was inundated in a wave of perfumes, feminine cries, and silk.

Taking a deep breath, he donned a smiling mask and chucked his curly-brimmed beaver to the family retainer before the five women swarming down the stairs could envelop him in hugs and tears. Accustomed to the tactic, the stoic servant caught the hat and dusted it off while the females swept Nick up the staircase, chattering nonstop and all at once.

"It's late. I'm so sorry, it's late, but we didn't know what to do," his stepmother murmured.

Restraining his haste, knowing it would only panic the women more, Nick handed over a lace-edged handkerchief to mop up tears.

"It is so very good of you to come. You smell like a perfumery." Abigail, the married sister next closest to him in age, sniffed in disapproval.

Maintaining his practiced insouciance, Nick tugged her blond curl in retaliation.

"Nick, you've been seeing that dreadful Bedwell woman again. How could you? She has no taste!" Bertrice protested. Just turned eighteen, she used her own handkerchief to hide her tears—and her reproach to hide her fear.

Nick hugged the scold's shoulders and whispered a naughty reply in her ear.

"You will be there for my come-out, no matter what happens, won't you, Nick?" Georgiana asked with the plaintive cry of a sixteen-year old. "Please, please? I will be a terrible wallflower if you are not there."

His baby sister had no understanding of death and thought only of the moment, which was as it should be. Undone by her innocent plaint, Nick surrendered his sophisticated reticence to tousle her fair curls. "You could not be a wallflower if you tried, Georgie. You will be a brambly rose bush catching every man in the room. And yes, I will be there, I promise."

"A brambly rose bush! That's dreadful, Nicholas." Georgiana smacked his coat sleeve, and lifting her skirt, fell behind with the rest of the brood of females occupying Atherton House.

Always fearing this would be the final call, Nick strode ahead to catch up with his stepmother. Without the girls close by, she finally lifted her tear-filled blue eyes to meet his.

"I think this time it may be..." Lady Atherton whispered.

He hugged her shoulders and pressed a kiss of reassurance to the top of her head. "He's too mean to die."

The countess weakened a little against him, enough to let him know she was in need of his strength, if just for a fraction of a second. He'd learned his cloak of nonchalance from the best. Lady Atherton would never let her daughters see her fragility, but she could not hide it from the son she'd never had. She'd raised him as her own after his mother died bearing him. Nick understood the enormity of the debt he owed her and tried his best to deserve her acceptance.

"He was unconscious," she whispered. "Do not let him tell you he's fine. He's not. He's just stubborn."

"Family trait, I fear," Nick said, keeping up his cheerful appearance for her sake. "It's why our houses are haunted. We refuse to leave."

His stepmother slapped his coat sleeve in the same manner as Georgiana had. "Disrespectful brat," she murmured, but she was almost smiling again.

His flock of twittering half sisters caught up. He removed protective Abigail from his path with a kiss to her pale cheek, then swung open the double doors to the earl's suite.

Unlike most sick rooms, this one was well-aired. A manservant read aloud from documents on a desk. The medicine tray was not visible. Only one lamp burned beside the bed, illuminating a broad-shouldered man propped up on the pillows, wearing a burgundy brocade robe. With a scowl at Nick's entrance, the patient finished signing a paper, and his right hand slid feebly off the desk.

Nick struggled to hide his dismay, signaled to his stepmother with a nod, and let her shepherd his younger sisters out of sight. Abigail tried to hiss her disapproval at disturbing the patient, but Nick tapped her nose and shut the door.

He squeezed the door latch hard enough to disable it, venting his apprehension before approaching the bed. "I see you're not quite at death's door just yet," he said lightly, striving for the right tone to appease a man he'd loved and feared all his life.

His father had grown old with the onset of the wasting illness, but in these past months he had been reduced to half the size of the huge man who had towered over Nick's youth. The palsy was new.

"You have to quit coming every time they call," the Earl of Atherton said with disgust, gesturing imperiously for the water glass beside his bed. "You smell like a brothel."

"Perhaps for good reason," Nick agreed, smiling and handing him the glass. "I think your countess demands my presence just so she can find out what I am doing at this hour."

The earl snorted. "Marry, and she will happily turn that role over to your wife."

Nick shuddered and perched on the edge of a gilt chair. "Who would escort my sisters about town if I was occupied by another female? Not Dabney. He's too busy counting cows."

"You need not remind me that my heir is a molly who dares not show his face in town." The earl dismissed the old argument with the lift of a brown-spotted hand. "But he has written that he's recovering from mumps he caught in the village, which means we must give up any remaining hope that he'll produce a son."

Nick swallowed, hard. He understood his stepmother's panic now, as well as the reason the earl looked more ill than usual. They'd all hoped Dabney would do his duty despite his proclivities.

The earl continued as if he hadn't dropped a cannon shell. "Dabney's a demmed good steward. I needn't fear he'll fritter away the estate and leave the girls homeless as long as he's alive. But damn you, you go the opposite direction and fritter and tup your way through life instead of doing your duty."

Nick let the old man grumble while frantically scrambling for a satisfactory reply. Viscount Dabney now lived happily with a former school chum at the family estate in Cheshire. Nick had made it easier for him these last years by representing the family as the ladies' man that his brother was not.

Only this time, Nick knew Dabney was warning him that it had been over the promised ten years since his return. He'd hoped to be better prepared by now, but time had only worsened his predicament. Every year, the marriageable maidens grew younger, until they were now the age of his *sisters*.

"If I married, who would come running at midnight when you have a fever?" Nick teased rather than argue at this hour.

"No one need come running," the earl muttered. "I'll die when I'm ready to die, and no one can stop me. Now go tell my wife to quit fretting and your sisters to get to bed, where they belong. Their fluttering only aggravates me."

"They keep us both ticking, and you know it." Nick would gladly die for his father, and nearly had in his youthful escapade to please the old man, but neither of them was much at communicating sentiment. "As long as I'm here, is there anything I can do for you?"

"You might ask your stepmother that. She is fretting over me for a reason. If anything happens to Dabney, Thurlow is likely to heave your sisters out of their home. If your stepmother is dragging you out of bordellos, it's in hopes that you'll see the light, marry Lady Ann, and produce heirs to keep Thurlow at bay."

Nick almost had a heart attack of his own. "Lady Ann?" He was hard put to keep the incredulity from his voice. Surely his beloved stepmother wouldn't be so... unperceptive... as to expect him to hold the reins on a duke's headstrong daughter. "The duke would have my head should I even glance her way."

"Don't be a sheep's ass, boy," the earl said wearily. "Should you ever settle down, you'll be the father of the next earl. And his daughter isn't getting any younger. He'd agree, all right. And Ann would obey."

"No sane woman would have me," Nick pointed out, warily, but even he knew he was delaying the inevitable.

"What, you thought you'd wait until you were too old to dally anymore, marry some poor widow, and magically produce an heir?" The earl regarded him with a mixture of amusement and impatience. "Your Cousin Thurlow will push you over a cliff before then. Ann's the perfect solution. She prefers her horses to town. She'd turn a blind eye to your mistresses, as long as you kept them hidden. Her dowry would provide enough for a dozen."

Appalled, Nick could only shake his head and offer flippancy. "I respect the lady too well. I'll let Thurlow reproduce, push *him* over a cliff, and bring his heir back for Mother to raise. That's the best I can offer."

Leaning his head into the pillow, finally showing his weakness, the earl chuckled. "You'll need to do it soon, then. And don't disgrace your sisters, while you're about it." He settled back, looking gray and weary.

Nick had spent these last ten years doing precisely that—nothing to disgrace his family or raise old rumors. Loyal to their father, he and Dabney avoided any scandal that could hurt the countess or ruin the chances of marrying off their flock of half sisters. He desperately wished to keep his family's respect.

But marriage to Lady Ann to ensure the succession? He shuddered at the grim prospect. "I shall be above reproach when Thurlow takes his tumble," Nick agreed fervently, "if that will keep you alive and well. I look dreadful in black."

The earl growled something irascible as Nick bowed his way out, wondering if he could manage to marry Thurlow to Lady Ann. At gunpoint, perhaps—and there was his whole problem in a nutshell. Civilization required he not use his weapons to force an issue. Or push his enemies off cliffs.

Quite indecent that he hadn't been appointed dictator—shouting orders had suited him well.

Outside the chamber, Nick determinedly maintained his good cheer even when the countess cornered him.

"He's worried about your sisters," she whispered. "I know you and Dabney will long outlive me, but your sisters need to know they'll always have a home."

"They'll all be married and have grandchildren before anything happens to us," he promised, praying fervently that wishes came true.

But he knew better than any that life was sometimes very short.

Collecting his curly-brimmed hat from the butler, Nick took the outside stairs at a rapid pace. He still had his other appointment to keep. The emergency summons had made him late.

His tension needed an outlet more physical than polite conversation. He was almost relieved to see the shadow lurking in the alley ahead. He rolled his shoulders and let his blood heat in anticipation.

Surreptitiously ascertaining that none of the beau monde lingered about to report his misbehavior, Nick sauntered onward, gripping his stick as if he hadn't a care in the world.

A blade flashed and the expected *Stand and deliver* emerged as a drunken mutter. Regrettably, the thief was too inebriated to provide much entertainment.

"Badly done, old boy," Nick said in disappointment, slashing his walking stick upward. A knife clattered into the darkness of the filthy alley.

A downward blow brought his moaning assailant to his knees on the cobblestones. Glancing about to verify no one noticed, Nick dropped a coin from his purse beneath the thief's nose. "Find a new alley," he warned. "I'll not be so polite next time."

With a sigh, he straightened his cuffs and proceeded up the steps to Knight's.

His tension lessened upon entering the hushed atmosphere of his club. He didn't belong to extravagantly expensive Whites or the bookish Roxburghe or political Brooks. The members of Knights were the lesser-known names of society, the less ambitious, the less wealthy, the less powerful, but not necessarily less disinterested. Nick and his friends called it the Younger Sons Club.

He met Blake Montague and Acton Penrose in the reading room. Penrose looked up first, and from his friend's worried frown, Nick feared he had not left all his problems at the door. He ignored the warning and signaled for a drink.

"You make me neglect my own lady while you pleasure yours," Montague snarled in greeting, setting aside his newssheet. Built large enough to be a boxer, with a silver streak through the glossy black at his temple, the Duke of Fortham's right-hand man disdainfully sniffed at the perfume clinging to Nick's coat. "One of these days, I'll tell Jocelyn what keeps me so late, and she'll cut off your ears."

"Or lower bits," Penrose added amiably, crossing his bandaged foot over his knee in an uncivilized fashion that would have outraged the elder members of more exclusive environs. Still wearing a black sling around his arm from the wounds he'd taken at Corunna, the ginger-haired ex-soldier sipped from a tumbler of whiskey held in his good hand.

Nick settled into a plump leather chair by the fire. "Blake's wife is much too polite to harm my anatomy. She would merely tell my sisters of my iniquities, and they would see me wedded before the day was out. Very effective. I bow to the lady's genius and pray fervently to stay in her good graces. To what do I owe the pleasure of your royal command, gentlemen?"

"His Grace is opening his home to Princess Elena of Mirenze." Blake folded his newssheet as he confirmed the gossip all London was buzzing about.

"And you want me to use my rusty language skills to translate for royalty?" Accepting the snifter a servant presented on a silver tray, Nick relaxed in the sumptuous chair and inhaled the aroma of his favorite brandy. He refrained from smoking for fear that it would interfere with his appreciation of the subtle tastes his palate preferred.

"I trust the princess is an ancient, doddering crone since you entrust me with the task?" Nick added in amusement.

Penrose scowled. "I told you Atherton's the wrong man for the position. He'll seduce the princess, and we'll have Napoleon's bullies on our doorstep in weeks."

"We already have Napoleon's bullies on our doorsteps," Blake pointed out. "It is because they're following the princess that we need someone we can trust. He was once a Naval officer. You underestimate Nick."

"I doubt it, old fellow," Nick said with a chuckle, enjoying the honorable ex-soldier's discomfort. Blake was a loyal friend, and Nick would help him in any way he could. That didn't mean he had to capitulate without a struggle. "But if the lady concerned is young and virginal, Blake's right. I need only think of my twittering sisters to flee in the opposite direction. I like my women wanton."

Penrose conceded the point with a nod. "After her father's exile, Princess Elena is not as sought after as she once was. She's been a royal pain in many arses since adolescence, but rumor has it that Bonaparte has offered her a crown in return for marriage to one of his many relations. I assume a woman in that position is wise enough to town ways to recognize a useless rake."

"And Atherton is smart enough to avoid a royal virgin, especially if she is to be the next queen on the Mirenzian throne. Our task is simply to offer hospitality and determine if there's more to this visit than seen on the surface," Blake conceded.

Nick rolled his eyes heavenward. "She's female. Of course there is more to her visit than visible to the diplomatic eye. And if she's young and pretty, it doesn't involve tupping Boney's fat cousins."

"That could be a problem," Blake said. "Since the princess is not currently on the throne, this is not intended to be a diplomatic visit. The word is that she simply wishes to see the sights of London and do a little shopping. His Grace has offered to house her and show her about. Your language skills should ease any communication barriers. Should she end up on the throne, her good will is needed for king and country," Blake explained.

The princess might be a good means of staying in his family's graces for the season, but that was his limit. Nick held his brandy up to the firelight to admire the rich amber. "I am not you, Montague. King and country are merely euphemisms for tedium and argument. I will translate for the lady because you ask me to and because I enjoy the company of pretty women. She is pretty, is she not? Otherwise, you would not be so concerned."

"It's more than that, old boy." Blake set his paper down and leaned forward so no one could overhear. "The princess's family has sent word that she may be in peril and requires an English bodyguard to protect her. We need you to be that bodyguard."

*Bodyguard*! That encroached a little too close to the line he'd been avoiding for years. Nick's profane response was not only colorful, but sworn in a dozen different languages.

# Chapter Two

ELEANORA MARONE Ballwin Adams precisely folded the edges of her linen handkerchief, applied the heated flatiron until a crisp crease formed, then repeated the process with a lengthwise fold. The fresh scent of newly dried linen and crisp starch blended refreshingly with the dash of rose scent she'd added to the wash water.

The scent made her long for the days when she'd bathed in rosewater, knowing her late husband's ship would be sailing into Brighton's harbor. It had been so long since she'd dressed in diaphanous chemises and felt that sensual excitement... Embarrassed at a tug of arousal, torn by old griefs and regrets, she dipped her head and returned to ironing.

Adding the square of linen to her meager stack, Nora decided the iron was cool enough, and removed a newssheet clipping from her apron pocket. Laying it out, she pressed it very gently, so it looked crisp and new again.

Princess Elena Marone of Mirenze to visit London read the headline.

"Is dat ta newssheet?" Viviana Ballwin glanced up from her bulky knitting needles. "Does it say ta princess has come?"

Nora frowned, wondering if she should stop encouraging her mother's fairy tales of the Marone family and the elegant Mirenzian court. But they had so little entertainment in their lives... "I have cut out the article for you. It doesn't say she's arrived yet."

"Have you heard from the marchioness?" Vivi asked eagerly. "She could help you meet ta princess." Vivi smoothed the still-warm paper across her lap.

Recently, Viviana had developed a bee in her bonnet about speaking with the princess she called niece, leaving Nora to fear for her mother's mental faculties. Given their finances, traveling to London was about as feasible as meeting a king.

Vivi's arthritis had prevented legible correspondence for years, but at her mother's insistence, Nora had finally capitulated and written to her father's aristocratic family.

"If the Beldens did not respond when Papa died, I cannot not imagine them doing so now," Nora warned. "And I don't believe we'll find a golden crown under the floorboards to finance a journey," she added, repeating one of her mother's wilder tales with amusement. "We will simply have to admire the princess from the newssheets."

She was almost relieved that a peremptory rap on the front door prevented her mother from replying with some new improbability.

"If dat is Mr. Connor, tell him you must go to London," Vivi said. "If he will not take you, he is not ta man for you."

Oh dear. Was that what was bothering her mother? That she might marry and leave?

She kissed her mother's frail cheek rather than argue. Then tucking wisps of hair into her cap, Nora hurried downed the dark stairs into the front parlor. It was a gray day, but she refrained from burning unnecessary oil.

Checking to be certain her cap was straight, she unlatched the door to discover Mr. Connor, her beau, on the step. The grocer's son was a strapping man of thirty, with a full head of brown curls. Nora encouraged him with a smile. She was older and more sensible now. Though she did not feel for him what she had felt for Robbie, Mr. Connor was not likely to sail off and die. He would own the grocery someday.

"Good morning, Mrs. Adams," he said formally.

On his lips, *Mrs. Adams* sounded so very respectable and boring. When Robbie had said it with his saucy smile, she had wanted nothing more than to be swept up in his arms and bussed thoroughly.

Fred didn't so much as smile as he handed her a sealed letter of heavy vellum. "The post just arrived and this looked important. Thought I'd best bring it myself."

The gold embossed seals alone justified his awe and haste. No wonder he had appointed himself a royal messenger. Simple schoolteachers did not receive sealed missives.

Although Mr. Connor knew her father came from aristocracy, most of the village accepted her at face value. No golden coach had ever arrived to cart her off, as Vivi's tales had suggested.

Nora was half afraid to touch such an impressive missive. She accepted the thick paper and offered an uneasy smile. "Would you like to come in? We have just made gingerbread."

"I need to go back to the store for the potato shipment," he said apologetically.

Conscious of her station above him, the grocer's son had always treated her as if she were a rare gem he admired from afar. His respect chastened her irresponsible fancies of stolen kisses.

Nora sighed. Fred's lack of imagination balanced her mother's vivid one, she supposed, but his insistence on keeping his distance was disheartening.

"Are you expecting bad news? I'll stay if you need me to," he offered.

"No, nothing bad, I'm sure. Just my father's family, I believe." Her heart beat a little faster in foolish anticipation—had the marchioness actually replied? Her father's distant family had never acknowledged her existence.

Better that she be realistic and expect rejection.

Fred Connor tugged his forelock as if he were still a delivery boy and strode off. His deference was one of those things that made Nora wonder if he would ever bring himself to propose. Perhaps she should heed her mother and discourage his suit, but she wanted children. And security.

Closing the door on the blustery spring day, Nora held the vellum as if it might explode. She didn't recognize the crest on the seal. Of course, she had never seen a crest on a seal.

Remembering her mother's tales of princesses competing to obtain the fanciest seals, Nora held her skirts off the floor and drifted up the stairs, studying the stately script of her name and address.

It was addressed to *her*. Someone wealthy and important had written to Eleanora Marone Ballwin Adams—someone who knew a lord and could have the letter franked.

She was trembling in fear and expectation as she approached her mother's sitting room. Her mother would want to see the seal. She hated to crush Vivi's expectations if the news was bad, but she equally hated to let her miss the excitement of a sealed letter.

"Who was at ta door, Eleanora?" Viviana Ballwin called.

Nora had been named after her Mirenzian maternal grandmother, Eleanora Marone, a woman she had never met due to Viviana's scandalous marriage to a British naval officer. As a gullible child, Nora had absorbed her mother's tales of Mirenzian ballrooms and swirled about the parlor in a fantasy of enacting the princess in silk stockings and elegant gowns.

Once she was old enough to study books on her own, Nora had learned that Mirenze was really no larger than a small grand duchy, one with no money, hardly a royal kingdom with glittering castles and knights.

After that, Nora had played out her mother's tales with irony— *And the grand duchess washes her cotton stockings in the basin before dumping the water into her chamber pot.*

She should not be impressed by sealing wax.

"Mr. Connor brought the post," Nora murmured as she entered her mother's chamber, unable to express the foolish hope trying to rise in her heart. It had been a very long time since optimism had ruled her world—

Three and a half years, to be precise, since the day they had learned her beloved Robbie had died at Trafalgar along with the heroic Admiral Nelson. She'd buried all foolish dreams with him.

"Well, open it, *cara*. Your father's relations may have answered dis time, no? It cannot hurt to look." Vivi sat beside the grate with a fire at her feet and a blanket over her lap despite the relative warmth of April.

"My father's relations don't know me from their scullery maid." Her father's relations were English and very real, unlike the fantasies her mother spun about her own family.

"Nonsense. They would know you the moment they set eyes upon you."

Like Nora, her mother was small and dark, but her expressive brown eyes and graceful, birdlike hands conveyed such warmth and charm that she exuded beauty, even now as her hair faded to silver.

Nora did not possess her mother's Mirenzian looks, but her father's placid Englishness. Unassuming and unremarkable, she blended into the woodwork. That was who she was—a plump brown sparrow who watched the world with curiosity while methodically going about the business of survival.

"It's sealed," she said, holding the letter for her mother to admire, trying to appear nonchalant when her heart raced nervously.

"Done *excellente*, too. None of dat candle dreeping people use dese days. It must be from ta marchioness. She will not ignore our plea. Open it, do, *cara*."

"If the head of Papa's family didn't respond to your requests after Papa died, I cannot imagine his widow has any interest in us all these years later," Nora argued.

"But perhaps ta marchioness writes about ta princess," Vivi said excitedly.

At least the lady had had the courtesy to respond to their silly requests. That seemed a practical assumption and made it easier to open the letter. Using her pen knife, Nora pried open the wax and unfolded two sheets of vellum.

She scanned the elegant writing then, gasping, she lowered herself to a chair and read more carefully.

"Will ta princess come here?" Vivi asked eagerly. "Will Lady Belden arrange it so?"

Certain that she had fully digested the incredible missive, Nora passed it to her mother and scanned the second one again. "It seems the marquess's solicitors have been looking for me. For *me*. Why me? I am at best a distant cousin, surely twice or more removed. I'm to inherit a thousand pounds a year!"

"Oh, dis is beyond all wonderful." Vivi sighed in ecstasy, hugging the first sheet from the marchioness. "I knew your fadder's family could not forget heem. He was such a fine man, a *hero!* My letters must have gone...how you say...astray. Or perhaps dere was some evil villain opening dem and trowing dem away. But ta villain has lost!"

"There are no evil villains in the offices of marquesses, Mama." Tranquil England did not have evil villains and stolen letters. Nora's life was not that of court chicanery, even if Vivi's stories of intrigue had entertained Nora's dull childhood better than any romantic novel.

She took the marchioness's letter back. Along with the solicitor's verification of the inheritance, the dowager had included an invitation to spend the London season with her. Why would the lady invite a nobody she'd never met?

Nora had very little experience at good fortune but a great deal at self-sacrifice, and she reacted accordingly. "What if she hasn't written before because our inheritance comes out of the dowager's portion? I don't think I can accept an inheritance this enormous if it means the lady must do without."

But she couldn't help wishing to be persuaded otherwise. With a sum like this she would never have to worry about her mother's medicines again....Viviana could even take the waters at Bath!

"You are a foolish child," Vivi said fondly. "And it is my fault dat you do not know ta ways of ta world. Dere are always villains at court and spies in wealty houses. Lady Belden is not poor. I have read ta papers and she attends balls and soirees. Dat is why I asked you to write. But she says notting of ta princess," she added with a measure of disappointment. "You *must* meet ta princess."

Nora had no real interest in meeting so exalted a personage as a princess, but the possibilities of an income... Heart pounding, Nora studied the impossible letters for meanings between the lines but could find none. Her hand began to shake until the paper rattled and she set it in her lap.

A thousand pounds a year. She gripped the vellum tighter, almost crushing it. After the important expenses of medicine and Bath... Moisture formed in Nora's eyes as she looked around her mother's shabby-genteel parlor. The draperies had hung on that window since she was a child and her father had been alive. The chamber pot had been scrubbed so often, it was hard to say what the original color might have been. Her beautiful, vivacious mother was reduced to wearing a bedcap without ribbon or lace. At some point in these past years, Vivi had even sold the gold band on her finger.

Tears blurred Nora's vision as she thought of all the ways she could use such an incredible sum. They might even move to one of the sunnier cottages near the sea where they could watch the waves—

"Wit a dowry like dat, you might find a better suitor, no?" Vivi said softly, intruding on her daughter's reverie. "You are only five-and-twenty."

There were days when she felt much older. And others when she longed to receive posies from admirers as if she were a child. But she'd been raised modestly, and Fred was more suited to her than elegant London gentlemen whose very sophistication terrified her country soul.

Still, she shivered with a thrill of expectation. She could indulge, just a little. Perhaps real perfume. Or a silk dress to marry in. She could be excused a small frivolity. The rest should be saved against a rainy day.

"I don't wish to be married for money," Nora said firmly. "I shall go to London and try to meet your princess. And then I shall give her any message you wish delivered and come home and we will look for a cottage by the shore."

Vivi leaned over and patted Nora's knee. "Dis is my home. Dis is where Teo brought me and dis is where his memory lives. You are ta one who must go out in ta world and make a new life."

Nora studied the magical paper and for the first time since girlhood, allowed a bud of wonder to bloom in her heart.

# Chapter Three

NICK SCOWLED at the short sword Blake held out to him and stepped away from the blade as if it were an anaconda. "Are you expecting pirates at the duke's dinner?"

Blake impatiently shook the scabbard at him. "You've been a sailor. We fenced together at school. I know you know how to use one. You're our first line of defense around the princess."

Gritting his teeth, telling himself he could behave while wearing a weapon through one miserable dinner party, Nick reluctantly strapped it on. He tugged his formal, forest green cutaway into a smooth line over his gold satin waistcoat and knee breeches, but judging by his reflection in the cheval glass, he couldn't hide the damned sword.

"One more embroidered flower and I could be planted in a field," he grumbled. "It is time the court entered the nineteenth century. Silk knee breeches are damned embarrassing."

Blake Montague's wife, the formidable Jocelyn of golden hair, curvaceous form, and devious mind, laughed in a throaty voice that could shiver timbers. "How do you say *very elegant* in Italian? The princess will be honored that you have gone to such trouble."

Leaning his black-clad, unembroidered shoulders against a doorjamb in the upper salon of the Duke of Fortham's London manor, Blake snorted. "From what I hear, once she arrives, the lady is likely to drag Nick off the parlor floor to test his manliness. I suspect her family merely wants a bodyguard to prevent her from getting into trouble. It's not as if a deposed princess is of any value to anyone but Bonaparte."

"Royalty is always trouble," Nick said with scorn. "If it was not for my father bursting his buttons with pride at my serving his majesty, and my damnable sisters near to fainting with joy at being invited to this crush, I'd tell you what you could do with king and country."

Jocelyn rapped Nick's arm with her fan. A duke's financial and political advisor did not earn enough to buy diamonds. Nick assumed Blake's wife had dressed her champagne-blond tresses in her mentor's, Lady Isabell Belden's, jewelry.

"You look dashing in frills, and you know it, you peacock,"

Jocelyn declared. "You must test your grandeur on Lady Bell's latest protégée. Mrs. Adams is apparently some distant relation of the late marquess and another recipient of his largesse. I have left the widow listening to the duke in awe and wonder. Quit admiring your pretty legs and let us make haste so we will be downstairs when the princess arrives."

Nick swallowed his discomfort with wearing a sword again—not a blunt decorative court point but a blade of finest Spanish steel, meant to be used. They actually expected him to guard the princess with steel and his life?

Setting him loose with a sword in a room full of feathered exquisites was not quite the same as setting a fox among the chickens, but he seriously resented the reminder.

Nick loosened his neckcloth and swirled from the mirror, resting his hand on the sword hilt to hold it in position with a practiced ease he had yet to unlearn.

If he must marry, he had to live with passive solutions to stressful situations. He squelched a shudder. "Lead me to Lady Bell's peahen, then, before His Grace puts her to sleep."

"You are not to remark on Mrs. Adam's resemblance to the princess," Blake admonished, holding the door so his wife might precede them. "We don't know why the princess is in London or why Mrs. Adams has just recently made her existence known. If there is a conspiracy, we must root it out."

Jocelyn shot her husband a look of wifely exasperation. "If there is any conspiracy, it is between Lady Bell and Lord Quentin. Poor Mrs. Adams is so grateful to be here that she would walk on water if asked. As a previous beneficiary of Lady Bell's generosity, I remember that feeling well."

"If Quent is leading me into a matrimonial trap with another of Lady Bell's heiresses, he is all about in his head." Nick snorted at the very idea of marrying a peahen. "He'll have to find someone more desperate for blunt than I. Better that they find husbands for Quent's cousins and my sisters."

Quent, the current Marquess of Belden's youngest son, was an interfering rogue who thought all his friends should be wealthy and married. So far, he and the dowager marchioness had possessed the sense to leave irredeemable Nick alone.

Nick was enjoying the new notion of marrying off his sisters so they needn't worry about Thurlow.

They proceeded downstairs just as the orchestra began setting up on the balcony overlooking the Duke of Fortham's grand salon. The pocket doors had been opened between parlors to receive the hundreds of guests on the exclusive list to be introduced later in the evening to the princess.

"Does one call a deposed princess Your Highness?" Nick asked idly, just to annoy his tightly wound friend—and possibly to remind himself that guarding an impoverished princess merely required diplomatic skills he used regularly on his sisters.

Montague was studying the salon as if Napoleon's spies might be hiding behind the potted palms. "Royal blood is royal whether or not it sits a throne," Blake said implacably, offering his arm to his wife so they might cross the salon together.

"Not if Napoleon has his way," Jocelyn protested. "He would marry all of Europe's nobles to his upstart family and make us all equal."

"Napoleon's an ass if he thinks marrying royalty will equalize the masses," Nick countered. "The aristocracy is bloated with incompetent idiots, present company excluded."

"You must tell me your story sometime, Mr. Atherton," the normally gracious Jocelyn said with asperity. "You are an aristocrat granted looks, family, and a reasonable income, yet you speak as if these gifts are insults."

"This time, your clever observations are wrong, my dear." Blake led them toward an anteroom curtained off from the servants scurrying about lighting candles and arranging flowers. "Nick worships his family. And probably his looks," he added, with sardonic humor. "But after his experience with the Navy, he lacks any regard for authority, which apparently includes all royalty and most of parliament."

"Which is why I should be the last man you want guarding a princess whose family can lay claim to Bonnie Charlie's throne," Nick reminded them.

"Really?" Jocelyn asked, wide-eyed. "An Italian princess is related to the Stuarts?"

"All European royalty is related in some manner or another," Blake said. "That's why Boney is spreading his family around. And the princess is Mirenzian, not Italian. The various states of Italy have no central government. Yet," he added ominously.

"The professor speaks," Nick taunted. "Regardless of her legal status, Princess Elena is female. She's royal. She can get me hanged. It's that last part that concerns me most. My neckcloth will not wrap properly if my neck is askew."

Jocelyn's delicious laughter turned heads as they entered the anteroom, reassuring Nick that this was a farce and his neck was in no danger.

He located Lady Bell's protégée with ease. He'd been told she was a timid brown wren, and he'd been expecting plump, dowdy, and nondescript. It took a moment to realize the strikingly poised young woman at Lady Bell's elbow could be in any way named a wren. Compared to pale, skinny, English misses, perhaps, but her golden honey coloring was so rich he wanted to lick her all over. Beneath curling chestnut tresses, warm chocolate eyes watched him enter with such astonishment that he wanted to strut like the peacock Blake's annoying wife called him. The newcomer had abundant curves in all the right places.

And she was a widow, unlike the virginal princess. Finally pleased with the evening's entertainment, Nick advanced on the confection garbed modestly in brown and gold and watched her dark lashes lower to sweep her creamy cheeks.

He would buy her gold and pearls as a parting gift.

* * *

By all the saints and heavens, the man was beyond delicious into the realm of godliness!

Fearing her thunderstruck wonder was obvious, Nora attempted to look away from the golden-haired aristocrat strutting across the room in Lady Belden's direction, but moths fluttered in her midsection, and her gaze was drawn to him no matter where he stood. His form-fitting cutaway revealed excessively wide shoulders and a narrow waist. His breeches... Oh my, she didn't think she'd ever seen a man in court breeches. She could see the curve of his legs!

Well, yes, she supposed now that she looked, many of the older gentleman wore baggy breeches and stockings and buckles. It was a quaint custom of respect for royalty, she supposed. But the golden god was strikingly... She cleared her throat. Robbie had been only twenty-two when he'd left for war. The sophisticated noble approaching was not a slender lad, nor a stocky grocer.

The scent of the lovely lilies on the table, the lavishly gleaming silk she wore, the powerful duke and his guests—all faded into wallpaper once the golden icon stopped before them.

"Lady Belden, *bellissima*," he murmured, bowing over the petite dowager's hand.

Nora swallowed hard and tried not to admire the muscled posterior revealed by the fall-away tails of his coat.

"Mrs. Adams, I would like you to meet..."

Nora scarcely heard Lady Belden's introductions. She had always felt dowdy and chunky next to her delicate mother, but this man made her feel feminine. He took her hand when she did not extend it, squeezing her gloved fingers in a reassuring manner guaranteed to melt her bones. He did not give her time to be embarrassed by the gaffe of not extending her hand first.

"Mrs. Adams, a pleasure to meet you," he said with such seductive smoothness that she nearly fainted at the image that the word *pleasure* produced.

Did men speak like that outside of bed? Not to boring schoolteachers. Flushed, Nora remembered to dip a slight curtsy.

"Mr. Atherton will be escorting the princess," Lady Belden was saying, jarring Nora from her stunned reverie. "He can help you speak with her about your mother."

"Yes, of course, Mr. Atherton! Lady Belden has mentioned you." The marchioness had warned that the gentleman was a notorious rake, as well as the master of numerous languages.

Nora could speak a rudimentary form of the Mirenzian dialect. Viviana had helped her brush up on it so she could pass the invitation to the princess in her mother tongue. She had not realized her performance might be critiqued by someone else. She hid a wince of dismay.

Her mother hadn't wanted anyone to know of her invitation for the princess to visit her. That wasn't difficult when Nora would prefer that no one knew of her presumptuous quest.

"I trust Lady Bell spoke favorably," Mr. Atherton said with a blinding smile meant to deceive and overpower.

He almost succeeded, but Nora had a better grasp of the dowager's warning now. Atherton used his looks and charm like weapons, probably with more effect than the sword at his side, she thought with just a touch of spite.

Her father had expended his excess energies in the winters by teaching his only child to use both rapier and small sword. Her mother had taught her how to use charm. Living in her confined world, Nora had never required either. She might enjoy taking out her rusty skills and polishing them for society.

Except she was relishing the notion of engaging in combat with Atherton entirely too much. Better that she play country mouse and pretend to be prey.

"Of course, sir, I shall be most appreciative of your expertise."

"How appreciative, *bellissima*?" the gentleman asked seductively, placing her hand on his arm as if to escort her from her chaperone's company.

Nora removed her hand from his coat sleeve and managed a brief, frank glare. "The message is from my ailing mother, not me. She is Mirenzian and would convey her condolences over the loss of the princess's mother. Not a message of overwhelming importance, I fear."

Well, it was of importance to her mother. She'd had time to wonder why, but Vivi had never explained. Still, Nora knew better than to let any gentleman believe he had the upper hand.

"I'm most glad to hear that we will not be oversetting the Continental balance of power with your presence," Mr. Atherton said smoothly. "Lady Belden, might I have the extreme honor of escorting your friend about the room while we await the arrival of our guests?"

"Mrs. Adams is a grown woman, sir. Ask her yourself," Lady Bell retorted.

"Madam?" he inquired, taking Nora's hand and placing it on his arm with a squeeze that was just shy of suggestive. "Might I have the pleasure?"

She had longed to better examine the beauties of the duke's salon. Against her better judgment, she allowed him to lead her from safety.

"Is that a portrait of the king in his youth?" she asked, steering toward a soaring oil of a young man in full regalia on a white horse. She filled with patriotic fervor for this royal personage who represented the country for which both her husband and father had died. "He and his family have sacrificed so much for the kingdom."

"And our country sacrifices much for their upkeep," he added dryly.

Startled, she cast him a questioning look. "Such as?"

"Our leaders sacrifice all the eager young men who believe as you do and take to war thinking king and country care about their welfare," he said, leading her away. "Let us speak of more pleasant things. The world is littered with Mrs. Adamses. May I have your full name?"

"I'm just called Nora," she said absently, bewildered by his jaded response. This wealthy lord did not admire Great Britain? Or was it just the king he despised? She didn't know how to take such treason.

"Nora, such an enchanting name, and not of the usual sort, I believe?" Atherton asked, maintaining the shallow conversation, letting his attentions speak for him.

He stopped before an enormous flower arrangement of lilies and roses so Nora might nearly expire in delight at the scent and color. His gallantry erased any confusion as to his true intent. He tucked a fallen bud behind her ear, and the brush of his fingers generated a heated rush she hadn't experienced in years.

"It is short for Eleanora, my grandmother's name," she answered, wondering if she could remember how to return his flirtation.

Nora followed where Mr. Atherton led, keeping up a polite pretense that this was no more than a social stroll about the salon rather than a simmering tempest she did not have the experience to handle.

She understood that Mr. Atherton merely sought conquest with his smoldering glances and intimate touches. Just because she'd been widowed for entirely too long and felt the impact of his masculinity did not mean she had to be his victim. She hoped.

"How did you learn to speak Mirenzian?" she asked, hoping for more meaningful discussion.

"Family genius and all that," he replied vaguely.

His evasion reminded her of Billy, the cobbler's son, when he hadn't wanted to tell her who had broken the slate. What wasn't he telling her? "Family geniuses teach Mirenzian?" she asked a trifle caustically.

He shrugged. "Travels in my youth. My sisters are excessively verbal as well."

He was definitely hiding something, but he would be no concern of hers once she met the princess. "Will your sisters attend this evening?" she asked, to avoid thinking of the way his hand stroked the gloved fingers she'd laid on his arm.

"Unfortunately, yes, so I must be on my best behavior. I was hoping to enlist you in their entertainment while I perform my duties with the princess. They have been practicing Mirenzian all week. My ears will fall off if I must hear more. I would be most appreciative."

She glanced up into deep blue eyes laughing with the depths of an ocean. She had almost made a cake of herself, thinking his suggestive tone meant this elegant aristocrat was actually interested in a country mouse like her. Instead, he'd pegged her for the teacher she was and wished her to guide his young sisters.

How appallingly embarrassing.

"Of course, I would be delighted to make their acquaintance, sir," she said primly, wishing the floor might rise up and swallow her whole. How would she ever survive an entire evening of London sophistication if she could not understand even one man?

"*Eccellente, mia cara.* And then later, you will allow me to show my appreciation?" He kissed her hand in a manner that suggested that wasn't all he meant to kiss, then left her in the company of the charming Montagues.

Nora didn't know whether to slap him or just melt into a puddle of sealing wax.

# Chapter Four

THE LITTLE WIDOW was perhaps a trifle too demure for his tastes, Nick thought as he abandoned her to Blake and traversed the salon at a discreet signal from the duke's butler. The angry flash of her big brown eyes when she thought he was too suggestive intrigued, but he dismissed Blake's fears that she plotted with the princess. He doubted a prim rural widow was a danger, no matter how close the resemblance.

Her unsophisticated rose-scent still teased his nostrils—fresher than the marchioness's musky perfume. Or the eau de stable of Lady Ann, the duke's daughter.

Unfortunately, the imposing Lady Ann was also responding to the covert signal. Statuesque, wearing her nondescript brown tresses in a knot without a single dangling curl, she marched across the open space like a soldier to battle.

Nick tried to imagine bedding the duke's daughter, gritted his teeth, and fingered his sword hilt instead. He'd be far better off finding husbands for his sisters.

He offered the lady his arm. She knew her duty, accepted it, and they followed the butler to the grandiose foyer. Once owned by royalty, Fortham's palatial mansion on the Thames offered more privacy and security than St. James, where the ailing king and his family resided.

Nick wasn't at all surprised to see His Grace pacing the marble floor like an angry tiger when they arrived. The duke was a large, thickset man in his fifties, with a mane of graying dark hair, and a temper.

"The prince has been delayed on the road and cannot accompany Her Highness," the duke announced. "We'll have no royal guards to surround her. It's a shocking lack of propriety. I don't know what this generation is coming to!"

The same decadence as prior generations would be Nick's guess, but he didn't think the duke appreciated his opinions. The idea of the man as a father-in-law caused an internal shudder and a sharp desire to run away like a lad. "I understood the princess travels modestly. Perhaps she requested a lack of escort."

The duke scowled. "We'll all be like the Frenchies shortly, rattling around in sailor's garb, spouting equality, and pretending upstart Corsican soldiers are royalty."

Nick's lips twitched. "German farmers are far better, agreed. If we let this laxity go too far, the ladies will be demanding trousers as well."

"Silence, Atherton. Montague vouched for you. It's his head that will roll should you fail me now."

Nick seldom scowled, but he wouldn't mind running his sword through a grumpy duke at this threat to his friend. Montague did a damned fine job of assisting the curmudgeon.

Ignoring their argument, the stately Lady Ann took her father's arm, and as if responding to a signal only she could hear, nodded at the butler waiting at attention by the door. The footman opened the double front doors.

Standing straight as he had countless times in his family's reception lines, Nick attempted the pompous solemnity required of him.

He tried not to register surprise when a young girl entered alone. She scarcely looked older than Diana, or Bertrice, at best. She was dressed more like one of his sisters' maids.

The drab personage swept toward them with the brash assurance of a princess, apparently recognizing the duke.

Nick surreptitiously glanced over her shoulder for some sign of an entourage, seeing only an unremarkable carriage and a post boy on the drive. Not even a maid? Or a lady in waiting?

He frowned. There should have at least been a Mirenzian guard or two. His instincts smelled rat.

He returned his gaze to the small female. At first glance, she looked remarkably like the country widow, as Blake's wife had warned, except the widow was dressed more royally than this drab personage bearing down on them with a determined gleam in her eye.

"Your Highness, this is a pleasure." Garbed in black, the duke made a formal bow to the half-sized creature before him, confirming the princess's identity if not relieving Nick's concern. "Will there be another carriage to follow? We were told to expect an extended stay."

"I believe the baggage wagon was delayed with His Royal

Highness," the princess said in a disdainful tone, apparently indicating her opinion of her retinue. "Sooner or later, they will make an appearance. It is quite kind of you to offer your home to so humble a guest as myself."

Despite her dowdy attire, Nick ascertained that there was nothing humble about the princess. He knew women well. Arriving alone and wearing that gown did not show any intent to enjoy an elegant social reception.

She was on a mission that did not include the duke or his guests. Or her bodyguards, it seemed. They had misinterpreted her family's warning about danger—the princess was the one of whom they need be wary.

He fought to keep his hand off his sword while he studied the princess's flimsy bit of gray muslin. He recognized the French style as more appropriate to a morning at home. The high waist suited the princess's plump bosom, but Nick preferred the widow's regal composure over this young hoyden's casual disregard for propriety.

And he couldn't believe he was thinking like that. He preferred loose women, didn't he? And he was all about lack of propriety.

Gathering his wandering wits, he bowed and offered a respectful greeting in Her Highness's native language. She narrowed her eyes and studied him more thoroughly. "I speak English and French quite competently. I do not need the services of a translator, thank you."

She was treating him like a servant instead of the son of an earl. It was scarcely a new experience, but a demeaning reminder that required retribution.

"With all due respect, Your Highness," he said in her native language, with more impudence than respect, "I doubt your father would approve of you traveling unescorted. His Grace and Lady Ann have gone to a great deal of trouble to provide you with appropriate company. The least you can do is show your gratitude," he said in the same tone he would use on a misbehaving younger sister.

The princess smiled sweetly, called him a Mirenzian equivalent of looby, and took the duke's arm.

Well, this was going famously.

Falling in behind the duke and the princess, again left escorting the duke's daughter, Nick studied the princess from behind. Her highness had hair the color of dirt, whereas the widow had sunlit highlights to add interest to her coloring. The princess wore heels to disguise her lack of height, but she was probably shorter than Mrs. Adams. And the princess had a wide rump and lacked the elegant carriage of the slightly older English woman.

But there was no denying a strong resemblance, and his instinct for trouble twitched.

"Our dinner party will be small," the duke informed his royal guest. "My daughter, my assistant Montague and his wife, a few family friends, and Mrs. Eleanora Adams, who I believe to be a distant relation of yours." The last was asked questioningly.

"My family is nothing if not prolific," the princess said with a dismissive wave of her hand. "And all the females are named in some manner after the sainted first queen of Mirenze, Eleanora Viviana. I am called Elena. My mother is Giovanna Elise. I think, should I ever be foolish enough to have a daughter, she will be called Hank."

"Henry, for Henrietta," Nick murmured. He stepped forward and scanned the salon out of habit. The sword on his hip aroused ancient survival skills. He had already inspected the musicians, but he glanced upward to verify there were no new additions. It was not as if cannibals or bloodthirsty pirates would swing, howling, from the balcony, but the damned blade had that effect on him.

"Bernie, perhaps, for Bernadette." A flicker of amusement crossed Elena's bored countenance. "And she will wear trousers."

Nick thought the duke's ears turned purple, but he refrained from snickering, just as the duke refrained from protest. The princess might be no more than a brat, but she appeared to have some semblance of a brain along with her willfulness.

The butler announced their presence, so Nick was not forced to find a polite response. As the duke and Lady Ann circled the room, introducing the princess to their guests, Nick sought the lady who was almost her mirror image. It must be freakish to meet a stranger so similar in countenance, but royalty was inbred and inherited features were often strong. It seemed the widow's vague claim to a relationship was based on fact.

The princess made small talk with everyone to whom she was presented, obviously experienced and bored with the etiquette. She did not even act as if she saw her older relation. Nick waited with interest for Lady Belden to produce her protégée for introduction.

* * *

Nora had known the princess was not quite three-and-twenty, but she had not remembered how very young that was. She'd been married to Robbie younger than that, and had already learned how to buy on credit and iron her own clothing on a sailor's nonexistent income. In the idealism of youth, they had been confident that he would someday make officer and earn prizes, and they'd have a house of their own and plenty of time for revelry.

Instead, widowed by the princess's age, she'd never experienced more of the world than her mother's home. The royal princess had seen Europe and danced with royalty, yet she retained the petulant pout of a bored youth.

Her Highness's resemblance to Viviana was so strong that Nora finally had to start believing in her mother's fairy tales. Discovering she truly had relatives she'd never met, she excitedly reached for her cousin's hand when offered. "You could be the little sister I never had!" she said warmly.

The princess squeezed Nora's fingers and looked momentarily relieved, before she assumed her bored expression again. "You are very much like your mother's portrait in the royal gallery. We must have a good coze, soon."

The impatient duke hurried on, carrying the princess with him. Stunned, Nora barely acknowledged Mr. Atherton's wink.

A princess recognized her from her mother's portrait? In a *royal* gallery?

She, plain Eleanora Adams, was *more* than distantly related to royalty? "Cousin" covered such a wide variety of shirttail relations, she supposed, but she had never presumed...

Viviana had a portrait hanging in a royal court! Surely palaces didn't exhibit portraits of distant relations? But why, then, was her mother living in near poverty in England? Probably because Mirenzian royalty lived on popularity and not money.

Thoughts whirling, Nora barely spoke to her table companions as dinner progressed. The princess was seated beside the duke, of course. Nora was half way down the table, not noble enough to even sit at the side of the duke's daughter. She preferred the obscurity.

"Mrs. Adams, how are you enjoying London thus far?" Mrs. Montague asked, trying to draw Nora into the conversation.

"I've not seen much yet, but Lady Belden says there is time. I'm still a little overwhelmed," she admitted.

Mrs. Montague laughed, drawing the attention of all the men in the vicinity as her diamonds bounced against her generous bosom. "Lady Bell adores squiring her late husband's relations about town to show them the best way to spend their new-found wealth."

Nora raised an eyebrow. "There is more than one of us?"

"Oh yes, I'm one. The Countess of Danecroft is another. The late marquess was a nip-cheese who wouldn't provide a farthing to help his relations. Apparently Lady Bell has interpreted his will to include all of us."

"Oh, I had wondered." Nora pushed her smoked flounder around the plate. "I suppose when my mother wrote after my father died, the marquess was still alive and simply threw our letters aside."

"Precisely," Mrs. Montague confirmed. "And then you wrote about seeing the princess, didn't you? Why is your mother not here to meet her as well?"

"My mother doesn't travel well these days, I fear. She's simply asked me to pass on a message to the princess." For some reason, Nora thought it best not to mention that Vivi was hoping a princess would visit. Both the divine Mr. Atherton as well as Mr. Montague were regarding her with suspicion as it was.

"You must stay for the season," Mrs. Montague insisted. "Lady Belden loves entertaining and she'll adore showing you off."

"I don't like to presume," Nora murmured. "And I cannot leave mother alone for too long. I'd rather go home and start improving our house and hiring servants to make my mother more comfortable. I'd thought..." She hesitated, fearing to sound foolish. "I thought perhaps I could start my own school."

She'd also hoped that perhaps, once she had a dowry to offer, Mr. Connor would finally come up to snuff and propose, and there might finally be babies in her future.

"You teach, Mrs. Adams?" the golden icon, Mr. Atherton, asked. He had a distinct upper lip that quirked charmingly in a manner destined to break hearts, and a strong chin that hinted at stubbornness. "Embroidery, reading...?"

"I teach basic reading and writing to young students, and I have a few older students who come to me for pianoforte or embroidery. Nothing terribly exciting."

She had once helped her father teach fencing, but those lessons had stopped when he died, before she married Robbie. She missed the exercise. She missed her father more. How he would have laughed at her foolish fear of this society!

Apparently catching part of the conversation, the princess leaned forward and asked in Mirenzian, "Do you teach the language of the stinking French pigs?"

Mr. Atherton looked amused but politely refrained from translating. He watched Nora expectantly.

"I am not adept at languages," Nora responded in English. "My mother taught me basic Mirenzian and some French, but I find little use for them."

"But you understand well?" the princess asked, again in Mirenzian, although she spoke in such a dismissive manner that anyone listening would think she'd ended the subject.

Uneasy with this odd inquiry, Nora wondered if she ought to start recalling the details of her mother's tales of court intrigue.

"Moderately well," Nora replied, in the same language, as if saying, "You're welcome." She'd picked up much of the language by communicating like this with Viviana, who enjoyed planning surprises for her husband by talking around him.

"Your accent is excellent," the princess said in English, before returning to converse with Lady Belden.

What had that been about? Nora caught Mr. Atherton studying her with interest, as if he, too, wondered if there might be more to the casual questions than appeared on the surface.

# Chapter Five

THE DUKE and his daughter broke up the dinner party shortly before the reception guests were scheduled to arrive. Nick offered his arm to the princess to escort her from the dining room. She touched his elegant coat sleeve as if he were a stick of furniture.

He would have been stung at being so ignored except he could tell the lady was intent on a pursuit that did not include him. Following her gaze, he could see she was studying her composed, older "cousin," if such Mrs. Adams really was. Intrigued, Nick maneuvered Her Highness through the lingering dinner guests in the lady's direction.

"Excellent, sir, my gratitude," the princess murmured in her own language. "I am most enthralled to discover Archduchess Viviana's daughter here. Can you arrange a private audience before the reception starts?"

Since the musicians were already tuning up, and aristocratic coaches were no doubt lined up in the drive, the conversation couldn't be long. Nick saw no harm in it. The princess had a right to be intrigued by a long lost family member.

Nick had once sailed with a Mirenzian seaman and knew the small duchy wasn't an influential nation so much as a silted-in port too poor to provide the upkeep of royalty. The family members he recalled hearing about had landed in comfortable palaces, not seaside villages. What did the princess know that others didn't?

The demure Mrs. Adams glanced up from a conversation with Lady Belden when they approached. She appeared grateful at being singled out by the princess.

"Perhaps the ladies' retiring room?" Lady Belden suggested at Her Highness's request. "Nick can stand guard outside the door so you are not disturbed."

The princess bobbed a curtsy of appreciation, proving someone had taught her respect, even if she didn't always exhibit manners. Assuming two young women couldn't get into any trouble requiring his sword while gossiping in a bedchamber, Nick escorted them up the stairs to the assigned room.

"I cannot prevent a battalion of dowagers from breaking down the door, so I fear your gossip session will not be private long," Nick warned.

"We will see one another over the next days," the princess placidly promised, "but I am too excited to wait."

"Right," he muttered under his breath, shutting the door after the two women slipped inside. She had an odd manner of expressing excitement.

Lounging against the wall, wondering if he ought to eavesdrop, Nick waited to see which ladies would arrive first to trim his ears for blocking their access to mirrors and chamber pots. His own stepmother might lead the execution.

* * *

"It is urgent that I speak with your mother, immediately," the princess whispered the moment the door closed. Perfume permeated the air from the lilies on a window seat, but she disregarded all the carefully chosen amenities that held Nora awestruck. "There are French spies everywhere. I cannot let them follow me."

The princess yanked pins from her coiffure and shook her hair free.

Nora's terror at the shocking start of their conversation descended into confusion at watching a princess descend into dishabille. Was this some foreign custom she didn't recognize?

She concentrated on *spies* over hair. "Spies follow you?" she asked. "Why?"

"I do not have time to explain. I need to see Viviana at once." Elena threw the pins to the dressing table and sought the fastening of her seed pearl necklace.

"My mother was hoping you might visit, Your Highness," Nora said, desperately attempting to assess this strange situation and failing. "She has sent me here expressly to offer the invitation, but it is a day's ride to Hytegate. We could leave in the morning—"

"*Non!*" the princess exclaimed, presenting her back. "Here, unfasten this miserable gown. I must leave now, before my bodyguards catch up with me. They will not stay locked in the stables for long, no matter how drunk they are."

Nora hesitated. The princess had got her guards drunk and locked them in a stable? Perhaps she'd misinterpreted.

The princess stomped her foot and began spilling her fears so fast, in a mixture of French, English, and Mirenzian, that Nora responded to the pressure. She began unpinning and unfastening as the princess spoke, concentrating on the more serious problem of spies and not what the princess was doing. Why would spies be interested in a deposed princess?

"They want me to marry the French pig who claims my father's throne when I come into my estate next month," the princess said, nearly spitting the words. "They will parade me through court and call me queen and call my obscenity-of-a-turd husband king and quell a righteous uprising of our people. This cannot be allowed."

A conventional lady might think the princess mad, but Nora had been raised by Viviana, and knew schemes lurked behind the madness. Unwilling to refuse a royal guest, frightened by her urgency, Nora helped the princess squirm out of her gown. What did her impetuous relation intend to do, climb from the room in her corset? Or would she wrap herself in the lovely maroon draperies first?

"I am sure England will welcome you and keep you safe," Nora said, seeking logic to counter the princess's dramatics, refusing to believe a princess could be in danger in tranquil England. "The duke will be happy to aid you. Or you are welcome to stay with my mother and me, although we live simply."

"No! We need a leader with the strength to stand up to Napoleon! You are very kind. I had not hoped to find you so easily, but Archduchess Viviana, she must have known that after my mother's death, I would seek her out. That is why she sent you." Kicking her gown aside, the princess spun around and began unpinning Nora's.

Bewildered, Nora grabbed her bodice and backed off. She wasn't surprised that her mother might be behind this madness, but she wasn't willing yet to believe in the necessity for drama. "I don't understand—"

"We must exchange places. You will be me for a few days. Go to parties and theaters and smile and laugh. It will be fun for you. I will be quiet Mrs. Adams, traveling home to my mother. This is what you meant to do, was it not? You only came to give me the invitation from Aunt Vivi, then to go home and await my arrival? That is what we must do, except you will remain here as me. You are a Marone. You will understand."

Nora might be a Marone, but she didn't understand at all. *Aunt Vivi?* The princess not only knew her mother, but thought of her as aunt?

Thrown off balance by this evidence that her mother's stories had not been fairy tales, Nora couldn't find the presence of mind to refuse a royal command.

Confused and more than a shade fearful, she allowed the princess to unfasten the first luxurious gown she'd ever owned. Stupidly, she resisted losing her beautiful gown more than being manipulated by a royal mischief maker. Perhaps if she applied reason...

"Traveling at night is difficult and dangerous. Why can you not just go home with me in the morning?" Nora sensibly asked. "We could be there by dinner. My mother will be delighted."

"Because the stupid French, they do not know Vivi is alive. They must not find out. If they see that the two of us look alike, they will be suspicious and follow us both. Vivi has what we need to help our people."

"Why should my mother have anything that you do not?" Nora protested, reluctantly stepping out of her gown.

"She is one of the four Royal Archduchesses! Do you know nothing?"

If the princess wasn't tale-telling, then obviously, Nora knew nothing. "Could we not wait until tomorrow?" she repeated with increasing alarm. "Let us talk with the duke. He can surround you with soldiers. If you must go in disguise, it would not have to be in such a havey-cavey manner."

A knock on the door intruded. "Ladies, guests are arriving. They wish to powder their pretty noses before being presented."

Giggles and female laughter followed Mr. Atherton's warning. Nora glanced frantically at the door, then at the gown the princess handed her. "I cannot be *you!*" she said in astonishment, finally grasping the real folly of the plan.

"Of course you can," Elena said. "My family is poor. I travel with no one who knows me. My bodyguard..." She spat the term with contempt. "They are stupid. They will not see the difference. You will have the very lovely Mr. Atherton to escort you about. It is an excellent plan. I am so relieved that you look like a Marone and not your English father. This is far better than running away to find Aunt Vivi on my own."

"You must take Mr. Atherton with you!" Nora said in horror, pulling on the flimsy muslin for fear of being caught undressed. "You cannot go gallivanting about the countryside without an escort. How will you find a coach? Do you have money? This is an impossible plan. Play at being me tonight, if you must, but reconsider, please. You may pretend to be me and go home with Lady Belden. We will work out a better solution tomorrow."

That would give her time to think, to decide who she might trust with this preposterous, impetuous plan.

"You are right. That is wise," the princess conceded. "We will fool the oh-so-charming Mr. Atherton tonight. Tomorrow, I will return here and we will scheme together. Let us simply test our thespian skills this evening, shall we? Do you think we will amuse?"

Relieved that the princess had come to her senses, Nora breathed again. She adjusted the wide ivory sash of her lovely gown to fit her cousin's more buxom figure. "You fill out this bodice better than I. The gentlemen will not notice your acting skills for staring in distraction. I don't believe I can act royal though."

Elena gestured dismissively. "No one knows us. This is the beauty. We can act as we will, and who will know the difference? The duke has offered me a ladies' maid. Does your Lady Belden offer you hers? Should I know her name?"

"Biggers. She is simply called Biggers. And I order hot chocolate and toast in the morning and like rosewater in my bath. But I have only been in London a few days, not enough to establish a pattern."

Nora belatedly realized she was agreeing to carry out this masquerade until tomorrow. By then, she might enlist others in aiding the princess. Elena was young. The princess might be misunderstanding some mishap. Or she was up to mischief, more likely. Viviana loved playacting, so the princess might also.

Nora didn't like it, but she saw no alternative except to see the princess to the safety of Lady Belden's until she had time to think.

Which meant Nora would be spending the night in a duke's palace. She really must warn someone. Who?

"Ladies, I will batter down the door for fear of your lives shortly," Mr. Montague warned through the panel.

"My hair has come unpinned," the princess called. "Please, I would not appear less than perfect before our distinguished guests."

"Five minutes, then, and you may make your grand entrance."

They could hear the foppish Mr. Atherton chatting amiably with the ladies waiting outside the door.

Elena looked pleadingly at Nora. "The fate of my country and yours depends on us. Do not give me away, please?"

Robbie had given his *life* for England. If there was any iota of truth in the princess's passionate plea, Nora could do no less. If nothing else, she must protect a foolish princess from acting even more impetuously and bringing harm to England's security.

For the first time in years, Nora felt purposeful and alive. With a quick twist, she rearranged the princess's brown curls into a style vaguely resembling the one Biggers had created for her. "I am very glad I am not really royalty."

"But you are," Elena murmured. "You are my older cousin. If the French knew of you, you might be wearing the crown already."

\* \* \*

The instant the retiring room door opened, the gaggle of impatient ladies surged past Nick, separating him from the princess. From his loftier height, he could see Her Highness in her dowdy gown graciously touching hands in greeting. The candlelight in the corridor was dim, and he couldn't see either woman well enough to discern how their private talk had gone from their expressions.

Murmuring she would meet everyone downstairs, the princess slipped past the crowd that held him trapped, with Mrs. Adams in the forefront, clearing a path for her. Whatever Mrs. Adams had said to her relation, it seemed to have brought the girl back to good behavior, he noted with relief.

Nick could not easily shove the mob of ladies aside to race after the princess. The weapons of civilization did not include swords.

"Fancy seeing you outside a ladies room, Nick," his former lover cooed, catching his arm. "Courting royalty these days? I didn't think virgins were your style."

"But widows are, my dear. If you will excuse me..." He peeled her grasping claws from his coat and took long strides toward the stairs, praying a shoe wouldn't strike him from behind.

Scanning the foyer and hall from the vantage point of the landing, he took the treads two at a time and caught up with the drab princess talking to Lady Ann at the bottom. At his arrival, the two women strolled to the reception line as if they'd been waiting for him. There for a moment, he'd feared the royal minx had meant to give him the slip. Glancing around, he realized it was the lovely widow who had eluded him. A pity.

Hand on sword, he checked behind the potted palms as he passed. No spies, such a pity.

\* \* \*

Nora nearly gave herself away by gasping when the duke's imposing daughter curtsied to her. She should have loosened her laces so she didn't faint from fear and lack of breath.

With her statuesque height and thick dark hair pulled back to emphasize Grecian features, Lady Ann looked more like a princess than her guest. The duke's daughter would be only the first of many such daunting aristocrats offering obeisance. Nora ought to go back right now and find her cousin and tell her she could not be a princess.

Except the princess had been frightened, and talked of saving entire countries.

Courage. She needed courage. And time to think.

"His Grace is waiting for us in the foyer, Your Highness," Lady Ann was saying while Nora fought her panic. "I fear my father is not a patient man."

Oh dear. She'd left a duke waiting. *A duke*! She'd never before met so exalted a personage as a duke, and now he was pacing the hall, waiting on *her*. And he didn't roar when they approached because he thought she was a *princess*. This couldn't be real. Perhaps if she pretended this was a masquerade...

The large, gruff duke bowed over her hand as if she were the queen. Boring schoolteacher Eleanora Adams' work-roughened hand. Thank goodness for gloves! She tried to think like her cynical, sophisticated cousin, but she had no experience in responding to a duke's bow. She could not make this work. She would tell the princess so the moment she saw her again.

In the meantime, she simply said nothing, and let the duke place her fingers on his coat sleeve and escort her to the receiving line. Elena would certainly yawn and say something about tedium. Nora could not insult her gracious hosts. They'd put so much work into this reception!

An army of elegantly-uniformed servants gathered in the

towering medieval hall. Every one of them looked thrilled at just a glance from a princess. Nora smiled at a footman, and he clapped a hand over his heart, before recovering and scurrying back to his duties. She clung to the duke's arm for support, and he patted her hand reassuringly. Everyone apparently loved princesses, far more than they loved sailors' wives!

Lady Ann whispered *bons mots* to keep her amused while the guests crowded in. Nora merely smiled in return. She was too nervous to act bored. She was too tense to speak. The chandelier over their heads contained a thousand crystal prisms, dancing rainbows and light over the immaculate marble floor. Footmen guarded the grand entrance doors with stately grace, bowing as their guests surged through, and Nora stood amazed, observing the glittering gems and gowns and aristocratic faces—all turned eagerly to her.

She couldn't faint now. She'd shame her host.

She would be cast from society forever if she made a dunce of herself. And she surely would. She scarcely knew the difference between a marquess and a duke, much less a viscount and a baron. Did one give one's hand to all of them? And to their ladies?

A smile froze on her face as the old lady first in line creaked a deep curtsy and had to be hoisted back to her feet.

\* \* \*

Resenting standing like a mindless statue behind the reception line, Nick made himself useful by scouting for royal assassins among the guests. Maybe he'd find a French spy under that ancient hooped gown worn by one of the *beau monde's* leading eccentrics. Good gad, the number of poor egrets that must have died for her plumes!

He concentrated on verifying the guests waiting to be received. He knew most of them. Society was small, and he was an earl's son. Both his father and brother served in parliament, although Dabney did not take his seat often. Still, Nick knew the Lords as well as most of the House of Commons. And their ladies. Some of the ladies did not take rejection well. Nick was far more likely to have his claret tapped for his indiscretions than to find a spy at a duke's reception.

Deciding any French spy entering with this crowd of peacocks would be laughing too hard to hide, Nick allowed his gaze to drift to the duke's party in front of him. He checked to see how the princess was behaving—and realized she wasn't there.

Her ugly gown was there, but that wasn't the princess wearing it.

His lungs clenched in his chest, and he thought he'd cough up a hairball before he recovered. He eased closer to the reception line to be certain his eyes did not deceive him in the candlelight.

That was the miserable gray gown the princess had worn, but not the plump derrière he'd observed earlier in the evening. The simple twist of dark tresses was lightened by the sun-bleached strands of Mrs. Adams.

He'd known it, dammit! He'd known the pair would be trouble. He'd expected it. But he'd grown soft if he let a throng of women blind him. Damn it, he'd wanted to die old in indolence.

Cursing, he scanned the parlor beyond, looking for the golden gown Mrs. Adams had worn earlier. But the women were petite and the crush was excessive.

He caught the faux princess's elbow from behind and whispered near her ear, "Where is she?"

Spectacularly thick velvet lashes fell across creamy cheeks. Rather than reply, Mrs. Adams reached for the gloved hand of the next guest in line, accepting pleasantries—while ignoring Nick.

In his fury and panic, he reverted to survival mode, inexcusably pressing her elbow hard enough for discomfort. "Newgate is a bloody unpleasant experience, Mrs. Adams. I think it is time we joined the party."

A noisy altercation in the foyer beyond disrupted the orderly procession in the hall, drawing the attention of the duke's stalwart footmen. Old instincts prevailed. Potential danger required immediate action.

Not lingering to determine the source of the commotion until he had the real princess safely in hand, Nick used the excuse of the distraction to firmly escort Mrs. Adams from the reception line into the mob in the enormous salon.

"She'd better still be here or we're both dead," he snarled, taking satisfaction in watching the rose drain from her cheeks.

"You will please to quit squeezing my arm, sir, and explain yourself." Despite her paleness, she courageously—or stubbornly— resisted his threat.

"You may fool all else in here, Mrs. Adams, but I have an eye for detail. What did you say to the princess to convince her to trade places with you?"

Rich brown eyes flashed furiously, then more warily, as if taking his measure.

"I am here to protect the princess from those who would harm her. I do not intend to fail in my duty."

Duty, she seemed to understand. Nick watched her fight an inner struggle, then reluctantly accept that her disguise couldn't fool him. She grimaced and began studying the crowd. "She made it seem as if England might be in danger. How can I trust you?"

"A duke and the Home Office have entrusted me with the care of a princess. What gives you the right to doubt them?" he countered. "She's played you for a fool for her own reasons."

Mrs. Adams sighed in surrender. "The princess is very young. Now that I've had time to consider the matter, I suspect she is merely engaging in minor theatrics over her proposed marriage, but I have no way of knowing for certain. She wished to run away. I told her to go home with Lady Belden until we can resolve her problem. Is the marchioness still here?" She stood on her toes to search over taller heads.

At least the lady wasn't a complete fool. Relieved that the situation might be saved, Nick tugged her down from her toes.

"Stop looking. Royalty doesn't do anything except wait for people to come to them. Pretend until we find her." Nick led her around the edge of the room, using the advantage of his height to look for the golden gown. "Why would a princess want to run away?"

"I am not a mind reader." Again, she cast him down as if he were an ill-behaved student. But this time, she did not argue or delay in offering her opinion. "But she was most insistent. I thought Lady Belden would be a sensible option until we could determine the source of her problem. But I believe she may have got her bodyguards drunk, so she is not entirely without resources."

Nick uttered a few well-chosen swear words. The Mirenzian for *stupid cow* was the least of them.

# Chapter Six

NORA ATTEMPTED to ignore the irate gentleman hauling her about as if she were an improperly trained hound. Mr. Atherton apparently had reason to fear for the princess's safety, but she didn't think the princess could fall into too much trouble in a ballroom, while wearing Nora's clothes. Elena was no doubt bored already with being treated as a sailor's invisible widow.

She had wanted to be dashing and brave, but Nora realized she'd been manipulated, in the same way as her mother enjoyed pulling her strings. The *Marones were puppetmeisters.* She could see it more clearly now that she wasn't befuddled by imperiousness.

She'd ruined her very first London appearance with this foolish deception. Consoling herself with the knowledge that she'd never meant to linger in society anyway, Nora scanned the room for her lovely golden gown or the marchioness's shot silver.

The salon and the guests were every bit as magnificent and exciting as she had anticipated. The music was angelic, the perfumes rich, the gilded decor far beyond any dream. She would like to simply stand to one side, savoring the beauty, for what little time she had left in this heavenly splendor.

Instead, she was anxiously searching for her dratted cousin so she might turn her over to proper bodyguards.

Obviously, if she could not fool a man who'd barely spoken to her all evening, she could fool no one for long. The princess—or whoever she was—should have seen that, too.

That realization brought Nora up short. The princess had lied to her! The lady had *known* they couldn't pull this off, which meant she might be long gone. To do what? Nora experienced a sinking sensation in her middle. Could she have put her mother in danger?

"I cannot believe she talked me into this," Nora muttered, seething at her own stupidity. "I have never met my mother's family. It all seemed so fortuitous..." Which made her wonder if her mother had known her family consisted of swindlers or frauds and that was why she'd run away to England.

"Royalty learns to dissemble from birth," Mr. Atherton said coldly, as if lost princesses were as common as stray dogs. He dragged her past an arrangement of enormous peonies, irises, and ferns Nora longed to examine closer. "I knew she was up to no good, and I still gave her enough rope to hang us. I will give you the benefit of the doubt and assume you are only guilty of ignorance."

At this acknowledgment of her own sentiments, Nora jerked her hand from his. "I appreciate your consideration," she said in a voice dripping icicles. "Pardon me for helping a relation I thought was in trouble."

"We'll discuss that later. There's Lady Bell. Let's see if the brat has spoken with her."

Nora caught the gentleman's elegant coat sleeve and tugged, forcing him to look at her. "Do not tell her the princess is missing," she commanded. "I have no desire to distress my hostess until we've sorted out this muddle. Let her continue to believe I am the princess."

"Contrary to popular belief, I like the way my head sits on my shoulders. I'd rather not have it severed because I couldn't keep up with a royal mischief-maker." Despite the ferocious scowl he bestowed on her, Mr. Atherton politely cupped her hand on his arm and sauntered nonchalantly through the crowd, in the direction of the young dowager marchioness.

Perceptive and deceptive at the same time was the elegant gentleman.

A petite brunette, Lady Belden represented the epitome of style and graciousness. Nora hated to disturb her generous hostess.

"Royalty speaks first," her escort warned before they reached her.

Nora had been in awe of the powerful marchioness since her arrival. She was taken aback now by Lady Belden performing a graceful curtsy for *her* benefit. It was awkward pretending she was a princess who deserved such deference.

"I did not have a chance to ask my cousin to call early tomorrow," Nora said carefully, trying to mimic Elena's bored tones. "Have you seen her?"

"She is the retiring sort, Your Highness. She asked to be excused, and I sent for my carriage to take her home. I can pass on your message."

Nora suffered a pang of guilt at deceiving her hostess. But until she knew if the runaway had actually returned to Lady Belden's, she dared say nothing. "That is thoughtful of you, my lady." She nodded regally and allowed herself to be led her away.

"The drive will be a tangle," Mr. Atherton muttered, his grip again tightening on her arm, as if he feared she would escape by melting. "I'll have the duke's servants go in search of Lady Belden's carriage." He caught the eye of a footman near the door and gestured.

"Send one to Lady Belden's directly as well," Nora suggested as the servant wended his way toward them. Hesitantly, she added her fear. "I must wonder if she's really royal. Could she be an impostor who resembles the princess? She arrived with no money, no coach, and no trunks. I own very little, but she may try to take what is mine. And anything else she can find."

"Observant," Mr. Atherton grudgingly admitted. He quietly commanded the footman to search for Lady Belden's coach and to send another to her house, before turning back to Nora. "I cannot abandon you to chase after the miscreant myself, much as I would like to wring her neck. We must call in reinforcements."

Alarmed, Nora realized he was heading for Mr. Montague. Dark and brooding, the duke's steward was formidable enough to be an executioner. She looked frantically for his more personable wife, but Mrs. Montague had not joined the circle of somber men in the corner talking politics.

"What if she was telling the truth?" Nora whispered in horror. "What if she really is a princess on a mission to save her people? Is it safe to let anyone know she's escaped her guards?"

She could feel the tension in his muscular arm, but the ferocious Mr. Atherton courteously kept his cursing to languages she did not comprehend. He had responded with authority when he'd thought the princess was in danger. Now, as they approached the group of diplomats, Nora watched in amazement as the fierce knight abruptly altered his appearance into that of an indolent fop. He straightened his neckcloth and lace, brushed off his coat sleeve, and donned a bland smile.

"Damme, Montague," he said, rudely breaking into the discussion by pounding Montague on the back. "Have you seen your wife about? Or Mrs. Adams? The princess is weary from her travels and would like to retire. As much as I would love to escort her—" He left the insinuation dangling.

Mr. Montague frowned and broke away from his fellow

diplomats. He bowed properly to Nora. "Your Highness, I apologize for my friend's extreme impudence—"

"Leave off, Montague, there is an emergency," Atherton said once they were out of hearing of the others. "We need to remove the lady from view and send out search parties. Can your wife keep secrets or do we call in Lady Ann?"

Nora could barely follow Mr. Atherton's rapid transformations from decisive knight to idle fop and back again.

Even though Mr. Atherton had not mentioned that she wasn't the princess, Mr. Montague sent her a look of concern. Rather humiliating that with all her mother's lessons in charm, she could not imitate royalty for more than a few minutes. Of course, the princess *had* been less than charming.

"You have utterly no idea how discreet Jocelyn can be," the duke's man murmured. "If you will follow me, Your Highness, she will be delighted to escort you to your chamber."

Jarred by his use of the honorific, uncertain whether Mr. Montague was play-acting, she refrained from speaking and making more of a ninny of herself than necessary.

* * *

Later that evening, Nora curled up on an ornate gilt arm chair in a far corner of the salon the duke had assigned to the princess. Exquisitely decorated in blue and gold, with draperies so rich they must have cost more than she could earn in a lifetime, the suite could have contained her entire cottage. And it was still not big enough to accommodate the two large, irate men who paced back and forth after she'd told her tale.

The wealth and sophistication of her surroundings intimidated her. She felt like a fish out of water. But men...apparently they were the same everywhere. After a while, their angry questions served only to raise her ire.

"I cannot tell you more than I know," she insisted for the fiftieth time.

"You said she would take Lady Belden's carriage, but she hasn't!" Mr. Atherton shouted, looking decidedly less pleasant than earlier.

"We've sent servants to all the coaching inns. I have a man riding for Hytegate, on the off chance she had a coach hidden. There's naught else we can do until we know her direction," Mr. Montague said placatingly, although he still looked worried.

Mr. Atherton headed for the door as if to follow the servants. Mr. Montague stepped in his way, blocking the door. "You can't abandon a princess."

"Servants won't know how to ask properly at the posting houses," Mr. Atherton protested.

"She can't have any coin on her," Montague argued. "We'll find her between here and Lady Belden's, I vow. We haven't enough servants to do more."

Flinging up his hands in frustration, Mr. Atherton stalked up and down the carpet. "What *precisely* did the princess say to convince you to accept this charade?" he demanded, not for the first time.

Nora merely lifted her eyebrows in response, refusing to repeat herself.

In embroidered waistcoat, with lace at wrist and throat, his golden hair still neatly combed, Mr. Atherton should have appeared a useless fribble, but he'd spent this last half hour ordering people about with ruthless precision, while brow-beating information out of her and anyone else he could find. He obviously hid his cold-blooded nature behind a gentleman's disguise.

"How certain are we that the woman we met was the real Princess Elena?" he demanded now, turning his interrogation to the duke's steward.

Nora had learned that Mr. Montague was more than a financial advisor. He also worked in conjunction with the government in some manner she could not discern.

"I assume there was some diplomatic exchange before her visit?" Mr. Atherton continued. "Was there any verification at her arrival?"

Mr. Montague glowered at him. "As much as you disdain bureaucracy, we have a purpose, and we're not all henwits. We still have ambassadors on the Continent. They're all familiar with Mirenze and the plight of the Marones. The princess traveled with an English diplomatic courier and a party of European nobility who vouched for her. She came with documents from both her father and the consulate. I was with His Grace when she was introduced to the queen."

That didn't mean her Royal Highness wasn't a thief and a fraud, Nora thought. She'd grown up in a harbor town. She'd seen her fair share of charlatans. The Marone resemblance was a reason to believe they were related, but for all she knew, the likeness was quite common. The Marones could have cousins and illegitimate offspring scattered across the Continent like Gypsies. Real princesses didn't do this!

*And she'd set this personage loose to find Viviana.* Would Elena go there as she said she would? Would her mother know if Elena was real or not?

Why would her mother be in danger if she was discovered? Nora clenched her hands and bit her dry lip.

"I take it the scuffle earlier was the arrival of her bodyguards. What did the duke do with them?" Mr. Atherton asked.

"You know His Grace," Jocelyn Montague answered with amusement. "He called them slovenly sots and ordered them to sober up before he would allow them in. The contretemps at the door kept us quite entertained."

"The princess knew they would follow her," Nora said, finally interrupting the male tirades now that Mrs. Montague had asserted herself. "She talked about spies and wanted to escape them, presumably to visit my mother in secret. Has anyone questioned the guards? Might there be some other reason she eludes them?"

"As in, did she rob them of their watches before she left?" Mr. Atherton asked sarcastically. "Charming relations you have, my dear."

"I am not your dear anything," she said crossly. "She has taken my best gown, possibly my identity, might be endangering my mother, and left me to an impossible situation. I had thought I'd persuaded her to wait until morning."

"She feared you were too honest to confuse her escorts. She needed a head start," Mrs. Montague said consolingly. "If she has only gone to your mother, the servants will catch up with her. The question remains, who else do we tell that we've lost a princess?"

"Not His Grace," both men said at the same time. They exchanged grim looks.

"His Grace would feel obligated to report to the Queen and the Prime Minister," Mr. Montague explained. "Losing a princess would be an embarrassment to him and to the state. Until we know more, it would be better for all concerned to keep quiet."

"Could we tell Lady Belden?" Nora asked. "I hate deceiving her. What will she think of me when she returns home to discover I've disappeared without a trace?"

"We don't know that yet," Mr. Atherton argued. "If she's smart, the princess left a note before she stole all your belongings."

"If she was terrified, she simply ran," Nora retorted. She'd lived without material things for so long, she felt only a passing regret for all her lovely new acquisitions, but she knew what it was to live in fear, too, and that was more important. "We do not know enough about her to reach any conclusions. Either way, I dislike deceiving Lady Belden."

"I agree," Mrs. Montague said. "Lady Bell has been too good to us to let her believe she's been abandoned so precipitously. I am persuaded we must tell her."

"Then we should tell Lord Quentin as well, as soon as we have something to relate. Lady Bell seems to trust her late husband's family." Mr. Montague drew out his watch. "The servants should be returning shortly. We can hope the princess, or whoever she is, is peacefully asleep in Mrs. Adams' chambers as we speak."

"The two of you go meet with the footmen," Mrs. Montague suggested. "Mrs. Adams and I will go through the royal trunk now that it has arrived with her drunken escort. Any way I see it, Mrs. Adams will have to pretend to be a princess for a while if we are to fool His Grace."

"I cannot do that!" Nora protested, terrified and humiliated by this turn of events. "I am very bad at pretense. Mr. Atherton saw through my disguise almost immediately. I will appear a great ninny and shame everyone!"

Jocelyn Montague laughed and her husband snorted. Both looked at Mr. Atherton, who leaned his wide shoulders against the wallpaper and studied her with a decidedly wicked gleam in his eyes.

"*Au contraire*, my little pigeon," her not-so-perfect knight said. "You make a far better princess than your hoyden cousin. If I am to escort you about town, all London will be confident that you are who you say you are, regardless of anything we might do."

Nora blinked, confused. She looked to Mrs. Montague for explanation.

"Nick is a notorious rake," Jocelyn said. "But he also knows absolutely everyone in town. No one would ever believe he harbored an imposter, not if the imposter was female, leastways. They'll be quite convinced he knows everything about you, right down to the freckle behind your ear."

Nora blushed clear down to her toes. A *rake*. An angry one. And he would be escorting her about, knowing she was not virgin royalty.

The possibilities for disaster were daunting. And maybe, just a little exhilarating?

She shivered and glanced nervously at Mr. Atherton, who was regarding her through narrowed eyes as if he would very much like to truss her up and heave her overboard. How had she thought him an elegant gentleman? Despite his outer elegance, he looked as ruthless as a...*pirate*.

And she was about to be cast upon society's waters with only him to defend her.

# Chapter Seven

"I CAN'T BELIEVE you got me into this bloody mess, Montague," Nick complained as they clattered down the duke's grand staircase after leaving the women to conspire in the bedchamber.

If Nick hadn't seen the flash of anger in Mrs. Adam's eyes when he'd insulted her questionable relations, he would have thought her an enigmatic sphinx, a da Vinci Madonna concealing secrets. His darker nature wanted to shake her until she told him all. His civilized veneer accepted she might know nothing.

"*I* got you into this?" Montague responded incredulously. "You were the one who lost the princess inside of five minutes of meeting her! I cannot believe it of you."

Well, neither could he, but that wasn't the point. "I'd be warm and happy in a lady's bed by now, instead of heading into the damp cold in search of wayward royalty, if you had not asked for my assistance. You really do not want to cross swords with me on this. You notify Quent and round up more men to search. If she's not at Lady Belden's, she must have planned another escape route. Ladies have a bad habit of hiding coins in corsets and hems. I'll start my search from the nearest posting house. Have some of your men start at the furthest known point, Hytegate near Brighton."

Not waiting for argument from the always argumentative Montague, Nick slipped out a side door rather than rejoin the festivities in the salon. Should his father learn of this disaster, the earl was likely to have an apoplexy and die on the spot. Nick refused to be the son who killed him.

In an effort to forestall using his puny sword to hack his way to the answers he wanted, he called up images of his worshipful sisters before commandeering a duke's stable boy. The lad was stupidly eager for adventure.

As Nick and the boy reached the inn, the Brighton coachman blared his horn and drove his team of horses out the inn gates to the open road. Nick had to yank his mount out of the way. Nora's mother lived in a village south of London, near the Brighton Road. The royal wench could very well be on that coach.

He was half out of the stirrups and calculating the distance from horse to coach roof, before he clenched his molars and restrained his reckless impulse. Other methods, old boy, he told himself. Don't let the pater down and all that.

He strode inside the inn in all his aristocratic hauteur. With rounded vowels and polite authority, he coerced the ticket seller into admitting a female, possibly foreign and traveling alone, had just departed on the Brighton coach.

If this was the damned brat he sought, he'd been minutes from catching her. His frustration rose another notch. At least she was heading in the direction of Nora's mother, as promised. Why the devil would a princess want to visit a rural seaman's widow?

Dusting off his lace, Nick dispassionately produced a few coins for the lad who'd accompanied him. "Be a good fellow and tag along after the Brighton coach, will you? You should be able to catch up at the bridge. Should a lady step off at any posting inns, send word to Mr. Montague and stay with her."

The youth eagerly clasped the coins, delighted to be paid for riding one of the duke's well-fed mounts.

After that, Nick rode hell-bent for Lord Quentin's townhouse, lathering his horse to release his excess of fury. He'd lost a damned *princess*. If he ever got his hands around her neck, he'd throttle the reason why out of the royal nuisance.

She was not in one shred of danger as far as he was concerned. She just had a royal bee in her bonnet that would have been better handled without terrifying her hosts.

If his father died as a result of this ridiculous disaster, he'd force the foolish Mrs. Adams to accompany the grieving countess and his spinster sisters about town for the rest of their lives, while he escaped to the wilds of Borneo and looked for a savage woman to produce heirs.

Concealing his rage behind his mask of indolent sophistication, Nick left his mount in the mews with Quent's servants, throwing them coins to rub down the gelding. He sauntered into Quent's study as if he'd misplaced a watch fob instead of royalty.

The youngest son of a Scots lord, Quentin Hoyt had come to London over a decade ago to make his fortune. Nick hadn't known him back when Quent had been a mere mister with a large extended family starving on a barren Highlands estate. Unlike Nick's society-bred relations, the Hoyts had not thought it appalling for their son to earn a living. Quent's quick wits and hard work had paid off extraordinarily well over the years.

With his father now a marquess, Lord Quentin lived successfully off his business affairs, offering his elegant townhome to a parade of sisters and nieces hoping to make good matches. The late marquess's wealth had stayed with his widow, Lady Belden, so Quent's fortune was all they had.

Unfortunately, London aristocracy still scorned Quent for being a tradesman. Nick thought that laughable, especially since Quent could buy his way into any home he liked with connections he always seemed to know how to make.

Apparently, meeting a princess hadn't been of enough interest for Quent to barter an invite to Fortham this evening. The Hoyt mansion was still well lit as Nick pounded on the door for entrance. A footman ushered him into the study where Montague and Lord Quentin were waiting.

"Brighton coach," Nick announced to his waiting friends. "I have a lad following. Send Penrose and a few of his cohorts in pursuit to be certain she doesn't depart unexpectedly. If it's our runaway, she'll not listen to a stableboy. We may as well let her reach the Archduchess Viviana, if that's her destination, but we'll need to send someone discreet to guard them."

Tall, distinguished, dark-haired, and several years older than either Nick or Blake, Lord Quentin tapped his quill against his desk and studied Nick's disheveled elegance from beneath one arched eyebrow.

Banking his simmering rage, Nick lazily flicked back the tails of his embroidered coat and took a chair near the brandy. He crossed his stockinged ankle over the top of his cursed knee breeches. He was fortunate he hadn't broken his neck riding in dancing slippers. For his audience, he offered a world-weary sigh and poured himself a drink.

"One would think you'd played spy before," Quent said without emphasis. "That was quick work. We've yet to locate Penrose, but we have messengers running about in his pursuit. Wouldn't hurt to send one to Fitz, as well. He's down that way and might be useful."

John Fitzhugh Wyckerly, seventh earl of Danecroft, was a family man these days, with a bankrupt estate and more to do than worry over missing princesses. But he was a good man and an excellent ally. Nick nodded agreement.

One more person who would know his failure to guard a princess. Soon, the whole world would. Nick took a healthy swallow of brandy.

Blake ran his hand through his hair and paced the room like a man demented. "I've read all the diplomatic correspondence. Princess Elena has a mind of her own, but she showed no particular rebellion when Napoleon's puppet arranged her marriage. All reports say she was quite content to live in her father's palace, continuing her usual pursuits, even after her father abdicated and retired to his island estate."

Nick made a rude noise. "And I suppose these reports were written by stiff-necked diplomats who know as much about women as they do elephants. A rebellious female does *not* suddenly become complacent unless she's getting what she wants or is plotting mayhem."

Quent snickered and Blake glared.

Penrose finally arrived, trailing several of his fellow ex-soldiers, interrupting the argument. The former military men were promptly dispatched to follow the Brighton coach, with instructions to keep an eye on the princess to be certain she made it to Hytegate and Nora's home without interference—if that's where she was headed.

"Penrose," Nick commanded, "let the others follow the coach. You head straight for Hytegate and the Archduchess Viviana. Stay out of sight unless you see trouble."

"Archduchess?" Penrose inquired doubtfully.

Nick waved negligently. "Mirenzian royalty stole their titles from both the Germans and the Italian states. If we believe the princess, then Mrs. Ballwin is actually a younger daughter of the late king, Elena's grandfather. The prince and princess crowns go to the eldest, but siblings are labeled archdukes and duchesses."

Blake studied him with suspicion. "How do you know this?"

Nick glared back. "I may be lazy, but I'm not stupid. Mrs. Adams would be Lady Eleanora had her mother stayed in Mirenze. For all I know, she still is. I'll leave appropriate address for you diplomatic types to argue."

Now that he'd made his point, Nick sipped his brandy and disguised his impatience while Blake and Quentin instructed

Penrose. As far as all London was aware, women were his one area of expertise, and in this case, that was exactly what they needed.

"You're asking for trouble," Nick predicted once Penrose and his men had clattered off. "If I know women at all, I know the princess is plotting, and I'll wager she's had more experience at plotting than all of you put together. Once you catch her, she needs to be trussed up and bound to a chair if your intent is to return her home as scheduled."

"We can't truss royalty. The king would have us executed," Blake argued. "Besides, if there's actually a plot afoot and the princess isn't just up to her usual misbehavior, we need to know what that plot is. I already have someone looking into Mrs. Adams and her mother to verify the connection with the royal Marones. We don't want Napoleon's spies knowing about them before we do."

Nick rubbed his brow. "Mrs. Adams isn't heir to a kingdom. Leave *her* locked up at Fortham before the pair of them can cause more trouble. And then I'm off the hook and can go home with a clear conscience."

A rustle of skirt and petticoats announced a new arrival, and he looked up in time to see Lady Belden glowering at him. The marchioness swatted the back of Nick's head with her fan. "That's for losing a princess." She swatted him again. "And that's for embroiling my protégée. You will *not* lock up that poor girl while you go off to play with your latest mistress. I invited Mrs. Adams here to learn more of society so she need not waste away in that dreadful little town forever. If she's actually royalty, then it's even more imperative that she gain town bronze."

Rising in the presence of a lady, Nick rubbed the back of his head and offered his usual smiling charm. "Lady Belden, and how lovely it is to see you, too. I could let my sisters overrun Fortham, and Mrs. Adams will learn more than she ever needs to know about London society. She will be grateful to return to that dreadful little town within days, if only to escape the rattlepates."

The dainty marchioness jabbed his waistcoat with her fragile weapon. "Women must experience the world just as men do, so they might know what is best for them. Marriage is not the only alternative when one has an income. Nora has an excellent mind. She can put it to any number of good uses."

"Like ensnaring Boney's henchmen?" Nick suggested grumpily.

"I'm quite certain she could do as well as you in that respect," the marchioness retorted.

Quentin pulled out a chair for the dowager so they might all sit again. "You don't think the country mouse has come to town simply to find a husband?" he asked, leaning back against his desk and crossing his arms after the marchioness was seated. Defiance gleamed in his dark eyes.

Nick sank back in his chair and exchanged glances with Blake that said *here we go again.* Quent and Lady Bell fought a contest of wills that dated back to the beginning of time and currently involved ridiculous matchmaking wagers.

"Mrs. Adams is dedicated to her mother," Lady Belden said with a huff, adjusting her skirt to fall properly over her dancing slippers. "She already has a suitor. I think she is far more inclined to start a benevolent society for sailors' wives with her inheritance. But first, I insist that she see what she will be missing by isolating herself." She glared at Nick. "And you will be the one to show her. As the escort of a princess, as promised."

Quent grinned. "I wager she'll prefer a London gent and marry him by the time the season ends. Women always fall for pretty graces over rural rusticity."

With a sigh of exasperation, Nick let the squabbling pair repeat their absurd routine, knowing by the end of it that they would have sealed the fate of Mrs. Adams.

Two seasons in a row, Lady Belden had wagered her so-called heiresses would not marry one of Quent's impoverished friends. Two seasons in a row, Lady Belden had lost the wager and agreed to chaperoning one of Quent's sisters as payment.

In Nick's educated opinion, Lady Bell was bored and loved chaperoning the girls. She simply wouldn't admit it to the man whose family had been wronged by the late marquess.

But Nick wasn't poor and didn't need a wealthy wife, so he refused to be part of their scheming. He knew the torture of *real* leg shackles.

As one of the pair's earlier victims, Montague impatiently interrupted their wrangling. "The princess has Mirenzian escorts who will insist on seeing her in the morning. If one of them is a spy, he will report any suspicious behavior. Our best recourse is for them not even to know Mrs. Adams and her family exist. The escorts did not meet Mrs. Adams tonight. Tomorrow, they will only see the princess, if we treat her as such. Sorry, old brick, but you'll be escorting the lady to all the diversions arranged for visiting royalty, as planned."

Nick could give him a thousand reasons why this was a very bad idea.

# Chapter Eight

IN THE DIM hours of dawn, Nora tossed and turned in her sumptuous bed in a princess's suite, unable to sleep while last night's events raced through her head.

In this past day, she'd met dukes and royalty, eaten elegant foods she didn't recognize, and sat at a dinner table sprinkled with noble guests. She'd walked through a magnificent dream wearing silk and lace in the glitter and glory of an exclusive London soiree.

And then she'd made a complete flat of herself and ruined it all.

As a child, she'd had idealistic dreams of adventure and protecting England with her daring, just like her father, but when it came right down to it—*argh*! She buried her face in her pillow in shame. She was out of her element and must admit it.

A maid entered to replenish her coals. Nora pretended to sleep until still another servant entered with a tray of clattering utensils, and she heard irritated male voices in the corridor. She might as well be sleeping in a public inn.

She listened as the chambermaid departed and closed the door after her, but the second woman bustled about, apparently laying out clothing. It seemed a princess had a busy life that started early.

A princess. She could not think of a masquerade more ridiculous for a country schoolteacher.

"Your Highness, His Grace is waiting," her lady's maid said softly, obviously fearful of waking sleeping royalty.

Nora thought she might like to learn to curse. Keeping the sheet pulled to the neck of the princess's virginal cotton nightdress, she sat up in the canopied bed draped in rich velvets and damask. Lady Belden had promised to send over Nora's own trunk when they could discreetly smuggle it in. Thank heavens the princess had not stolen it.

Trying to think generously of a cousin who had taken advantage of her was a strain, so Nora sat silently while the maid arranged a tray containing hot chocolate and rolls on the bed. Hot chocolate was a rarity she could not remember having since a Christmas before her father died. She wanted to savor the pleasure, but the duke's well-trained maid rattled off her daily appointments and tarnished the moment.

At least her cousin had undergone the ordeal of meeting the Queen and her court, and Nora did not have to go through that. Otherwise, it seemed as if all London meant to entertain the princess while she was here.

After finishing her chocolate, Nora bathed and donned an insipid, pale pink muslin. Elena either had exceptionally bad taste or had hidden her favorite clothes elsewhere. Given their brief encounter, Nora would wager on the latter.

With her hair stylishly dressed in pastel ribbons suitable for an unmarried maiden, Nora was escorted to the breakfast room by a sturdy Mirenzian soldier who bowed stiffly and followed at her heels. She was so miffed at her own cowardice that she didn't care if the soldier knew she was an impostor. What could he do? Scalp her?

That thought stiffened her backbone. She had no more reason to fear sharing breakfast with a duke than she had of the bodyguards. His Grace didn't know Elena or Nora. To a man that powerful, a deposed princess was merely a pawn on a chessboard.

As long as she was assured Mr. Montague and Mr. Atherton were guarding her mother, she would face whatever the day brought.

At least Lady Ann was present to act as buffer. "I think perhaps we should send apologies to our first appointment," the duke's daughter said after taking one look at the dowdy pink gown. "Our first appearance should be with my modiste. She will be ecstatic."

Since Nora assumed a princess would require a wardrobe far beyond her own needs, and she had no intention of spending precious funds meant for her mother's comfort, she politely demurred. "My budget is limited, my lady," she said, sipping tea, imitating the elegance Viviana unconsciously employed in her every movement. "The war has hurt the people. I cannot justify such expense on my poor self."

Both duke and daughter looked startled at the concept, and Nora hid her smile. If she was to be a pawn, she would be one with a mind of her own.

She would simply keep telling herself that there wasn't a thing anyone could do to her after placing her in this ridiculous position—unless there was a law about aiding and abetting runaway princesses.

"Nonsense," His Grace blustered. "You need only use my name, and the accounts will be forwarded to the Exchequer when I receive them. What you wear will be in high demand for months and will generate income for our hard-working English tradespeople. That is how it is done. The wealthy owe a responsibility to the less fortunate by sharing their wealth in a productive manner."

Nora puzzled over that concept as she nibbled kippers basted in a delicate lemon sauce and crepes rolled in finely milled sugar and stuffed with scrumptious marmalade. She could buy her mother's medicine for years with the cost of this one meal. His wealth had bought fine food for his table, but she did not understand how that would feed a soldier's widow.

Still, if he wanted to buy a wardrobe for a princess, so be it.

By the time she'd cleaned her plate, she'd decided if the wealthy spent their funds on education instead of gowns and lemon sauce, seamstresses and servants could better themselves instead of working their fingers to the bone for little or nothing. But the duke would not appreciate her revolutionary notion.

Although if Princess Elena was to live among French radicals, perhaps espousing their cause would serve her cousin well. It would not enhance her popularity in England though. Nora had to twist her mind to think like a diplomat.

So Nora smiled and nodded and agreed to a shopping trip. When she was done, Elena would be stuck with a wardrobe that suited Nora's taste. Let her cousin learn how it felt to be taken advantage of.

That thought sustained her until Mr. Atherton arrived.

The dandy was even more resplendent in buff pantaloons and gleaming, high top boots. He looked as if his valet had sewed the navy tail coat onto his wide back, and the crisp, snow-white cravat at his throat must have come fresh from the linen-makers.

"Good morning, ladies," he said cheerfully, helping himself to coffee and a chair without invitation. "What is on the schedule today?"

"Nothing for which we need an escort," Nora said coolly, enjoying borrowing Elena's arrogance to needle this annoyingly self-confident coxcomb.

"On the contrary," Lady Ann said enthusiastically, "Nick will be able to advise us on what all the other ladies are wearing, and what you need to exceed them all!"

"Ridiculous extravagance," Nora protested. "A walking gown or two, a new ball gown, and I shall be fine. I am not a peacock."

"One hopes not, Your Highness," Nick said with a wicked leer. "But I would not recommend being a peahen either. I must insist on escorting you, if only to fight off all the suitors two such lovely ladies will collect when seen on the street."

Nora wondered if princesses were allowed to say *balderdash!* Ignoring his inappropriate jest about cocks and hens, she sipped her tea and attempted to look regal. "Nonsense. We will have footmen. I'm certain you have better occupation than warming the chairs at a milliner's."

"No, actually, he doesn't, Your Highness," Lady Ann said with a smile. "Nick is a useless fribble who idles his days away, so let us employ him to a purpose."

Perhaps Lady Ann was not as astute as Nora had thought, if she did not recognize Mr. Atherton's sharp mind and arrogant character. Beneath the languid gestures and silk and lace, he radiated the intensity of a seething male who would like to strangle them both right now. Very odd.

Without expressing agreement, Nora finished her meal in silence, wishing she had a newssheet to hide behind as the duke did.

Her uniformed bodyguard stood straight with his back against the far wall, properly watching everything she did from behind the concealment of a rather disturbing mustache.

* * *

Nick pushed back his coat tail with one gloved hand and kept his other occupied with his walking stick rather than risk reaching for the blade in his boot every time a stranger approached the ladies. Of course, with a flick of his wrist, the cane would become a sword, but that was expected of a sporting Corinthian. The hidden knife...that would be harder to explain in a dressmaker's shop.

Civilization was an entertaining challenge.

"The purple one," Nick suggested vaguely as Lady Ann studied several bolts of satin. Playing the part of dandy, he waved at a fashion doll the modiste had suggested. "In that style there. With jet beads."

Lady Ann actually considered the ugly purple-brown. The mock princess, however, gazed on him with imperious disdain and removed a different bolt of fabric from the shelf. "The marigold velvet for the bodice, please," she told the modiste, "with gold tambour embroidery, and the white muslin with gilt threads for the skirt. With pearl beading."

Nick hid his grin of satisfaction. She had contradicted every single one of his choices, until he had taken to choosing the worst possible combinations so she would buy the pretty ones.

"Really, Mr. Atherton, you are being of no help at all," Lady Ann protested. "Puce is not purple, and black and puce, indeed! One would think you wished the princess to look like a dowager."

The *princess* was actually a widow and probably ought to be wearing black and puce, but if he was to escort her about, he wanted her in gold and pearls. And perhaps some of that peachy color she'd admired earlier and had disdained after he'd pulled the bolt out for her. He was determined to get her into that color—after they found the princess and she returned to widow. For now, she was stuck with the boring whites of a maiden.

"The fashion will be for higher waists than that," Nick said, knocking over one of the dressmaker dolls. "So any bodice will be very limited. If Her Highness wishes to save coins, then relegate the more expensive fabrics to the bodice."

If he wasn't so annoyed with her, he would enjoy the way the little widow blushed whenever he mentioned bodices. She wasn't used to men noticing her breasts, more fool she.

"I will only need the one evening gown," Mrs. Adams said with quiet authority. "I should like to see a half-dress gown with higher décolletage, please. We are more modest in my country."

Nick stifled a snort and pointed out a doll with ruffles around her neck. "Perhaps that one? In crimson?"

"Nick!" Lady Ann cried. "A maiden cannot go to the park wearing red! I do believe you are being ridiculous on purpose, so we will release you from your obligation and tell you to go away."

Oops, not quite what he had in mind, not while that damned stiff Frenchie with his saber waited outside the shop. Mirenzian, he was not. The soldier might know the language, but not the accent. He reeked of Napoleon. Nick hoped Montague had located the bodyguards' credentials in one of those massive diplomatic folders the government accumulated.

"I give up then," Nick conceded languidly. "The princess must do as she wishes in gowns, but I want to be there for the milliner."

He had spent weeks of his life affably entertaining his sisters and mistresses in shops without a thought in his head beyond their pleasure. He would sip whatever beverage was provided, offer advice when asked, and happily carry their purchases to waiting carriages. He'd vowed long ago to never be bored if he had a full stomach and his luxuries, and so he indulged himself.

Why was he grinding his teeth now and all but pacing the floor as the pretend princess hesitated over the purchase of the perfect cloth or a cheaper variation? He wanted to grab the expensive bolt, shove it at the modiste, and order the daring gown he'd suggested earlier. There wasn't a doubt in his mind that the willful baggage escaping to the coast would have chosen half a dozen of the most expensive fabrics given the duke's *carte blanche*.

But the widow was not accustomed to wasting coins. With malice aforethought, Nick placed himself between Mrs. Adams and Lady Ann. He stepped closer to the widow. The widow scurried to examine the bolts on a different shelf. Step by step, he cornered her where no one could overhear.

"A princess would not be hesitating over pennies," he murmured, pulling down a fine muslin liberally woven with glittering metallic threads. "She would have ordered a dozen gowns of the most expensive materials and be on her way to the next shop by now. You are behaving like a shopkeeper, my dear."

The warm velvet of her eyes hardened to brown diamond as she haughtily took in his proximity and the manner in which he'd cut her off from Lady Ann. "I am even less than a shopkeeper, sir. And if my cousin is so wasteful, I will not be the one to publicize it. Have fabric from this bolt sent to my mother." She dropped a rich royal blue into his arms.

Nick carried the expensive bolt to the counter, almost laughing at her ability to turn the tables on him.

She might annoy the hell out of him, but he was starting to enjoy the contest of wills. It distracted him from wondering how many spies were hiding around the corner.

# Chapter Nine

"FOR TONIGHT, the duke has accepted an invitation for the princess to attend a ball in her honor held at Lady Jersey's and hosted by several of the Almack's patronesses." Back in the princess suite in late afternoon, Lady Bell held up the ball gown they'd appropriated at the modistes and had altered to fit Nora. "I think you will enjoy that far more than a stiff royal dinner."

Nora had been appalled when Lady Ann had usurped a prepared gown, as if royalty could have anything that caught their eye. The poor woman who had been trying it on hadn't argued with a princess and a duke's daughter. Lady Bell equally seemed to think they'd done the right thing. And even the woman had seemed flattered.

Nora simply couldn't adjust to such selfish notions. Perhaps if she'd had a lifetime...

The shoes she'd had to buy to match the dress had cost another small fortune, and they didn't fit all that well—just as she didn't fit this exalted company.

"Have we heard anything from the men following my cousin?" Nora asked nervously, once the maid had left the room to find thread to tidy a piece of lace. She was growing painfully aware that every word she spoke was overheard. "Perhaps the princess will return in time to attend."

"If I had anything to say about it, Princess Elena would be turned over my knee and spanked once she returns." The charming marchioness looked unusually miffed. "True royalty respects their subjects and does not put other people to the test as she has done. She has ruined your debut. No one will know you as yourself, and no gentleman will even attempt to know you better as long as they think you're out of their reach."

Nora shook her head to dispel such fancies. "I did not expect gentlemen to pay attention to me. I merely wished to see the sights and go home happy to have done so. This way, I'm seeing far more than my humble self could have expected. I simply worry that the princess will come to harm on the road."

"You are a better cousin than the wretch deserves, but you are not to be concerned," the dowager admonished. "Mr. Montague and his friends have seen to everything. She will have a quiet coze with your mother and will be back here by tomorrow. You have just to smile and enjoy the dancing tonight."

Her new corset pushed her breasts higher as Nora sighed and prayed the lady was right. She'd love to have no worries beyond remembering the next step. She simply wanted to be on the dance floor, enjoying the gowns and the music. She resolved to do so and trust in her more sophisticated London acquaintances to deal with the mysterious etiquette of retrieving Elena.

"I shall simply pretend to be the fairy tale princess who disappears at midnight," Nora agreed. "I hope these gowns can be adjusted to the princess when she returns. I will have no use for them again."

"Don't be ridiculous. The princess can find her own gowns. We'll add vivid underskirts and ribbons to these, then introduce both of you at some function or another, and everyone will have a good laugh. We'll worry about that when the time comes. Here, Lady Ann sent up these pearls. They will work well with that neckline. Tonight is your night to shine."

Nora hoped she was shining by the time she was dressed and escorted down the duke's stairs to meet her waiting retinue. Her hair had been dressed with curls and flowers. The rope of pearls had been wrapped and re-wrapped until the diamond pendant snuggled between her breasts. She wore a white gauze overskirt, but the pale gold silk underskirt was more suited to Nora's married status than the princess's. Elena was European royalty. People could assume her country's fashion was different. The fabric draped in crisp but elegant folds just above Nora's ill-fitting embroidered slippers. The effect had taken hours to produce.

Her self-consciousness evaporated the instant she saw Mr. Atherton lounging against the mantel. He'd been with her most of the day, garbed in a gentleman's pantaloons and tailored coat, sartorially exquisite and verbally inane.

Tonight, with his attention on a note in his hand, he'd returned to dashing. She scarcely noticed the duke and his daughter. Her handsome escort took her breath away.

Apparently squiring a princess required silk breeches and sword and lace. His golden hair gleamed in the lamplight. At the sound of their entrance, he slipped the note into a pocket and straightened. Having caught him unaware of her observation, Nora felt her breasts tighten when he did look up.

His aquiline nose and sharp cheekbones were a trifle too carved, adding a harsh cast to features normally disguised by the seductive smile of full lips. The flare of male appreciation in his eyes aroused long dormant desires. It was unfair to finally discover attraction again in a man she'd never see after she left the city.

She couldn't flee or avoid his presence, and if the truth be told, didn't want to. For one night, she could pretend and live a fairy tale.

She graciously laid her gloved hand over his silk-coated arm, and smiled up at him as if she had no other thought in her head except the picture they created, her gold against his black.

"The gown is fit for a queen," he murmured as he bowed over her hand.

"And it can go back to one after her servant has worn it," Nora replied wryly, so no one but he could hear.

His lips cocked in wicked appreciation, but the interlude disappeared all too quickly.

"Your carriage awaits, Your Highness." The leader of the Mirenzian guards stood at attention near the door, eyeing them with suspicion. Tall and dark, with a formidable mustache, he never smiled.

Nora wondered if she was supposed to know his name. But playing the part of princess, she merely accepted her wrap from her escort, lifted her gown above her new slippers, and with her retinue following, allowed herself to be led to her coach. She hoped it wouldn't turn into a pumpkin at midnight.

The duke and his daughter took a separate carriage so Lady Bell could travel with Nora as chaperone, Mr. Atherton as her personal escort, and her soldiers as bodyguards.

A uniformed guard rode with the driver. Another assumed a postilion's seat. More waited on the street, apparently prepared to follow on foot. After seeing the three passengers inside, the mustached leader checked the door's lock, then stood at attention on the footboard, clinging to the door handle as the carriage lurched into the street.

"Can he hear everything we say?" Nora whispered.

Nick nodded, touched a finger to his lips, and produced a snuff box from his coat pocket. "I took the liberty of providing a few peppermint candies in case you wish to sweeten your breaths," he said in a normal voice.

Nora didn't comment on the unusual use of the box but widened her eyes at the calling card note beneath the candies. She and Lady Bell helped themselves to both card and candies, exclaiming aloud over the treat while surreptitiously straining to read the note hidden in their gloved palms.

*Lt Gerard Martine, Imperial Guard* was scribbled hastily in an elegant script.

Nora gestured to indicate the tall soldier guarding the carriage door. Nick nodded.

The Imperial Guard! One of France's finest soldiers, guarding her cousin. *Her.* He ought to be in uniform!

Nora blinked as she realized what the lack of uniform meant. He was one of Napoleon's spies! The seriousness of the charade they played destroyed any hope of engaging in pleasant fantasies.

"The candies are delicious, sir," she simpered, returning the box and the card. "You are so very kind."

Palace intrigue, just as Viviana had warned. Nora's heart beat a little faster. What could the French do to her if anyone discovered her deception? She was an Englishwoman, after all.

But the menacing man at the door didn't look as if he cared about such niceties. England was at war with France, so he was the enemy.

She, plain little Nora Adams, was being watched by a dangerous French spy! Was this how her father and Robbie had felt when they sailed into enemy waters? She could scarcely keep her hands still.

"The prince will not be there this evening," Lady Belden said in her most officious tones, for the benefit of the spy. "Lady Jersey and her friends will meet you at the door. Lady Ann and the duke, as your hosts, will then take you to the reception line. Your hosts will choose your dancing partners."

"Or I will be your partner," Mr. Atherton said wickedly. "Then you need not bother with all the other drab and boring men."

Would a princess acknowledge his outrageous flirtation? Would the spy know how a princess would respond? Most likely not, Mr. Montague had said. She could behave as she pleased.

"I think I shall take my chances on the other gentlemen of London rather than waste my time on a peacock," she said loftily. "A lady does not wish her elegance to be surpassed by her partner."

Lady Belden sputtered. Mr. Atherton grinned. "You have no idea what you're asking. Don't come begging to me later when your toes are sore and bruised."

"I think I shall choose my partners by how they dance. Lady Anne will no doubt be of inestimable aid."

Nora thought her companions approved her haughty attitude, but the carriage arrived in Berkeley Square and no more was said in the bustle of footmen and the mob outside number 38, straining to catch a glimpse of royalty.

Once, she might have been in that crowd, dying to gaze upon a distant and more glamorous world. Those poor people had no notion that a princess was just like them, except in fancier—and less comfortable—clothes. She'd never look at fairy tales the same way again.

Footmen pressed the mob away as she climbed the stairs, her gloved hand on Mr. Atherton's arm. She noticed he kept his other hand firmly around his decorative sword hilt, as if expecting trouble. The carriage had outpaced her foot soldiers, but the three guards who had arrived with them formed an outer barrier. What did one do with royal guards once they were inside? It wasn't as if she'd seen Elena with any—although she now sympathized with her cousin's desire to escape their constant presence.

By the time they reached the reception line, Mr. Atherton had released his sword, but he radiated tension. The charming dandy had transformed into an arrogant stranger who abandoned pleasantries to curtly post her guards where he chose. He made this game too real. She pretended he didn't exist as she entered an enchanting storybook scene.

Crystal chandeliers blazed. Granite columns sparkled. Polished marble floors reflected light and color. Enormous flower arrangements scented the air, along with exquisite perfumes—pure enchantment. Nora wished she could paint the tableau.

Lady Anne and the duke introduced her to her famous hostesses. Nora had read about the Almack patronesses, but in person, they weren't the paragons of wealth, beauty, and sophistication that she'd imagined.

Had they been stripped of their expensive garments and flashing jewels, they would be little more than the vicar and mayor's wives, filled with self-importance, in charge of their own small world. She supposed these ladies must help with benevolent societies just as the vicar and mayor's wives aided the poor, but on a grander scale befitting their fortunes. But one was frumpy, one was silly, and another looked as if she suffered permanent frostbite. Human.

If she kept in mind that the elegant creatures crushing through the hall were not gods and goddesses but people just like her, she might breathe easier.

Once past the reception line, they entered a ballroom lit with wax tapers scented with lilac. Bouquets of lilac and other blooms graced the gleaming Sheridan tables. The most important matrons of society had decorated a ballroom in hopes of impressing *her*.

She was certain Elena wouldn't have noticed or cared. At least Nora appreciated the beauty, although she did wonder at the extraordinary expense when the widows and children of His Majesty's forces went hungry.

"It's so artificial," she murmured with an odd disappointment, mostly to herself since Lady Ann was speaking to Lady Belden.

"It's civilized," Mr. Atherton countered. "I'd much rather wage war on a dance floor than in a mud field."

"Is that what we're doing? Waging war? How? That sounds much more intriguing."

He cast her a surprised look. "Veritable soldier, are we? Perhaps we should have fed you sooner so you aren't feeling so bloodthirsty." He snapped his fingers and a liveried servant arrived with a tray of delectable morsels from which to choose.

"I am too excited to eat." Although she did savor a bit of pastry and cheese she could never have at home. She'd heard about the French custom of providing small bites before dinner but had never seen them served. "But I must admit, being followed by French spies and bowed to by dukes is far more thrilling than ironing handkerchiefs. How did you learn who Martine is?"

"Montague's diplomatic friends are well-informed," he said with a shrug. "I believe the duke is about to introduce you to your first partner. Rothbottom is a pompous ass, controlled by his mother's purse strings, but I am told he dances admirably."

In anticipation of finally dancing to beautiful music, Nora ignored her escort's insults. She held out her hand to a gentleman with receding hair and a sagging jawline. He could have been a rabbit for all she cared. She wanted to join the dancers.

Tapping her toe, she dismissed Lord Rothbottom's hand-kissing and relaxed only when he led her to the floor.

The orchestra was sublime. The other dancers glittered with jewels and silk and feathers. Nora glided through the set as if in a dream, with a nearly invisible partner who regarded her with solemnity and caution. Knowing she need not waste time impressing him, she was free to float on winged feet, enrapt in the music alone.

Being carefree for just this stolen moment was worth every minute of terror she'd suffered since Elena's deception. By tomorrow, Nora would be a seaman's widow again. But tonight...tonight was divine.

Until the moment she noticed Mr. Atherton conferring with his friends in a far corner, and their agitated gestures and frowns indicated the subject wasn't pleasant.

When they glanced at her, she tripped.

# Chapter Ten

"THE PRINCESS has fled," Montague reported. "She visited with Mrs. Ballwin as expected, but no one saw her leave. The archduchess insists the princess only visited an hour and left."

Hearing this latest catastrophic development, Nick had to deliberately peel his fingers from his sword hilt and force his usual expression of unconcern. He still wanted to bash heads and slice necks.

*Relax,* he ordered himself, *smile, say something witty.*

"Lady Bell has already offered to spank the brat. Perhaps we can send the princess to bed without supper after we find her," Nick suggested, nonchalantly removing a sticky candy from his odd snuffbox, while his companions continued to look grim.

"I don't think you understand the seriousness of losing a princess," Montague protested. "She's eluded French spies and the best soldiers in the kingdom. We need to discover what maggot she's got in her head. I think we need to return Mrs. Adams to her mother and demand explanations."

Mrs. Adams had been smiling as if she'd been gifted with heaven just moments ago. Nick had relished watching such naïve happiness. Now, glancing in their direction, she stiffened as if she heard every word they said. Had someone stomped her toe?

"Leading French spies to a Mirenzian archduchess, an enfeebled one at that, is not one of your better ideas," Nick protested, straightening the lace at his cuff while studying the other dancers for anyone who might have insulted a princess. "I propose we simply tell Mrs. Adams that the princess has been delayed on the road."

Nick knew Montague hated lying and dishonesty, but the world revolved so much more smoothly when everyone heard what they wanted to hear.

He offered Mrs. Adams a sweeping bow and a smile of appreciation when next she glanced in his direction. Instead of looking relieved, she frowned. No woman could be that discerning, could she? His family always fell for the reassuring gestures he used to hide his scheming.

The set ended and she was led back to the duke, on the far end of the room. He waited with interest to see with whom she danced next. The duke had his task cut out for him, choosing between politically expedient candidates and men who wouldn't break her toes.

"And while you're dangling after the widow here in London, the rest of us must scour the roads of England for a straying princess?" Acton Penrose asked with a scowl. "You're the one who lost her. Why do you have the comfortable task?"

Because if the task was left to him, he'd slay a French spy, hijack a coach, hold Mrs. Adams at gunpoint, and threaten the conniving archduchess in order to find a princess.

But Nick resisted terrorizing friends and family. Instead, he gestured insouciantly. "I'll happily ride up and down the byways calling her name while you attend these charming gatherings in the company of His Grace. By all means, please."

Penrose scowled even more at mention of the tyrannical duke.

Montague intervened. "We need Nick close to the widow to detect anyone unknown attempting to reach her. The princess is most likely running from danger, so we are jeopardizing Mrs. Adams by continuing to use her."

Nick hid his displeasure by turning back to face the ballroom as the music struck up again. He sought the widow where she'd last stood, but she wasn't there.

He didn't go into full alert until he traced the path she should have taken with her next partner and didn't see her anywhere near the dance set forming.

He had already left behind his friends and their argument and was almost half way around the outskirts of the ballroom before he found her—bearing down on him with a look as grim as his own.

She trailed a nervous Lady Ann, who sent him a glance of relief.

"Her Highness claims she promised this set to you," Lady Ann declared, her narrowed eyes clearly expressing her disapproval.

"I make it a point never to argue with a princess," he said ambiguously, bowing and taking the widow's hand. "It would be my pleasure."

"What is wrong?" the widow whispered as he led her into the first open set under the critical eyes of her hostess.

"Why must you believe anything is wrong?" He performed his most elaborate bow, while she curtsied in line with the other women.

This was a *contre danse* that required paying attention to who was doing what, which meant that all around them could and would watch and listen. And they were dancing with the lesser nobles who had yet to make her acquaintance and who were inclined to stare in awe.

Aware of their audience as they promenaded down the floor, through the line of dancers, Mrs. Adams murmured through a carefree smile. "I can tell something is wrong because I'm not a six-year-old selfish child blissfully ignorant of the world around me."

"Or arrogantly unconcerned," he offered, deliberately diverting the topic by referring to the princess. "You have all London at your feet. You are to be admired for your integrity by not taking advantage of the fact."

"My integrity, or lack thereof, is not in question," she responded angrily. "But you are insulting my intelligence and testing my patience."

The next couple in line threw them startled looks, but Nick laughed and pressed a daring kiss to his partner's knuckles. Everyone expected him to flirt outrageously. An older couple shook their heads in disapproval but returned to concentrating on the steps.

"There is a time and place for everything," he said soothingly. "You are to enjoy the evening and not fret over what you cannot change."

"My mother?" she asked, her gaze anxious.

"Is fine. Probably having a roaring good time if she's at all like you. You learned to manipulate a duke's daughter pretty quickly."

"Apparently audacity is a family trait," she said dryly.

She looked as if she'd like to say more, but with the set moving quicker and closer, it was simpler to let conversation move on to the music and the conviviality of the company.

The lady was as quick of mind as she was fleet of foot, Nick noted with approval, admiring her slender ankle revealed by her coyly lifted skirt. Under other circumstances, he would delight in dancing with her. But as long as she portrayed a princess, flirtation led nowhere.

His friends had reported that the princess's bodyguards were stationed at every exit, and even though he'd ordered Martine to guard the front, the soldier was even now watching from the ballroom entrance.

Elena had been right to fear her bodyguards. These were not men under her command.

"We are being watched," he leaned over to whisper as he led her back to Lady Belden after the dance ended. "Bamboozle the sapwits by acting as if you're having the time of your life."

"I *am* having the time of my life," she replied unexpectedly, flashing a glorious smile. "Just as long as you can reassure me that no one has come to harm, I can dance the night away and disappear at dawn, if need be."

He could offer no such assurance, but he couldn't tell her the princess had gone missing, not while all the world watched. "The lady is dangerous," he told Lady Belden as he handed over the humble widow. "Don't let her out of your sight for an instant."

Which was just daring the chit to do something reprehensible, Nick could tell from her challenging glare. He should have laughed her off or teased her into submission, but instinct had him shielding her against unseen dangers. He wanted to lock her in a closet and stand outside, pistols drawn.

Why, of all the women willing to play a princess, did this one have to be an independent, intelligent sort instead of an obedient, empty-headed doll?

Because no other woman of his acquaintance would have daringly—or naively—traded places with a princess.

Damnation, she would drive him to drink or murder if they didn't sort out this cock-up shortly.

* * *

At the end of the evening's last dance, Mr. Atherton was flirting with Lady Bell and Lady Ann. Nora had half a mind to elude him and run home to her mother to be certain all was well, but she knew that would be dangerously foolish. The exhilaration and freedom of dancing all evening had simply gone to her head, making her rash.

She took Mr. Atherton's arm and nodded regally in reply to her hostess's questions, ignoring the foreign spy hovering just to one side as they left the ballroom with the rest of the departing guests. She *felt* like a princess in this elegant attire, so it was not difficult to pretend to be one. And her antipathy for the Frenchman came naturally. Her husband had died protecting England from reprehensible murderers like Martine.

"The modistes again in the morning," Lady Belden said as they entered the carriage. "You will be available for limited morning calls tomorrow afternoon, before we all set out for a soiree at Melbourne House."

"I don't suppose the opera is on our agenda?" Nora asked, dreading the stilted conversation of morning calls and soirees.

"Too public," Mr. Atherton said irritably, glaring out the coach window as if he expected assassins in the street. "Perhaps we can suggest to Lady Melbourne that the princess would like to see one of the singers tomorrow evening."

Nora still did not know what was happening that had the gentlemen looking so grim. Were they confirming that the real princess would not have returned by the morrow or were they simply play-acting for the sake of the guard at the door?

"Have Lady Ann send around a note to this lady." Mr. Atherton produced pencil and paper and scribbled a note. "Once she has agreement from the performer, the duke can speak with Lady Melbourne, and she might arrange for musicians, if she wishes."

The lamplight was very poor and Nora had to strain to read what he'd written. *Cuz ran away again* she thought it said. She wanted to crumple the note in fear but had to tuck it away as if it were vital information. So, they were play-acting to deceive the guard who watched through the window and listened to every word.

The princess wasn't coming back?

"We are appreciative of your efforts on our behalf," she said stiffly, trying not to panic—although her heart beat so erratically, she thought she might be having an attack.

She must have succeeded in hiding her fear. Lady Bell and Mr. Atherton gossiped about the evening the rest of the way back to the duke's mansion as if they hadn't a care in the world. Unaccustomed to the long hours or exhausting emotions, Nora simply froze in place.

Not until she realized both of her companions were joining her in entering the duke's mansion did she wake from her reverie. The three bodyguards on the carriage were dispatched to the servants quarters while a good, solid British porter shut and locked the doors behind them.

She raised her eyebrows questioningly.

"Since the hour is late, the duke has invited us to stay," Lady Bell said. "I've had my trunks sent over. We might as well make the best of this while we can."

"I believe the duke's invitation was phrased more along the lines of 'Keep those demmed Frenchie spies out of my house,' but it amounts to the same," said Mr. Atherton with an offhand shrug. "One does not question the commands of dukes."

"May we talk now?" Nora asked cautiously as they headed up the stairs together.

"You may wish to stop in my suite for some of that face cream I told you about," Lady Bell suggested, leading the way down the upper corridor, creating a safe topic for the benefit of any servants listening. "Mr. Atherton will have to retire to the gentlemen's wing after he sees us to our chambers."

The corridor seemed interminable but at last they were in Lady Bell's suite with candles flickering and servants out of sight. Nerves taut, Nora turned to Nick with the note he'd slipped to her in the carriage. "What does this mean?"

"It means the princess was seen entering your home disguised as you and has not been seen since." There was a decided look of suspicion in Mr. Atherton's expression as he regarded her.

Nora almost resorted to hysterics, until she recalled Viviana's devious ways. Wearily, she shoved a straying wisp of hair behind her ear.

"My mother was raised with court intrigue. When I was young, she used to amuse us, and herself, by appearing at our door as a Gypsy or a fairy godmother or a royal duchess, depending on her mood. She can't get about much these days, but her costumes are still in a trunk in the attic. I don't suppose your spies noticed a hunch-backed maid departing through the kitchen gate?"

Lady Belden collapsed on a settee with her hand at her throat. "She could be anywhere!"

"We've lost a royal princess—*again*." Mr. Atherton paced the floor. "We ought to send you back to Mirenze in her place. Serve the wretch right."

"That's probably what she fully intends," Nora replied.

# Chapter Eleven

"WHAT DO YOU *mean, 'that's what she intends'*?" Nick forced his voice to a low rumble instead of the explosive shout working up inside him.

Losing a princess would create shocking repercussions. Nick was the one responsible, but the duke couldn't execute an earl's son. Montague would be the one to pay, with his position and the loss of the duke's support in Whitehall. Blake had a wife and family to feed, and the country *needed* his encyclopedic mind, even if England didn't deserve it. The damned princess had to be found.

"You're asking why would the princess want to send me to Mirenze in her place?" Mrs. Adams asked in surprise. "Isn't that rather obvious?"

"She's a blamed princess with a castle and loyal subjects, despite Napoleon. Why would she throw that away unless she's sitting on a pile of gold elsewhere?" Nick couldn't conceive of a young female flinging away her family and home to flee into uncertainty. Women didn't *do* that. Surely the princess would reappear on their doorstep once she'd had her little flight of fancy.

Mrs. Adams regarded him with disbelief. Apparently, her opinion varied.

"Because she's young and rash and doesn't wish to marry some fat old man forced on her by Napoleon?" she suggested. "And that's just the most obvious. We could follow with—her family is scattered to the winds, she hates a moldering old castle, she has a lover somewhere, she longs to visit Egypt... Want me to continue?"

Nick ran his hand through his hair. None of his sisters would do such a thing. No woman he knew would have traded places with a princess—even for a day, as Mrs. Adams had. It must be something in the exotic Mirenzian blood that craved mad escapades.

"You need to speak with your mother and find out what the princess told her," he said. "But we can't risk letting the French know the archduchess is alive or where she lives or they'll learn about you."

"Besides, if my mother is protecting Elena, she won't tell us anything but nonsense," Mrs. Adams said dryly. "I can write a note, if you can have it delivered, but do not expect a sensible reply."

Nick knew what it was like to live as if everyone was an enemy. He almost admired the crafty old lady. "Write the note, and I'll see it delivered. Then let's keep up the playacting until we have a response."

Accepting Mrs. Adams' hastily scripted missive, he bowed out of the ladies' parlor.

He would have run to his chamber had he known where it was. Instead, he had to stow his impatience and saunter after a footman to where his clothes had been taken. His trunk had already been unpacked and the bed warmed. A fire crackled in the grate and hot water waited behind the dressing screen. This was how he'd meant to live the rest of his life—in comfort and luxury and appalling laziness.

Not chasing after escaped princesses in the middle of a cold foggy night.

He stripped off silks and lace and hunted for his riding breeches even as he cursed his fate.

He was still cursing as he took the servants' stairs down to the kitchen. He appropriated an old cloak hanging by the kitchen door and took the outside stairs two at a time. If any of the Frenchmen noticed him striding through the fog into the mews, they gave no indication. A moment later, he was slipping down the alley to the river.

The tide was with him. With the aid of the duke's watercraft, he was in Chelsea by dawn. Montague had said he would take his family to their country estate so he could conceal from the duke his frantic directing of the search for the princess. Nick wasn't looking forward to the menagerie that was his friend's home life, but he didn't intend to handle a fraudulent princess all on his own.

Rather than wake the household in the early dawn, Nick used a slender blade from the bad old days to pick the conservatory door lock. By the time the family began wandering down to break their fast, he had taught the parrot a new word, helped Blake's odd brother-in-law add bars to a monkey cage, and helped himself to a plate of bacon and a cup of coffee.

Jocelyn Montague raised her lovely blond eyebrows at finding him at her breakfast table, but Blake's wife was as devious as Nick. They'd come to a comfortable understanding once she understood that Nick had her husband's back at all times.

"We're not to escape the Problematic Princess even out here in the idyllic countryside?" she asked.

"Your husband got me into this. The least he can do is help me out," Nick agreed, slathering his toast with jam. "We need to speak where there aren't a thousand ears listening."

"That's not here," she said blithely. "Even the parrots talk. And Walter will repeat every word if he finds them at all interesting. And let's not start on my mother or the babbling infant."

"Better than Frenchie spies and the duke's snot-nosed servants. We can hire a boat and sit on the river, I suppose, but I need fortification before heading back to another round of dressmakers." Yesterday, he'd enjoyed watching the modest widow brighten with wonder and excitement over the variety of fabrics—when he'd stupidly thought it would be just for a day.

Montague entered with one of his wife's feathered friends on his shoulder. He scowled at Nick and poured a cup of coffee before speaking. Nick leaned back in his chair, crossed his legs, and waited for his cranky host to oil the cogs.

"Don't tell me the widow has fled with her cousin," Blake finally said after a few gulps of the inky beverage. "The duke will have me beheaded."

"The widow thinks her cousin has permanently fled, leaving Mrs. Adams to go back to Mirenze in the princess's place. We need to find out what the royal brat discussed with the archduchess." He handed his host the widow's note addressed to her mother. Wordlessly, Montague tucked it in an inside pocket.

"You don't think I've had my men ask?" Montague bit savagely into a boiled egg without bothering to take a plate. He fed the rest to the bird on his shoulder. "The archduchess simply says they had a lovely coze and caught up on family matters and claims to have no idea that the princess meant to run away."

"The princess knew where to find a disguise," Nick pointed out.

"The archduchess said her family goes about in peasant clothing all the time. She claims that the princess simply meant to have a little fun while letting her cousin enjoy London. The archduchess appears to approve."

Nick bit back his curses and threw back another gulp of coffee. He had no desire to publicize the misdeeds of his youth by revealing the depths of his eccentric knowledge, but he couldn't withhold information that might aid Montague. And Mrs. Adams.

"As you're aware, the Marones are the hereditary rulers of Mirenze, through either the male or female line. What you might not have bothered to learn is that the last Marone king had *four* daughters. Elena's mother, Giovanna, was the eldest and hence became the queen and the one everyone knows."

Blake nodded acknowledgment. "We knew there were more sisters, but Mirenze is too small to bother tracking the powerless."

Nick snorted at this underestimation of the power of women. "The three younger archduchesses scattered. The next eldest sister married some obscure Austrian noble and had a son. The third eldest disappeared into Prussia years ago, but rumor has it that she, too, had a son. Viviana vanished mysteriously at the same age as the princess is now—no one even knew she was alive. I suspect Elena is following her example. Which means—what are the chances that one of the male cousins is plotting an overthrow?"

"I'll not ask how you know so much about an obscure European duchy any more than I asked how you know the language, but yes, we're aware of the cousins." Blake sipped his coffee with a scowl. "Inquiries have gone out. But it's difficult enough to send messages through the fronts. Sending royalty is another matter entirely. We should have been informed if the cousins were on the move."

Nick rolled his eyes heavenward. "You are thinking like a pampered British noble who sends soldiers into war with a target on their chests. Believe me, the Mirenzians are survivors. And apparently, masters of disguise," he added with disgust.

Blake shrugged. "I can't see how the obscure cousins matter. I don't think Napoleon will allow challenges to his plans. As the daughter of the queen, the princess is crucial to the alliance he wishes to forge in the Italian states. Elena must know that. Chances are good that she's doing just as the archduchess says—going out to play until she gets caught and has to face her responsibilities."

Nick had seen the princess in action. He was pretty certain *playing* wasn't in her vocabulary.

He rose to refill his coffee cup. "Then I propose that we post notices in the paper that the princess has come down with a dreadful contagious illness, lock Mrs. Adams up somewhere safe, and start scouring playgrounds for your lost princess."

"You know better," said Montague, adding bacon to his plate.

"The duke would hear complaints from the queen if the princess is sequestered," Jocelyn Montague said with a desultory wave of her hand. "Blake would suffer the duke's wrath. Modistes and milliners throughout London would rise up in arms at being deprived of this occasion to dress all the ladies for the round of entertainments planned."

"My sisters would personally behead me," Nick agreed.

"Besides, Mrs. Adams deserves her whirl through society," Jocelyn continued. "Lady Bell would enlist Lord Quentin's aid, and together, they'd twist arms until they forced you to unleash Mrs. Adams on London."

"Blake, you'll owe me into eternity for this," Nick muttered. "I'll be old and gray within the week if you don't find the princess and haul her back here at pistol point."

"I'm trying to find out how much coin she had on her," Montague said, unperturbed. "The royal jewels were sold long ago."

"She only needs a man with money," Jocelyn pointed out. "I suggest looking into her former suitors."

Nick and Blake both uttered their favorite expletives.

# Chapter Twelve

"HAVE YOU recovered your lost cartwheel yet?" Mrs. Adams asked politely that evening as Nick escorted her to the carriage for their nightly round of entertainment.

Since he had lost a princess and not a cartwheel, it took a quick twirl of his brain to follow her question. He had to hide his amusement when his thoughts caught up with hers. A cartwheel was cant for a *crown* coin. Clever wordplay, a crown for a princess.

The mustached faux-Mirenzian guard bowed and held the carriage door for them. Nick could swear the pointed tips of the man's whiskers quivered like a cat's as he eavesdropped.

"Nary a trace," he replied with a carelessness he was far from feeling. "If it were worth the effort, I would start where I last remember seeing it." And ride straight to Hytegate and her mother, but he'd been overruled on that score. Blake should have had the note delivered by now.

"A coin that large means a lot to some people. Could it have been stolen?" She settled her skirts and cloak so Lady Belden could join her on the forward-facing seat.

"A cartwheel is only worth a few shillings," Lady Belden said dismissively, not following the path of their conversation. "Nick loses the like at the tables every night. It's the price of entertainment."

"I leave gambling to Fitz, who has a head for numbers. I've better ways to idle my hours," Nick said, stretching his legs to annoy the demure widow by brushing suggestively against her slipper-shod toes. "I have a dislike of misplacing hard-won coins and feel compelled to track them down."

"Or replace them," Mrs. Adams replied, obviously deriving some wicked pleasure at his expense. "Too bad one cannot inquire of everyone within your vicinity when you last had it in your hand. Perhaps someone noticed what you did with it."

"And pocketed it," he said gloomily. "It could be on a ship to India for all I know."

Finally understanding that Nick wasn't cast in gloom due to a coin, Lady Belden shook her head. "It's foolish to ponder the impossible. Have your servants hunt about where it was last seen. They're more competent at such things."

Nick sent her a glare, but his part of irresponsible fribble did not allow him to insult a marchioness. He preferred it when he could actually *be* a careless fop.

"Did the opera singer agree to perform this evening?" the faux princess inquired, diverting his blue devils.

"What performer would refuse to entertain royalty?" he asked, more irritably than he liked.

"Oh," she said quietly, before sinking into the cushions. "I had not meant to coerce a performance."

Nick shot her a look of exasperation and shoved her slipper, hard. "The penalty for being royalty is lack of privacy and security. Others must help alleviate that price."

Teaching a seaman's widow to become royalty might have been amusing under other circumstances, but he'd rather leave those lessons to her deceptive archduchess of a mother. He wanted his life back.

Disgruntled, he glared out the window at the ugly guard clinging to the door. Perhaps he could arrange an accident.

That's what Devil Nick would have done—removed any danger to his survival.

The Honorable Nicholas, Lord Atherton's son, would never slit a throat. Damned nuisance, that.

The widow kicked his shoe in return and spoke in her haughtiest royal tones. "Then we should dispense with useless royalty. When was the last time your monarch did you any favors?"

Nick had to chortle at that. "Prinny buys pretty architecture. Does that count?"

"Paying for creative genius is the price of being wealthy. Monarchs should *rule*. Your Parliament has tied your royalty's hands, rendering them useless. A country should be loyal to its monarch."

To England's mad Georgie or to the Marone kingdom or who the devil was she talking about? "Only to the extent that the monarch is loyal to his people," he said grumpily. "And how often does that happen? Unfortunately, royalty is as human and selfish as any other creature on God's earth."

That made her frown. He didn't usually argue with women he

meant to seduce.

*So that's what this argument was about.* Despite her annoying independence, the widow was lovely and intelligent and he'd enjoy sharing her bed. And he couldn't while she played the part of virginal princess. Damn, he used to be better at doing two things at once.

The carriage arrived at Melbourne House and their little tempest in a teapot dissipated. Out of sorts, Nick turned his back on the Imperial spy to aid the ladies out of the carriage. Not until Mrs. Adams laid her gloved hand on his arm and darted him a small smile did he realize his irritation wasn't at her, but at having their argument interrupted.

\* \* \*

Forced to appear calm, gracious, and slightly bored for the benefit of Lady Melbourne's guests, Nora feared she might burst her seams with nervous energy. She extended a gloved hand whenever Mr. Atherton pinched her elbow, nodded graciously at curtsies, and wished everyone to Hades.

She could not even take too deep a breath for fear of bursting out of the modish gown Lady Belden had insisted she wear. Despite—or because of—their earlier squabble, Mr. Atherton's attention kept drifting to her bosom rather too frequently. And she wasn't insulted but excited.

The dark carriage had offered an intimacy that had allowed her to speak freely, as she could not here under a thousand candles with people all about—and with her escort peering down her bodice, keeping her flustered.

The dastardly efficient cad positioned her guards while greeting half society and reminding her of names she'd already forgotten. He nudged her into proper courtesies, while steadily steering her through the crush to the throne set aside for her at the front of the room.

A throne. Nora wanted to turn and run. Mr. Atherton blocked her path and urged her into the gold-embellished armchair. Hand on his sword hilt, he stood slightly behind her, his sharp gaze assessing anyone who approached.

"I can't take much more of this," she muttered in between bowing guests. "I cannot blame my cousin for fleeing. I trust she is having a great deal more fun than I am."

"If you decide to don a disguise and flee, please be so kind as to notify me first," he grumbled *sotto voce*. "It would be unutterably cruel to force me to hunt for two of you."

"I am unfortunately too practical to risk the lives and positions of others for my own fancies," she said with a resigned sigh. "But I do worry about my cousin."

"If even mild-mannered Lady Belden is threatening to spank the chit, you have reason to worry. Splendid gala, Lady Melbourne," he segued into Prince Charming mode without hesitation as their hostess approached. "You look ravishing, as always."

The lady tapped his arm with her fan and made her curtsey to Nora. "Madame Radicati has agreed to a solo performance for your highness this evening. I believe she is known on the continent as Teresa Bertinotti. She's been widely acclaimed at the King's Theatre for *The Magic Flute*. Is your highness familiar with the story?"

"My mother follows..." Nora corrected herself. As the princess, her mother had recently died—another reason to sympathize with her lost cousin. "My mother followed opera enthusiastically. I simply enjoy listening."

The notorious Lady Melbourne, said to be the mistress of Prinny and numerous other nobles in her day, was little more than a stout old lady in grandiose clothing, Nora noted with disappointment. The viscountess would have been a peer of her mother's, had Viviana cultivated noble circles.

Perhaps wealth did not provide the happiness and freedom Nora had enjoyed while growing up. She'd loved fencing with her father and standing at the harbor, watching the ships come in. She wouldn't have liked to have been raised by nursemaids while her mother slept with other men. But then, she was her mother's daughter. Viviana had apparently chosen a quiet life for a reason.

As Lady Melbourne prepared her guests for the arrival of their entertainment, Nora whispered to her escort, "I begin to understand why an archduchess and a princess would seek a different life than this one."

"It's a splendid life," Mr. Atherton argued. "You would rather starve?"

"There is no middle ground?" she countered. "May I not have pretty gowns and good food and not sleep with the prince?"

He coughed and didn't come up for air until Lady Melbourne shot him a glare from the front of the room.

Nora smiled and nodded regally as the pianist was introduced and bowed to her. She thought perhaps her mouth might crack at the corners if she must do this much longer. Only Mr. Atherton's company let her sit back and enjoy a few moments here and there. She was too tense with worry and too self-conscious unless he was whispering information and gossip in her ear. He provided a marvelous distraction.

So did Madame Radicati. Fascinated, Nora fell into the glorious song as if it were a spell woven around her. Thirstily, she drank up every note as one whose soul had been parched. Never in all her life, had she imagined such magical majesty produced by a simple voice. She almost vowed to do anything so she might hear such beauty again. *This* was why one would wish to be a princess.

At evening's end, Nora applauded enthusiastically, standing before anyone else, forcing the gentlemen to wake from their naps and their yawning companions to hurriedly set aside fans and accoutrements to applaud.

"She's not that good," Mr. Atherton whispered, "But you'll own her for life after this performance. You've permanently filled her theater."

The singer was, indeed, in tears. Bowing nearly to the floor, she wiped her eyes and threw kisses before her husband led her away.

Nora had done that. Stunned to realize she could influence an audience of jaded London sophisticates, she hastily took Mr. Atherton's arm and indicated she wished to leave.

"The guests will be disappointed," her escort murmured. "They were hoping to bend your ear for a few hours more."

"To what effect?" Nora asked. "To let them know my dress designer? What musicians I would recommend? I'm sure they don't want my opinion on the Poor Laws."

"And I'm sure I don't want you offering them," he agreed. "Not in public, leastways. Play emotional collapse. Wipe away tears. I'll steer us out of here."

Nora had no difficulty wiping tears. The music had been elevating, and tears of joy were no different from any other kind. She clasped Lady Melbourne's hands and murmured her sincerest gratitude. She plied her fan as if unable to find words as others crowded around her.

Lady Belden caught on and quickly aided Mr. Atherton in guiding her through the throng. So much attention for someone as inconsequential as Robbie Adams' widow!

A tall dark-haired gentleman joined them in the crowded hallway, adding his broad shoulders to the cadre forming around her.

"Lord Quentin Hoyt, your highness." Lady Belden hastily introduced them. "My late husband's younger nephew."

Lord Quentin wore a worried frown and looked as if he would say something, except the Mirenzian bodyguards began forming an impenetrable barrier. Trusting Mr. Atherton to inform her of any news from the worried Lord Quentin, Nora looked for an opportunity to help the two to speak privately.

She donned a flirtatious smile, tapped one of her younger guards on the arm with her fan, and exclaimed her pleasure over the evening. She danced playfully out of Mr. Atherton's reach, forcing her guards to hurry her in wake.

Mr. Atherton frowned, but she noted over her shoulder that he managed to exchange a few words with Lord Quentin. In consequence, Mr. Atherton's pleasant demeanor formed an even more ferocious scowl that should intimidate anyone daring to cross his path.

She really didn't want to hear unpleasant news after so marvelous a performance, but if the princess wasn't returning soon, it might be time to take matters into her own hands.

# Chapter Thirteen

ISABELL HOYT, Lady Belden, swept up and down the boxwood path behind the duke's terrace. "This is ridiculous, my lord. I haven't attempted an assignation since I was sixteen years old! I'm much too old for this foolery."

She vibrated with such energy that any overlong branches danced out of her path without touching. A pity to leave all that vitality locked away, Quent thought, watching her from afar, as always.

"You are barely older than my younger sisters," Quent reminded her. "And I'd not qualify this as an assignation—unless you wish it to be," he added suggestively.

Returning in his direction, she tapped him with her fan to express her annoyance. "You are practically my nephew. That's laughable. Why did you call me out here?"

Equally annoyed but not revealing it, he replied with his usual composure. "We are in no way related except by nature of the wealth you hold, which rightfully belongs to the marquessate."

"And which also belongs to every other poor relation Edward refused to support and to every merchant and tenant he robbed. Stand in line, my lord. The list of people who deserve my riches is long, indeed. Are your sisters enjoying their London debut?" she asked with a hint of spite.

Since Lady Bell was financing their debuts, Quent acknowledged her direct hit. "They are, my lady, and we've a young cousin eager to do the same. Our usual wager if your protégée finds her match among my friends?"

"That's scarcely a fair wager while Mrs. Adams is disguised as a princess," she argued. "Our last wager was a tie, and I'd like to prove myself this time. If you're foolish enough to make one, I do unabashedly enjoy your matched bays. I might keep them another year."

"As long as they're available for the use of my sisters, agreed." He glanced over the hedges, verifying no one had followed them. "We have reason to believe our missing *cartwheel* has gone to ground somewhere in the vicinity of Brighton. We need to keep our... guests...busy and distracted while the others search. Perhaps a house party at your country estate in Essex?"

"At the height of the season?" Sounding appalled, Lady Bell fluttered her fan and paced the walk. "What about His Grace's country estate?"

"The duke's estate is in Surrey. We want to distract the guards *away* from Brighton. Essex is well out of the way."

"The place is a medieval barn," she protested. "Your father might appreciate it, but no one else."

"You know perfectly well that my father won't leave Scotland to take up residence in England. You're the one who has life possession of the Hall. I'd offer up his home in Scotland for a house party, but I daresay we'd hear considerable objections," he said wryly. "Crofts aren't much better than barns. And your barn is closer to London. Society can travel there easier."

"Society would sooner spend the winter in London than travel to *Essex* at any time. Are you certain this is necessary? Perhaps we could arrange a series of entertainments. Her Highness might wish to tour Oxford. The duke could open up Blenheim. Really, Windsor would be so much safer—"

"Really?" he interrupted dryly. "You want to let Her Highness's spies loose in the king's corridors? Better that they go hunting in your fields."

"It's not hunting season," she said grumpily. "They'll have to hunt each other. This is not at all what I wished of this season," she added with resignation. "Rural solitude, my word!" She shook her head in dismay, then took up plotting. "The medieval hall is large enough for state dinners, of course, and balls and such. But the chambers... You do not appreciate how miserly Edward was."

"I do appreciate that you're not Edward," Quent corrected. "We'll call it an idyllic retreat to the pastoral countryside to clear the palate for more regal affairs later. Just a few days."

"I'll send the servants ahead," she agreed with a sigh. "We'll have to offer our regrets to every important hostess in London. They'll see me hanged. My reputation will be in tatters."

"Blame it on the duke, then invite all their daughters and sons. And Sally and Margaret, of course," he said wickedly, naming his sisters. "If nothing else, they will have your chambers cleaned and refurbished for pennies within days of arrival."

"And is your young cousin equally wise in household matters?

Best send her along as well. There could be birds nesting in the canopies for all I know. Mice in the larder. I shudder to think."

"We'll send the girls out with the servants. The girls are all the managing sort. The princess may buy out London tomorrow, order heaps of gowns for next week, and depart the day after. Our duty will be done toward the merchants."

"But scarcely to the hostesses of London. Their wrath will be on your head, my lord. I've had quite enough of their tittle-tattling as it is. You would not like it if I could no longer give you access to the wealthiest nobles in the kingdom." Distressed, she stalked back toward the duke's mansion, no doubt already making lists of things that must be done.

Quent admired the way her mind worked even more than he admired the sway of her simple gown. He was more than happy to bear the burden of society's scorn. He'd done so most of his life. It was the fair lady's scorn he didn't wish to earn. Why had she acquired that brittle shell?

He'd always loved a good mystery. He should have done a little research sooner. He'd start on it after the princess was found.

* * *

While Nora sipped her delicious tea and nibbled at a delicate, buttery pastry in her chamber the next morning, maids bustled about, lighting the fire, heating water for her bath, displaying a scrumptious collection of walking dresses from which to choose for their shopping expedition. She needn't stir a finger.

She might not mind this part of being royalty. The maids liberally sprinkled her rose powder into the bath water, and the chamber smelled heavenly. She was warm and cozy and— not in the least content.

With a sigh, she poked her bare foot from beneath the silk sheets and the down counterpane. She could not be content while worrying over her cousin and her mother. She had not slept for thinking of Mr. Atherton and his broad shoulders and impressive smile—and his concern for others. And his wicked tongue and sharp mind and...

She had been living with dull minds too long, she decided, and that's why she'd taken a fancy to Mr. Atherton. It was ridiculous to fan the flames of infatuation over a lazy rake just because she suffered the pangs of desire for the first time in years. But it had been so long...

She had never given virtuousness much thought. She'd been loyal to Robbie because she loved him dearly. After his death, no other had appealed to her. She and Fred Connor had a mutual respect and understanding that both expected to become more, perhaps after his father let him run the grocery. She expected to be loyal to him. Virtue had just happened because she had no alternative.

Did she dare...? Not yet. She was too wary of her new role.

The news that Elena might have been seen in Brighton only reinforced Nora's hope that her impetuous cousin had run off with a handsome, wealthy young suitor. Then she wouldn't feel quite so guilty feasting at the sumptuous tables prepared for royalty, or buying gowns that the real princess couldn't wear. The brat owed her for this torture of spies and worry, if she was out honeymooning.

When Nora was finally downstairs and ready for the outing, she noticed Mr. Atherton looked as if he hadn't slept well either. Barely shaved and looking surly he handed her into the duke's carriage without his usual engaging charm—but crushed a note into her glove.

Once inside the carriage, with the Mirenzian guard just outside the window, Nick produced an assortment of newssheets. "I thought you might enjoy the lovely reviews of last night's performance—yours as well as the singer's."

Nora took one of the sheets and opened her note behind it.

Her mother's cramped, illegible writing was unmistakable, as was her chronic misspelling. Should she hand the missive to the guard, he was unlikely to make even a bit of sense of it. In this light, Nora could scarcely hope to decipher more than a word or two.

*Out...nettle...pluck...tontine ...soon.*

She tucked the note inside her reticule and let Mr. Atherton and Lady Bell discuss the newssheets while she ran the words through her mind.

*Tontine?* Out, nettle, pluck teased her mind with familiarity, but *tontine* worked in no quote that she knew. She needed to look again to see if she misread a letter or misspelling.

*Out of this nettle, danger, we pluck this flower, safety.* Shakespeare. The quote flared in Nora's mind as one Vivi had used frequently when speaking of her husband's career.

The quote did not relieve her mind.

Once they reached the dressmaker's, Mr. Atherton argued with the guards, curtly smacking his walking stick against the stones when they dared contradict him. In officious Mirenzian, he ordered the imperial spy to stay with the carriage as it circled the block.

And cursed under his breath as the towering, mustachioed guard ignored his orders by standing on a corner and watching while they promenaded from shop to shop.

It was exceedingly difficult to read and discuss the note while pretending to shop.

"You cannot fault him for doing his duty," Nora whispered to her escort.

"He is no better than a ruthless pirate guarding his prisoners," Mr. Atherton retorted. "This is English soil. I'm in charge here."

He steered her into a milliner's, and his deceitful smile returned as he nodded at the proprietor. "Good morning, *madame*, and I have returned as promised."

"*Oui, monsieur*, you are all that is noble and proper and our gratitude is great at being able to serve her royal majesty." The black-garbed milliner dipped a deep curtsy.

Fascinated by her escort's changing facades and by the glorious inventory of hats and bonnets, Nora ignored her school-teacherish urge to correct the honorific. She was no queen. But then, she wasn't a princess, either, so who was she to argue? "May I see the white and primrose straw, please? I think I shall make primrose my signature color. Perhaps with the addition of a few violets?"

As she tried on bonnets, with the note burning in her bag, Nora watched her escort from the corner of her eye. He paced the front of the shop, occasionally exchanging pleasantries with Lady Bell but mostly watching out the windows. The petite milliner ignored him as she added ribbons and flowers to her creations at Nora's request. But Nora noticed the tension in Mr. Atherton's shoulders, the alert way he kept his hand on his sword, and the way he narrowed his gaze at any movement on the street.

His powerful muscles alone proved this man was no indolent rake. Was he a British spy? Had he read her mother's reply? Or understood it?

"Mr. Atherton, your opinion, please." Nora managed to phrase it as a royal command. "Does this color make me sallow?"

He swung on his heel and regarded her with icy blue eyes that warmed to summer skies as he admired the pert bonnet she'd chosen. "Ideal! It frames your lovely cheekbones. What a pity it must hide her your beautiful hair."

There was the rake—but was he the façade, or the tense soldier underneath? "You are a flirt, sir." She reprimanded him as she untied the ribbons. "I shall need new gloves for the new evening gown. Pearl gray, I think. May we walk? It is such a lovely day."

"Not pearl gray," Mr. Atherton said with a frown. "Never gray on you. Always the colors of autumn. Do you not agree, Lady Belden?"

"Cream, I believe," the marchioness said as she prepared to leave.

"You have a door in the back, *n'est ce pas?*" Nora inquired sweetly of the shopkeeper, adding her best steely undertone as she swept past the counter without waiting for an answer.

There was little a poor shopkeeper could do to deny a princess. The milliner hastened to remove boxes and hat stands so the royal entourage could sweep through her dusty workshop and out into the narrow alley.

Caught by surprise, even Lady Bell and Mr. Atherton refrained from scolding until they were out of earshot of the milliner and her staff.

Nora, using royal privilege, spoke first. "I think we should make our imperial spy earn his wages. I cannot believe my cousin ever made it easy for him. We will alleviate his suspicions and keep him busy so he has no reason to look for the real princess."

For the first time that morning, Mr. Atherton appeared genuinely amused. "I do believe you are correct, your highness. Shall we head to Gunter's for ices? I'll have the glove maker come by with some of her wares while you dawdle in the street and drive the spy mad."

"It would be better to have the carriage to eat in," Lady Bell fretted, lifting her gown and regarding the alley with disdain. "A princess cannot stand about in the street. She'll collect a crowd."

Did Lady Bell know of the note? What was expected of her in these circumstances? None of her mother's anecdotes involved racketing about London with spies in pursuit.

"If we call the carriage, I'd rather go farther than Gunter's," Nora declared. "A park, perhaps? I would love to see more of London than ballrooms and shops."

Apparently approving, Mr. Atherton led them to another street, avoiding the corner where they'd last seen the imperial spy. He gave a boy a coin to chase down the duke's carriage. "Such impropriety," he said with a gleam in his eye. "You ladies shock me, *shock*, I say."

"Leave off, Nick," Lady Bell said. "It is nothing you wouldn't have suggested had His Grace not terrified you into behaving."

"It is not the duke who terrifies me, it is my mother," he declared, handing them into the coach. "If I'm caught scandalizing a princess, she will decide it is time a wife take me in hand, and I will be inundated in virtuous misses."

"A fate to be feared, indeed," Nora said mockingly as the closed carriage pulled from the curb. "Oh, I do prefer this freedom!" She gazed approvingly out the window with no bodyguard in sight. "I can appreciate how poor Elena must feel, trapped in a box day and night. The ability to speak freely is a prize I had not appreciated so much until now."

"You have many things to say that you don't wish others to hear?" Mr. Atherton asked with interest, while he studied the passing scenery as if expecting pirates to leap from the curb and attack.

"I dislike curbing my tongue, admittedly. I've not had to do so, except with the children. With my students, it's easy enough, because they have inquiring minds and other interests to distract from the unpleasant. But I should be able to speak my mind to adults, who don't need to be treated like children."

"You overestimate adults," Mr. Atherton said dryly.

Scowling, Nora removed the note from her reticule and lifted a skeptical eyebrow at him. At his nod, she unfolded the paper to attempt closer perusal.

"I do not understand *tontine*," she admitted. "I cannot think of any other word this could mean."

"I had hoped it was a code word," Nick said, revealing with his admission that he'd read the note. "The rest appears to be a mangled quote from Shakespeare?"

"King Henry," Nora said absently. "One of my mother's favorite quotes. But I'm quite certain *tontine* isn't in Shakespeare."

"It's French," Lady Bell said unexpectedly, "a financial term, I believe. The participants in a tontine contribute and share equally in some prize that is ultimately awarded to the survivor. A rather foolish concept developed a few decades ago. The French are all quite mad."

*Survivor?*

Nora tried to restore her breathing by studying the greenery as the coach turned into Park Lane—Hyde Park, the place where the fashionable went to see and be seen, a wonder she had only been able to dream of visiting.

The carriage slowed to make the turn through the gates. Mr. Atherton shouted "Down!" and slammed her to the floor.

A sharp noise rang out, shattering the coach window where Nora had been sitting.

# Chapter Fourteen

AS THE COACHMAN lathered his horses into a reckless dash to escape any further shots, Nick bit back his fury and frustration. His task was to protect the ladies with his life, not leap from a galloping coach in futile hope of throttling a villain. He pried his fist from the sword and pushed up on his elbows to assess the damage.

The jarring bounce of the wheels still brought him into intimate contact with rose scents and yielding feminine flesh. But the widow seemed unhurt, and so did the shocked Lady Belden.

Curbing his rage, he breathed deeply of flowers and forced himself to think in civilized terms instead of irrational violence.

Any gunman would be on foot, able to slip into the crowds in the street before Nick could reach him. The experienced coach driver was whipping his horses into a frenzy through the empty park, out of range of pistols. He heard no more shots.

There was absolutely no reason to leap out in hopes of thrashing anyone within an inch of their lives, no matter how much he'd like to indulge in physical violence instead of this damned subterfuge.

Fighting his insane urge to shoot back or climb out of the carriage to take the reins, thereby terrifying all London plus his paralyzed companions, he almost forgot the slender woman he'd nearly crushed into the floorboards. When she elbowed him, he forced his muscles to relax and let the duke's coachman handle the horses as he'd been trained to do. Devil Nick knew ships, not coaches.

"I think we may be safely away, sir," Mrs. Adams said dryly from beneath him.

He heard her well enough over Lady Bell's epithets and tears. He simply wasn't ready yet to stir. Her calming presence could very possibly have prevented him from drawing his blade like a berserker.

He'd never been over-fond of flowers, but he could learn to appreciate roses. The scent calmed his racing pulse. With more nonchalance than he felt, he shifted his elbows and moved his hip to remove his weight, if not the protection of his body.

"Are you all right? Were you hit anywhere?" Taking her chin between his fingers, he turned Nora Adams' delicate face to be certain there was no blood. She did not have the pale complexion of an English rose, but the more Mediterranean one of her ancestors. He'd never liked white anyway. "There's a scratch." He wiped at her hair line. "Not serious, it appears."

"I'll be fine if I might sit up and find a handkerchief." She elbowed him again. "I appreciate your dedication to duty, sir, but I don't think we've been followed by an army."

"This is dreadful," Lady Bell was saying above them. "Nick, perhaps you ought to keep Nora down there until we return to Fortham. There could be anarchists on every corner!"

"I doubt that seriously, my lady," Nick said, biting back a sigh.

He eased up from the floor and helped the little widow into her seat. She looked luscious even when disheveled. And her gaze was mutinous. Interesting.

"Anarchists, or French spies?" she asked with shrewdness.

Nick scanned the interior for holes. He located the trajectory from window hole, to Mrs. Adams, to a tear just above Lady Bell's bonnet. "If you will excuse me..." He removed a knife from his boot and pried the lead ball from the upholstery.

He examined it with a whistle. "Pistol ball, not flintlock. No sporting man would carry one of these."

Both ladies went pale and silent. Nick mentally slapped himself, pocketed the lead, and smiled cheerfully. "We only need hunt for a drunken duelist who overslept dawn."

"And mistook a duke's carriage for his opponent?" the ever astute Mrs. Adams asked. "I don't suppose it's possible to determine if it's French or English?"

Worse, this size only fit a Prussian pistol, one of the deadliest weapons in Europe. "If one makes one's own ammunition, then it could be anything," he said evasively. "We shouldn't refine too much upon it, but leaving for the country suddenly has its appeal," he lied. He despised the countryside. "If anarchists are after a duke, then we'd best warn His Grace."

Nick didn't think he'd diverted Mrs. Adams, but Lady Bell frowned and nodded agreement. English politics were rife with enough violence that assassins were credible. The duke didn't work hard at being liked.

Nick was just fairly certain the Whigs hadn't taken to shooting dukes with Prussian pistols.

Someone European had been shooting at a princess.

The word *tontine* took on a more immediate meaning. Coupled with the quote about danger, the message left him wanting to package the would-be princess up and ship *her* to Borneo.

Lady Bell checked the scratch on Mrs. Adams' forehead, and the two women reassured each other as the coachman ran his cattle ragged to reach the safety of the duke's London estate. The gates to the estate swung open without the carriage halting and swung closed again after they entered. His Grace's servants operated like well-oiled machinery.

The princess's bodyguards would not be pleased at being left behind.

Nick relaxed a trifle at the thought of the plaguey mustached Martine having to tramp across London not knowing where his prisoner was. He'd told the man to guard the coach. A good walk served him right.

He ushered the women inside, ordered extra footmen at all the doors, and cursed Montague's absence. No one should have left him in charge of guarding royalty. He dispatched messages to Montague's home in Chelsea and to Lord Quentin here in London. They would have to investigate shooters and tontines.

He sent maids to start packing trunks for the ladies. It was a pity that he couldn't show the little widow the city sights, but keeping her alive had become more important than seduction.

This was why he didn't gamble. His luck was all rotten.

* * *

"Your new gowns will follow later. It's more important that we remove you from London now," the officious Mr. Atherton told Nora as maids rushed about, packing trunks.

The guardian angel who had protected her with his life had not taken time to repair to his room and smooth out his blond locks, nor dust off the dirt smears on his elegant coat. He shouted orders and commanded his troops while wearing a crumpled stock and a ferocious glint that did not bode well for someone.

Nora very much feared he would slice the draperies to ribbons with his small sword if she denied him. Which she fully intended to do, if only to see how he would react. She didn't need theater when she could watch the fascinating Honorable Nicholas Atherton in action.

He had saved her life today. She ought to be having fits of the vapors.

Instead, she forced her trembling hand to lift her teacup. She shook her head placidly as a maid held up her new nightshift of the softest cambric with exquisite embroidery and lace ruffles, asking if it should be packed.

"We are staying here tonight," Nora insisted. "We are perfectly safe behind iron gates, and I will not run like a coward."

"You're a damned princess! You need not hold your ground like a common soldier," Mr. Atherton argued, pointing at the trunk.

The maid looked confused.

"He does not belong in here, Marie," Nora told the maid. "He cannot tell royalty what to do. Have a footman show Mr. Atherton out if he continues to question my commands."

She bit back a laugh—probably of hysteria—as Mr. Atherton appeared ready to have an apoplexy. Apparently women did not often argue with him. He was obviously having second thoughts about having given her the power of a princess.

The maid obediently removed the shift from the trunk and returned it to the wardrobe. Lady Bell had departed to oversee packing her own trunks, but apparently princesses were never allowed to be alone. Nora put her feet up on a stool, and studied her mother's scribbles while admiring Mr. Atherton's simmering fury.

She was pretty certain the cryptic message said just what she'd suspected: *Out of this nettle, danger, we pluck this tontine, safety.* Except, of course, her mother's misspelling read more like *Outta dis neddle, danejer, we plucka ta tontine safely.* Had Nora not known the quote, she'd still be puzzling over the handwriting. Even an encryption expert could not have deciphered it.

"If I say it is necessary to leave London now, then we will go now," Mr. Atherton raged as she nibbled her toast. "I cannot be put in charge of your protection and be countermanded. That's mutiny."

"Interesting chain of command," Nora mused. "Does all royalty do as they're told? I shall take your suggestion under advisement and give you my answer in the morning."

He flung his long arms up in the air in frustration, unable to repudiate her orders in front of the servants. "I'll have the duke turn you out tonight," he threatened. "You could be a danger to him and his family."

"It would be better if I were a danger to Lady Bell and her servants by traveling tonight?" she inquired. "You are thinking only of yourself and not all the consequences. Marie, I'll need a travel gown for the morning, an evening gown for dinner, and the rest may be packed, thank you." She didn't care if royalty never expressed gratitude. She did.

Although she supposed she ought to be offering gratitude to Mr. Atherton for his quick actions this afternoon. Of course, she also ought to be shaking in her shoes and having fits of the vapors, but strangely, now that she'd had time to think, she was intrigued. She'd been handed a puzzle to solve.

*The better part of valor is discretion* came from that play, she remembered. What else was her mother telling her?

Finished with her tea and toast, she stood up and walked out of the bedchamber's parlor, into the hall where a footman waited. She needed to speak privately with the frustrated gentleman stalking after her, but she was surrounded by anxious servants.

"Let us discuss this with Lady Ann." She nodded regally at the footman, as if accustomed to having dozens at her disposal. "If you would fetch your mistress, we will be waiting in the gold salon."

Nora waited for Mr. Atherton to contradict her command. To her relief, he nodded acquiescence to the servant, who scampered off, leaving them alone for a few minutes.

"You adapt too easily to the habits of royalty," he complained, taking her elbow and steering her toward the salon. "You'll have the duke crawling at your command. You'd better hope he never discovers you're no more than a seaman's widow."

"I am extremely proud to be a seaman's widow. And daughter of a navy captain, who himself was the great-grandson of an English marquess. *And* I am apparently also the daughter of an archduchess of Mirenze, who is adept at intrigue," she added with just a touch of wryness. "I have no idea of my precedence over an earl's younger son, but I am not stupid. I do know that it's safer here than traveling to Essex in the dark in a slow-moving coach."

"You are not safer if your fake Mirenzian bodyguard has taken it into his head to assassinate an incorrigible princess," he asserted.

Nora had to admit that she hadn't thought of that possibility. She considered it now. "Did you see the shooter?"

"I saw a man in a broad-brimmed hat raising his arm in our direction. I tend to react without thinking," he said with a shrug. "The cut of his coat might have been foreign. Beyond that, I did not recognize him."

"Which means he wasn't one of our guards, and most likely no one hired by them," she decided. "If Gerard Martine is truly an Imperial Guard, he would rather die than impede Napoleon's decree."

"He's a damned Frenchie! They're not to be trusted," he argued as they strolled through the corridor.

"If I'm to understand my mother's absurd warning, there is safety in the tontine. Since the Marones are penniless, I cannot believe the prize is wealth."

That shut him up for all of half a second. "The crown," he muttered. "The prize would be the crown."

"The survivor wins the crown. That does not sound particularly safe," she said dryly. "Who could be partners in a crown?"

Frowning over her question, he opened the salon door and let her pass.

For a few brief minutes, they were alone. Nora tried not to reveal her suddenly rapid breathing. Had she engineered this meeting just so she might be alone with Nicholas Atherton? She was a fool, if so.

Of course, she was about to suggest worse.

"The river at the foot of the garden goes in to the London docks, does it not?" she asked the instant the door closed.

"When the tide runs out, yes," he said warily.

"Do you have access to a boy's clothes, something about my size?" He would refuse, she knew. She was insane to suggest this. But all her life she'd wanted adventure, and here was the perfect opportunity to protect herself, Elena, Lady Bell, everyone. Just for a few hours.

"If you think you will look like a boy in—"

"It does not matter what I look like so much as that I can move freely. Women's clothing is too confining. We have all the afternoon and half the night to plan this. We will need to know when the tide turns. We will need a small sailing ship willing to take us to Essex. I would very much like a small sword of my own, since, as you say, my disguise will not be good."

"Wait a minute!" He grabbed her arms and all but shook her.

He smelled of an enticing male musk and hid very strong muscles beneath his frills, she noted with interest. It would only take a second's work to step into his arms and place her hands against his chest...

"You must play a princess," he continued, intent on his own goal. "Royalty does not carry swords. You don't know how to use one. You are descending into the hysterical."

As much as she was enjoying his proximity, Nora jerked from his grip. "Far from it. I'm having the time of my life. Indulge me, please. I was once quite good with both sword and rapier. I'm sadly out of practice, but I had an excellent teacher. I daresay I can use a weapon more effectively than most thieves."

He ran his hand through his hair, loosening a lock that fell over his forehead. "You can use a rapier," he said flatly, in disbelief.

"Only child of a navy captain," she reminded him. "I was not brought up as your sisters were. My father and I fenced for sport. If we can depart before dawn by ship, we will leave behind my bodyguards and elude any assassins. Lady Belden will be safer traveling in her own carriage than in the duke's. The bodyguards may travel with the servants and our baggage, where they belong."

"The princess will be compromised beyond repair by traveling with me!" he nearly shouted.

Nora thought he looked interested despite his gentlemanly protests. A very intriguing man. "Lady Belden will claim that I traveled properly with Lord Quentin's sisters and maids and that she simply followed behind in the comfort of her own carriage. Do you really think any of them would report otherwise?"

"They would all rather die than acknowledge that they've been involved in anything improper," he agreed with a long-suffering sigh. "I could send my own sisters today and they would do the same. We will have so many carriages traveling in that direction that no one will know the difference."

"Except the bodyguards," Nora said with satisfaction. "And they're not about to report their own incompetence. They'll simply have to follow orders for a change if they wish to find me. Once they see me in Essex, they'll just assume Elena is up to her usual trickery."

"You needn't look so smug," he pointed out. "You will be traveling alone with me in the company of thuggish sailors. A rapier is a flimsy weapon."

She shrugged. "I'm the widow of a thuggish sailor. Test me."

# Chapter Fifteen

DEVIL TAKE the woman! Had she no idea what she looked like strolling down a dark garden path in those sailor's trousers? Even loose as they were, Nick could see every well-rounded contour in this lantern light, and the roll of her hips was even more delicious than in skirts. And he'd been fantasizing about those hips for nights.

In frustration, he flung a cloak over her, although it dragged the ground and the night was relatively warm.

Mrs. Adams cast him a look he was glad he couldn't see.

"Your ship awaits, your majesty," he said dryly, purposely irritating her. She might pretend to be regal, but she was a teacher through and through. He'd seen the way her lips pursed when she was addressed incorrectly. His life had once hung on the balance of reading subtle body signs.

As they reached the duke's wharf, she warily studied the skiff and the two oarsmen awaiting them. Nick hadn't been about to spend a few hours leisurely rowing a princess, if that had been her intent. He needed his arms free for weapons, so he'd hired help. He threw their portmanteaus down to the waiting crew.

"I'll climb down first and lift you in," he cautioned.

Wordlessly, she tugged the cloak's hood over her face. Before he could act, she leaped into the skiff as if she truly were a boy.

She remained ominously silent for the entire journey to the docks. Nick examined the sailors he'd hired for fear she'd recognized them as scoundrels. They'd come highly recommended by his many acquaintances, but it made him itchy if Princess Nora was seeing something he couldn't. He'd expected her to chatter excitedly all the way down the river.

She never did anything he expected. That was ominous, but admittedly, intriguing.

His companion remained silent upon disembarking at the docks. Her soft contralto couldn't possibly pass for a boy's. She held the cloak close as he signaled the mate awaiting to sail them out to sea and up the coast to Essex. He'd far rather sail than trudge along dusty roads in a parade of carriages and servants. Here, *he* was in control.

Again, in the dawn light, the lady seemed perfectly comfortable scrambling up a rope ladder into the small yacht he'd borrowed from Lord Quentin. His sisters would have fainted had he requested such physical activity. He noted she managed the short sword on her belt with reasonable ease. He kept his distance, just the same. As much as he enjoyed watching her in trousers, he'd rather not be skewered for following too close.

Instead, he placed himself just below a very well-turned, delicious ankle. He could wrap his hand around it twice over. He tested his restraint by not doing so.

Once they were safely on board, he led her to the luxurious captain's cabin while the sailors ran about, preparing to set sail.

"This is more like it," he said with satisfaction at the table already laid with linen and silver and an assortment of prepared breakfast dishes. "Quent travels in style."

With the door closed, his companion relaxed sufficiently to shake back her hood and admire her surroundings. "I commend you for your choice of transportation," she said with a warmth that probably melted the butter on their toast. "I had expected a smelly fishing boat."

"That is no longer my preferred mode of travel." He poured coffee and sipped it with pleasure. "I have a decadent nature that demands the niceties. Shall I take your cloak and weapon, my dear?"

He watched in amusement as she shed them herself, hanging them neatly in their place on a hook at the door. Self-sufficient was Mrs. Adams. She poured her own tea, too, and seated herself, leaving him to roam about. The cabin might be luxurious, but it was barely larger than a barouche. He was well aware of the big bed tucked under the stern window.

"I apologize for my silence. I recognized one of the men rowing the skiff." She added marmalade to her toast and bit into it with every evidence of ecstasy.

"I had wondered," he said, unable to draw his gaze from the way she licked her lips of every morsel of sweetness. "I did not think silence your natural state."

She darted him an amused look. "You have no idea. Did the bodyguards raise a great fuss last evening when they arrived? The duke keeps me isolated from any events of interest."

"Bodyguards cannot roar at a duke. They extended a formal

protest. The duke reprimanded them for not following my orders. They were reassured when they were allowed to watch you dine last evening and when told they might accompany you today. They are no doubt spit-polishing their boots and oiling their swords this morning in anticipation of riding in all their uniformed glory in a duke's retinue. I doubt they'll find the baggage wagon worthy of their magnificence." Nick finally settled in a chair to sip his coffee and help himself to the bacon.

"I'm glad you talked Lady Anne into riding with Lady Bell. The duke needs to cover the crest on his carriage before he goes out again." She carefully divided the bowl of eggs in half and ladled them onto both their plates.

Fascinated at being served by a princess, or an archduchess, or whatever, Nick didn't protest. "You do realize the duke has no such intention, don't you? I daresay he'll order his driver to wheel him all over town today, daring someone to shoot at him."

"That's his problem. His daughter shouldn't suffer for it. She's taking her horse and will probably ride ahead of Lady Bell once they're out of London. Now tell me if you believe the shot was meant for the princess or the duke."

"It's impossible to say with certainty. We must question your mother and preferably the princess. They're the ones playing with smoke and mirrors." He sampled his eggs without really tasting them.

"A tontine would need to be written down, would it not?" she asked, devouring her eggs with apparent delight.

"Most likely. I've done nothing except try to think how a financial arrangement would have anything to do with the princess, but it keeps coming back to the *survivor* part to me. If the crown is the prize, who would stand next to claim it if Elena is assassinated?"

"One would assume if the direct descendant of the queen is dead, that the crown would then revert to the next surviving archduchess. Napoleon would have some difficulty wedding his relatives to a married old lady who could produce no heirs."

He slumped in his seat and drank his coffee while pondering the puzzle. "The French would prefer that Elena be kept alive in that case. They wouldn't shoot her. This is getting us nowhere."

"It is getting us out of London until we can find the princess. You have done a positively brilliant job of arranging transportation, thank you."

He grimaced. "Had I known there was any possibility of seamen recognizing you, I would no doubt have had a dozen failures of the heart. One of your father's men?" He had the urge to learn everything about her, which was ridiculously foolish.

She rapped his hand with her fork, whether at his glance toward the bed or his question, Nick failed to tell. He returned his gaze to her delightfully luminous eyes. Very definitely pearls and gold against that creamy skin.

"One of my late husband's crew. I daresay if I appeared on deck, I'd find a few more who might recognize me. We entertained generously when ships were in the harbor. What do you plan to do if Elena is not found?"

"Ship you back in her place," he said morosely, picking at his eggs. "You'll bring Napoleon to his knees."

She laughed. She actually laughed. The damned woman probably would enjoy ordering half of Europe around. If her cousin was anything like Nora, Elena had probably done the shooting. What better way to escape than to be dead? He didn't think he'd tell the little widow of his twisted suspicions or she'd realize the darkness of his mind.

"Were it not for the war, I might enjoy ruling Europe for a few months. But I reserve my right to choose among Napoleon's family for a husband. What about you? Would you enjoy being royalty?" She checked the other pots on the table and decided on the honey, smearing it liberally on her cold toast.

Nick laid a slice of bacon across her sugared repast. He enjoyed watching her indulge her appetite. "If I can be the kind of royalty with money and no responsibility, most certainly. I might consider holding court, knighting a few daft soldiers, accepting a few bribes, nothing too tedious."

"But if you had to marry to retain your royal status?" She lifted her arched eyebrows and bit into the honeyed toast and bacon.

Nick envied the bacon's proximity to such a petite, pointed tongue. He drank his coffee cold. "Never," he affirmed. "I would abdicate. I have more than enough family already."

"*Irresponsible* Corinthian," she concluded. "One who arranges yachts at the drop of a hat. And responds to bullets faster than the bullets themselves. I will admit interest."

Nick didn't know whether to sputter a protest or preen. "This from a modest widow who orders dukes about," he scoffed. "If I admit interest, too, will it gain me any favors?"

"Possibly." She eyed him with decided *interest*. "Just to be clear, what kind of favors do you have in mind?"

"As many as you'll grant me." He offered his best wicked grin.

"A practice session with the sword?" she suggested, her eyes sparkling knowingly.

So, she didn't wish to give away her charms too easily. Nick respected that. He wiped his hands on the linen napkin. "I am quite good," he warned.

"I used to be, but probably not so much now." She wiped her hands as well. "We'll have to be good so as not to draw blood with real points."

"There's not room for adequate offensives anyway. We'll practice our defense, standing behind marks. No footwork, just arms." He rose to examine her weapon. He'd chosen the shortest blade from his collection, one that wouldn't hamper her, without thought to her actually *using* it.

She pouted but rose and took the short sword from him. She laid it across her palm, then flipped it up to check its balance like an expert. "I'll be handicapped by the smaller reach, but that's practical, I suppose. It's not as if I would grow long arms in a real battle."

"Bloodthirsty wretch, I don't intend to let you near a real battle, but you are welcome to use my weapon, if that evens the odds." He held out the sword he'd had specifically forged for his reach and weight.

She tried it with curiosity. "This was meant for use, not looks," she said with irritating surprise. "I'm better off with the cheaper weapon, and now I know to be very wary."

"Insult me one more time and I'll relieve your coat of all its pretty gold buttons." He retrieved his blade and plucked at the threads of her boy's coat with the point.

She grabbed her hilt and riposted neatly. The clang of metal in the narrow cabin exploded memories Nick would prefer to forget.

He hastily inscribed lines on the floor. "Stepping beyond the line is a forfeit."

They both cast off their coats. She removed her neckcloth, and

Nick nearly surrendered as her graceful throat rose from the open neckline of the shirt. When she moved, he could catch glimpses of her cleavage. She didn't wear a corset.

She raised her weapons, forcing his mind back to the moment.

Amazingly, he enjoyed the exercise that followed. He'd never fenced with a woman before, so he was easily distracted by watching her breasts bounce beneath the boy's shirt.

When she started throwing her hilt from hand to hand, fighting from both sides, his eyes nearly rolled from his skull, and his excitement intensified. He wanted a second sword to fend her off, not because he was afraid, but because he relished the challenge. He'd never considered swordplay a *pleasure*.

She wearied faster than he did, however. He caught the outer edge of her hilt, meaning to tip it from her hand and end the game. She reacted with astonishing swiftness, bringing her hand down and catching his weapon by the forte, slamming his blade away.

In the process, his point sliced her palm. Blood bloomed.

Horrified, he threw aside his sword and ripped off his neckcloth in practically the same motion. He grabbed her hand before she'd even laid down her weapon. Horror raged through his veins, horror and blood, fear and fury.

"It's only a scratch," she insisted, trying to pull away. "I need only wash it a bit."

He couldn't let go. *He'd* done that. Not Devil Nick, but the Honorable Nick. Blackness engulfed his miserable soul. What the devil was *wrong* with him?

He poured water into a basin and dipped her small hand into it, watching ribbons of blood float to the surface. Appalled, he tried to scrub the wound with Quent's shaving soap.

"Mr. Atherton!" She spoke sharply and finally succeeded in jerking her hand from his grip. "The cat has done worse. It is all my own fault for being so slow. Go pour yourself some wine. I promise not to bleed to death."

She turned her back on him, cutting him off from the basin so she might attend herself. Nick staggered back, unable to grasp what he'd just done.

The Honorable Nick, the man he worked so hard to be, made love to women. He didn't stab them. He needed to *fix* what he'd done.

Wrapping a rough cotton washcloth around her palm instead of his expensive linen, she turned around and studied him quizzically. "Mr. Atherton? Perhaps you should sit down. You look a bit pale."

It made no sense, but Nick lost his calculated seduction. He simply grabbed her by the waist, hauling her from the floor and against his chest where he could feel her heart beating next to his. She strained backward for a moment, but he kissed behind her ear and along her throat and within seconds, she was kissing him back. Despite the rolling of the water beneath the yacht, his world steadied.

On firmer ground, he let her take the initiative. She held the cloth wrapped about her palm and rested it against his chest, but she slid the other one behind his neck and urged him to lower his head. Once he obeyed, she rewarded him with further kisses, tentative at first, and then more eager. The excitement generated by their match returned.

Nick shifted his stance to support her. Her snug curves pressed intimately just where he needed them, and he allowed himself the pleasure of caressing the round buttocks he'd admired too long. He thought she moaned, but he was feeling nothing but delight in her response, so he took it as a moan of pleasure.

Her tongue blatantly teased his, at which point he lost all responsibility for his behavior. He carried her to the bed and laid her back so her knees dangled over the edge. Propping himself on his elbow, he came down beside her. With his free hand, he tugged her shirt loose and caressed the soft, giving flesh of her waist while murmuring Italian endearments.

She briefly fell still, and he sent a frantic prayer that he hadn't gone too far—before he went further. He cupped her breast through the soft cambric of her chemise. She responded by tugging his head down to hers again, where their tongues tasted and implored and all reason fled.

Given her acquiescence, Nick took his time in offering all the exquisite sensations two people could bring to each other. She lay like one stunned when he whispered kisses down her throat to her collarbone, but she was soon eagerly participating again. She untied his shirt and ran her uninjured hand beneath the fabric, caressing him with the warmth and gentleness of a summer breeze. He *needed* that reassuring touch, as well as the life-affirming rise of his cock.

He was rigid and ready and anyone could interrupt at any

moment.

She buried sweet kisses against his throat and ran an exploratory hand down his chest, aiming ever closer to that part of him straining to be free.

Stopping wasn't in his power.

# Chapter Sixteen

IF NORA had only known a little scratch could stir a gentleman to show her such an excess of sensual pleasure, she'd have drawn blood much sooner. Oh, Lord, but she loved the aroma of shaving soap and pure male, loved the slightly salty taste of his skin, and most of all—she loved being touched again.

It had been so very, very long since a man's hand had caressed her with need and urgency. Mr. Atherton's caress was assured and confident, without the inexperience and hesitancy of her infrequent encounters with Robbie. He didn't give her time to consider rejecting him, but he didn't rush her either. He simply kissed and touched and led her on until she was the one undressing *him*. It seemed so right and natural and *beautiful*.

He was all powerful male with wide shoulders and a taut strength that he'd repressed when they'd fenced. He held back even now, balancing his weight on his side so as not to overwhelm her despite the ship's bobbing and dipping. She wanted to be overwhelmed, but maybe, not just yet. She needed to know that she'd gone into this with eyes wide open.

He removed his shirt at her insistence. In the flickering shadows of lamplight, she admired a chest chiseled from hours of practice with sword and fists. She'd known he wasn't as indolent as he pretended.

His male organ pressed demandingly against her hip. The place between her legs was damp with need. She need only press a little more... She licked his collarbone and twisted a curl above his nipples, enjoying the texture of crisp hair against heated flesh.

He growled deep in his throat, making her insides quiver with delight. In the next instant, he'd parted the ties of the chemise she'd worn under the boy's shirt, and his mouth found her breast.

On wonder of wonders! *This* was why she loved bedplay. How could she have denied herself for so long?

Casting aside the cloth covering her scratched palm, she ran both hands through his glorious dark blond locks and held him while he licked and kissed and teased until her nipples were hard pebbles, and she could stand no more. Audaciously, she reached for his trouser buttons. The time had come to end this drought of the senses.

Before she could unfasten him, he pushed up her shirt and chemise and ran his kisses down her belly, pushing aside her hand so he could undo her trouser placket. Long, incredibly agile fingers slid beneath the fabric to caress her where she was wet and ready.

"Oh, please," she murmured. "Hurry. I need—" She couldn't say what she needed. She was so tense with it that she feared she might explode.

"This," he whispered, pulling her trousers down and inserting a finger to the place that ached the most. "And this." He rubbed the magic button.

And she came undone. With just a touch. She cried out with the force of the quake, wept, and grabbed his arms for support as the shuddering release swept her away.

"What an incredible beauty you are," he said, holding her tight and continuing to lightly caress the responsive flesh as she shivered beneath him. "We need to free your dragons more often—and unleash your inner wench." He nibbled her nipple teasingly.

She was too shaken to reply. She stroked his hair and tried to gather all the scattered pieces of her senses and remember just exactly what it was she thought she was doing.

A sharp rap at the door shattered the interlude.

"We're to sea, m'lord, and there's a squall to the nor'east. Need to fetch the captain's china before the blow hits."

Startled, Nora gazed at the man hovering above her. The relaxed smile vanished, replaced by a tight frown. He straightened and began tucking her clothes back in place, with no sense of urgency but with expert efficiency.

"One moment." He tossed back the covers, swung her onto the mattress, and covered up her dishevelment. "I'll be back, *mia cara*." He pressed a kiss behind her ear that shivered her straight to her toes.

She wanted to protest and fling back the covers and leap up to clear the table as if she hadn't just committed a wicked sin. Lord Quentin's crew knew only that they transported a disguised passenger, but a tousled and flushed female would arouse unnecessary curiosity.

She'd almost committed a carnal act with a gentleman she hardly knew! And she'd loved every minute of it. And wanted to do it again. Wanted far more than the little piece of heaven he'd offered.

She feared there would never be another opportunity. She listened to the men murmuring as they gathered the dishes. Felt the wind catch the sails and the cold seep through the wall.

The door closed, and a strong male hand rubbed her shoulder. "Best get some sleep. We're in for a bit of squall and I need to be topside. We've a long day ahead."

If there was regret in his voice, she didn't hear it. She flung herself over and glared up at him. He'd donned his coat and neckcloth and looked all that was proper, the wretch.

"Why do they need you?" she asked with as much curiosity as frustration.

For an instant, she thought she recognized a flash of some emotion behind his gaze, but he composed his features into his usual insouciance. "Because their captain was dead drunk when Quent called for the yacht to be set to rights. Quent values his expensive toy, and I had to promise to step up to his place if needed. It's a sturdy vessel, and the squall is slight, but the crew needs someone at the helm. As a sailor's wife, you know that."

"As a princess, we are not amused," she said mockingly. "You have more expertise than the first mate?"

He looked as if he wouldn't answer but finally nodded an acknowledgment.

How odd that he was reluctant to flaunt his skill. "Go on then. How long until we reach Essex?"

"A few hours, no more. We'll take on a local pilot to guide us upriver to the harbor closest to Belden Hall. We'll easily be nibbling a noon meal while the others are still rattling their way through town."

She would not say it. She narrowed her eyes and glared at him rebelliously.

He tipped an imaginary hat. "As much as I have enjoyed your company and would love to continue as we were, I value my neck too much," he replied to her glare, apparently reading it correctly. "The Hall will be full of Quentin's scheming sisters. But once the princess is found..." He left his message dangling temptingly and departed.

If she wanted more bedplay, she'd have to find that damned

Elena herself.

* * *

Nick welcomed the cold north wind cooling him off as he manned the wheel and ordered the sheets hauled. The yacht was a sleek design, far better than the bulky brigs he'd once navigated.

He and his unhappy John Cock would rather be in the warm bed with the luscious widow, but paradise must wait until she no longer played a princess. Everyone knew his reputation too well. Circumspection was all about keeping his head, literally.

He was utterly shocked that he'd gone as far as he had. And that she'd let him. He'd thought her a little more prim and proper and had expected to employ all his wiles to persuade her into bed— which proved circumstances were everything. After the fencing, he'd been hot enough to forget his restraint. It was only good luck that she felt the same.

He tried not to think too hard about the perfection of her firm breasts or how amazingly she'd responded. He didn't do regret these days, but leaving an amazing woman lying tousled and delicious on that bed had taken a severe toll on his sense of duty. Montague owed him for the sacrifice.

He spent the hours fighting the squall and sailing into the harbor wondering how the lovely widow would retaliate for his neglect. Shoe flinging didn't seem her style, but he'd learned to expect the unexpected from her. He was actually anticipating the tussle to come.

Wrapped in her cloak, she emerged from the cabin once the winds died down, planting herself at the rail without glancing around at him or the crew. He'd like to see her with the hood down and the breeze flying in her hair, and had the odd notion that was the way she was meant to be—as free as the wind. She was as trapped by society's expectations as he.

He turned the wheel over to the helmsman to steer into the harbor to pick up their pilot and strolled over to stand beside her. "I can't keep calling you *your majesty* or even a proper *your highness,* except in public, of course. But now, when it's just us, what should I call you?"

"Easy," she suggested wryly. "Starved for attention. I'm sure there are less pleasant names you could summon, but I refuse to regret what we did."

"We're adults. There is no reason for regret. It's only the awkwardness of the situation that comes between us. I would like to know you much better once your cousin is returned to her proper place." He'd never installed a mistress in a love nest, but he was considering it now. Traveling to her home on the coast just to enjoy her company wasn't in the cards.

She shot him one of those long-lashed, knowing looks that saw straight into his wicked soul.

"As you say, I am unfortunately an adult, with adult responsibilities. I'm grateful for the inheritance left to me by the marquess, but it must go to help my mother and educating the children of the sailors lost in His Majesty's service. I will not be living in London." She turned back to admire the sun peering from the clouds and spilling across the village ahead. "This visit will be my one and only chance to see something other than my home. I must take every advantage offered."

That put him surely into his place. He was an *offered advantage*. Well, fine. Two could play that game. Knowing she meant to leave him behind might even be easier than looking for ways to rid himself of her. He might not even need gold and pearls.

He *wanted* to give her gold and pearls.

Uneasy, he merely admired the shoreline with her. Except he'd seen more than his fill of derelict fishing villages. They offered nothing of interest to him, not the way this woman did. "Then we must arrange to see as much as possible," he said affably, hiding his irritation.

"I would enjoy that," she replied. "I would enjoy it more if I could do so without four bodyguards and a retinue. But I'm grateful for every opportunity. Thank you for arranging the yacht. In private, I would be pleased if you called me Nora."

"And I am Nick, when I am not *idiot, sapskull,* or *beast.* I have no purpose other than to please, but occasionally, I rub people the wrong way. I regret that." He didn't really. He only regretted if he was inconvenienced. But honesty had its limits.

Her melodious chuckle tickled his innards. The woman oozed sensuality, right down to her laugh.

"I suspect you regret nothing, sir. But it's a pleasure to meet a man who enjoys life and admits it. Sailing this yacht and your fencing skill prove you are a *useful* ornament. And if I say more, I will embarrass myself. I will try not to make your duty too difficult."

He didn't know if he should be pleased at being labeled an *ornament*. Gathering the schoolteacher had enjoyed his bedroom skills, he chose to view her comment as admiration. "Duty is always difficult. Your company is a pleasure, however. Lady Belden will have a carriage waiting at the local inn when the ship reaches Maldon. We'll mix with the crew entering the tavern. I'll escort you to a private chamber where you may change into your princess attire, and we'll properly arrive at Beldon Hall with the marchioness's footmen as guards. Confusion, obfuscation, and never answering questions works well, I find."

She traced a gloved finger over the hair on the back of his hand, arousing him as easily as if she'd covered him in kisses. "Life is so very complicated. I appreciate that you know how to navigate it." She glanced longingly at the shore. "I only wish I knew how to find my cousin and help her gain what she wishes. It's frightening to think someone may be shooting at her. She must be very alone to have done this."

"More likely, she has an entire army at her disposal, and she deserves shooting. Trust me. Pampered royalty does not run off unless they have someone to run to. They're not used to fending for themselves." He turned his hand over and squeezed hers. "You are to take this time for enjoying. Let others worry about the reprehensible princess."

She glared at his insensitive remark about shooting her cousin. He shouldn't have said it, but the princess had put a lot of people into a difficult situation. Even if she was raising an army to save a country, he couldn't find sympathy for her.

Instead of scolding, Nora merely replied, "Thank you. I should like to think that if my mother isn't worrying, then there is no reason for my concern, but my mother does not always live in the real world. I would like to see that Elena is safe and happy. It is very strange to have family after so many years without."

"I can tell you from experience, it is very strange to have family, period. I must go do my duty now. You will pardon me if I return to formality?"

She nodded regally, and Nick strode off, fighting the whirl of confused emotions she engendered. It was just the situation, he assured himself. Once life was back to normal, he'd forget all about the pensive beauty and her deceptive relations.

Acting as master of the ship was second nature to him. He greeted the pilot coming aboard, ordered the sails, and discussed weather conditions as if he had never left all this behind.

The woman clinging to the rail, raising her face to the sun, was an entirely new experience, one of which he should be wary. He feared she had the ability to turn his comfortable world inside out, and he couldn't allow that.

Of course, it would be most excellent if he did not get shot in the process.

* * *

The exchange at the inn went as planned. Nora smoothed the wrinkles out of her luxurious emerald traveling gown and was a bit shocked to realize she regretted changing into it. She'd enjoyed that brief interlude of being herself with a handsome man. *Nick* had secrets he hid well and that she'd like to explore sometime.

She would take his advice and not suffer regret. She had just enjoyed the most exciting sensual experience of her lifetime, with a gentleman so handsome she could hardly believe her good fortune, and she was still feeling the pleasure.

She was wearing a beautiful gown and being treated like a princess. Elegant, uniformed footmen helped her into an aging carriage. A maid waited to hand her a flask of lemonade and neat little squares of cheese and bread to pacify her hunger until she reached the Hall. She could admire the rolling Essex countryside, tidy little villages, and distant manor houses from the ease of upholstered seats. It was a comfortable adventure.

But it wasn't exciting, as fencing with Nick had been. Or what they had done after. She hadn't felt so *alive* in years.

Nora teased at a piece of an idea. She didn't know what Elena was up to. She didn't know if Elena knew she might be in trouble. But somehow, they had to find a way of communicating with the missing princess, to let her know they would protect her, if she needed it. How could she force Elena to reveal her location, or at least correspond?

She could think of one way. A princess had to have a modicum of care for her reputation. If Nora began behaving like a wanton, wouldn't Elena fear the news would get back to her father? Her aunts? Her suitors?

Would that force the princess into sending her a message?

Insides churning at the thought of acting so out of character, Nora pondered the probabilities all the way to the Hall.

# Chapter Seventeen

BELDON HALL rose grandiosely above rolling acres of green on the only hill in the area, Nora observed as the carriage rumbled up the rutted drive to her father's ancestral home—now Lady Belden's country estate. A wooden bridge allowed them to cross the old moat, currently dry and filled with uncut wildflowers and weeds.

As they approached the hall, she studied the arrow slits in the medieval tower in the center. Windows had been added in the solar above and in the newer wings out to the side. But the hall itself, where knights had once slept and eaten and defended their lord, would be gloomy, indeed.

Nick had chosen to ride beside the carriage so all would look innocent as they rolled through the entrance. Just watching his straight back, broad shoulders, and easy hands on the reins had left her in a state of semi-arousal all morning. She had to find other paths for her straying mind, so she studied the Hall.

A bleak, three-story tower with more arrow slits for windows guarded the gate. Nora wondered if the late marquess, as magistrate, had once kept prisoners in the daunting structure. She was rather glad she was only a distant relation and did not have to visit here often.

At the manor, a footman waited to open the carriage door.

Looking polished and handsome in his dark blue coat, with his hair now tidied and his boots gleaming, Nick handed Nora down. Even through gloves, the strong pressure of his hand recalled what he had done to her, and she had to swallow hard and try to remember who she was supposed to be.

"Quent's females came early to tidy up. There will be a gaggle of women watching from the window above," he warned softly as he placed her hand on his arm. "They are oohing and ahhing over your gown and your hat and keeping an eagle eye on me to be certain I do nothing worthy of gossip. Are you ready?"

His warning served its purpose. She straightened and pretended his hand had never encountered her breast. "As I shall ever be, I suppose. Had circumstances been otherwise, I'd have been up there in that window with them, excited at the glimpse of real royalty. It's a bit disheartening to realize royalty is human."

"Painfully so," he agreed. "And occasionally subhuman. But I suppose we all must have our dreams."

"Are your sisters above, too?" she asked. "I believe I met them the night I was introduced."

"They offered to help. We are awash in women, all of them eager to report back to my parents. You need only mention a tiny misdeed in passing, and I will be banned from all society on the morrow."

"And this matters to you?" Nora asked, fearing this would ruin her delicious scheme to drag Elena out of hiding.

"It does. My father is dying and has placed his trust in my upholding the family name and seeing my sisters properly married off. My older brother cannot escort the females about as I can. So I must be what I am not, for their sake."

Interesting that he admitted he was acting a role, as she had surmised. "Commendable, sir," she said, and she meant it, although he'd just destroyed her hopes. "Not too many gentlemen would give a fig what the women of their family thought."

The doors opened and they entered into a flurry of bows and curtsies, feather dusters and mops, and a rush of feet from all directions.

"You are early, Nicholas, you terrible fiend," one young voice cried.

"Hush, Georgie," another lady said in a raised whisper. "Make your curtsies."

Nora recognized the lovely blond locks of three of Nick's young sisters. From a different direction raced three slightly older ladies, all garbed in old gowns and aprons and looking distinctly disheveled.

"Mr. Atherton, you did not warn us—"

"It's the princess, Sally. Curtsy," one of the young, fair-haired maidens warned in a whisper.

"Your highness," the dark-blond Sally said, falling into a grand curtsy while wearing an old muslin morning gown. She ruined the effect by standing and glaring at Nick. "We were told we'd have all day to set this dust heap to rights."

"I fear that's my fault," Nora said, restoring her escort to good reputation. "Precautions require that I not be where people think I am."

Nick made hasty introductions to the three slightly older ladies. Lady Sally and the dark-haired Lady Margaret were Lord Quentin's sisters. Elizabeth, the third lady, seemed more the age of Nick's sisters and was apparently a cousin of Lord Quentin. Nora vowed she'd work out all their names before the day ended.

To that purpose she nodded at their curtsies, then stripped off her gloves. "We have a few lovely hours to come to know one another before the company arrives. Let me change my gown, and I can show you an excellent mixture for polishing silver, if that's needed."

Gasps filled the musty air. Ignoring the rising protest, Nora simply regarded the medieval hall with its high wooden ceiling, enormous fireplace, and threadbare carpets and found the most likely doorway to the kitchens. If she couldn't shock society with Nick, then she'd find other ways. She hoped that would bring Elena running back.

"Let me change out of this gown, and I shall be right down." Holding her gloves so her work-roughened hands were visible should anyone look, she waited expectantly for someone to lead the way.

"Georgie, show the princess to her room while I pick the rest of the ladies off the floor," Nick said jovially. "Her Highness is unique, so you may as well become used to it."

Bless his hard heart, he might actually understand that she couldn't tolerate sitting on a throne all day. She followed behind a chattering Georgie who was evidently too young to have had her come out but had been allowed to attend the Hall with her sisters to help with setting the house to rights. Not that the chatty Georgiana had a high opinion of her sisters' abilities to direct the servants. Nora was hiding a grin by the time she reached her suite.

"We cleaned here first," Georgie said proudly, indicating the unadorned tester bed and Queen Anne wardrobe. "We hid the bare spots in the carpet under the bed. The footmen had to lift the bed for us. The one called Nate is lovely," she added with youthful blue-eyed innocence.

"I shall have to watch out for him. Perhaps he'll carry up the rest of my trunks when they arrive. If you would unfasten the hooks at the top of this gown, I think I shall be able to find a morning gown in my portmanteau. My maid won't arrive until later." Nora tossed her cloak on the crisp white embroidered bedding.

"I'll call my sisters' maid. I'd be all thumbs. Oh, this is so exciting, a real princess! I shall be right back, Your Highness."

Even a fifteen-year-old knew more about how to go on than Nora did. She unfastened what hooks she could reach, tidied her hair, and was impatient to see the rest of the house by the time the flustered maid arrived. Apparently, royalty was difficult to have about.

Ignoring suggestions that she have a lie-down, have some tea, or be seated in the equally-unadorned parlor to await visitors, Nora dressed in her loose gray morning gown with the appalled maid's aid. She then gleefully set out to explore.

She could hear feminine voices up and down the cold stone corridors, but she saw no one until she descended to the hall again, where she found Nick. Looking majestic and practically edible, he sat sprawled in a throne-like chair near the empty fireplace, drinking coffee if she was to judge by smell. He winked at her entrance, then properly stood, set his cup aside, and bowed.

Her heart skipped a beat just from the heated gleam of his eyes.

"Hideous gown, that," he said unrepentantly. "Perfect for silver polishing and rag bins. You'll have the tabbies nattering incessantly. Is that your plan?"

"So much as I have a plan," she agreed, trying to maintain her composure. "I dislike idleness and prefer to be useful. Perhaps if rumors fly about my unprincess-like behavior, Elena will have to return."

"Not likely, but as good a plan as I've got. Shall I show you the silver or give you a tour of the premises first?"

Nora raised a wicked eyebrow at him. He looked momentarily startled, then grinned so charmingly she almost dissolved into a sentimental puddle.

"Not a chance of visiting bedchambers, my lady," he declared, taking her arm and leading her toward one of the doorways. "The house is teeming with females who won't stay put. They'll be tracking us down as soon as they've tidied their hair and donned their newest gowns. Does one address daughters of archduchesses as *my lady*?"

Nora tried to breathe evenly as Mr. Atherton strode beside her, while her mind and his were on bedchambers and not titles. "I have no idea how daughters of archduchesses are addressed. I've barely sorted out daughters of earls. And please don't start me on the wives of second sons of earls. While I may be a staunch monarchist, I have a notion that we could de-nobilize half aristocracy without causing harm."

"Better than shooting them like the Frenchies did," he agreed. "My poor non-existent wife will only be a Mrs., and since I'm a mere Honorable, would you de-nobilize me?"

"What is the point of being an Honorable?" Nora scanned the formidable dining chamber to which he introduced her, wondering if she could order the seating arrangements so she could have his company during dinner. "So that one's hostess knows where to sit you at this immense table? It must be tiresome to always sit next to the same people, as if tables should be arranged by alphabetical order. I would much rather sit next to someone with whom I have something in common."

"An anarchist!" he crowed. "I knew it. You may profess to be a monarchist all you like, but you'd smack the prince if you met him. I'm so very sorry your cuz offended Prinny and left him in the lurch so you never had the chance to meet him. I don't think you're likely to shock her into returning, you know, especially if she's in trouble."

"I am trying not to think about it," Nora whispered as they entered the butler's pantry where one of the servants was scrubbing hastily at the silver. She picked up an ancient gleaming piece and admired it. "Oh, *perfetto*."

The footman flushed bright red and bowed deeply.

"He'd rather cut his own throat than let a princess polish," Nick whispered in her ear, disturbing her in so many ways that she practically felt his voice on her skin. "So much for equality. Your place is to make everyone proud of their positions."

"And then go home and polish my pewter," she retorted as they passed through to the next chamber—the men's salon, she assumed from the heavy dark furniture and decanters. Her escort would be right at home in here. "I hate that everyone is working themselves to the bone while all I do is wander about looking approving."

"No, you don't. If you'd loosen up, you'd realize you're enjoying yourself. You may occasionally be bored, but I'm sure pewter polishing isn't all the kick either."

"Nick!" a horrified gasp resounded from behind them. "Are you talking cant?"

"Ah, Diana, my disapproving sister. You remember her, Your Highness? She probably doused you with tea if you dared come too close." Nick fended off a sisterly swat and a muffled sigh of irritation as his eighteen-year-old sister dropped into a deep curtsy.

"Please, we shall accomplish nothing at all if everyone is forever bowing and curtsying," Nora protested, trying to adjust back to the real world and not the intimate web Nick's voice wove.

She studied Diana and determined this sister had gray eyes and a slight pock mark marring one pale brown eyebrow. "I'd rather have a few friends. It's very convenient that your brother has sisters and acquaintances close to my age. Did your Queen Elizabeth not have ladies in waiting who gossiped and worked with her? Could we not pretend to be a coterie of courtiers?"

Nick snorted, but Diana held out her hand and smiled, revealing a slight gap between her front teeth. "We can try, until our elders arrive, at least. Come upstairs and we will show you what a maze of rooms we have to set to order. There isn't enough linen, and we've had to send word back to Lady Bell. Where is she? Did you leave her behind?"

Not looking back, Nora left Nick in the men's salon, to do whatever it was men did. No regrets, she reminded herself. She would have fun wherever she could find it and never, ever look back.

* * *

In his normal routine, at noon Nick would have been just climbing out of bed to face the day and pondering what coat to wear. He'd stop at his club to see if anything entertaining had happened over night, perhaps cruise Brook Street in search of company, take a ride in the park, and then go home to dress for the evening.

He'd already been up more hours than that today. Time stretched dauntingly without his usual pursuits. What the devil did one do in the country?

Devil Nick longed to sail a yacht to Brighton and strangle a wayward princess.

The Honorable Nick wandered about a library of ancient tomes, flipped cards on the moth-eaten felt of a whist table, and joined the chattering ladies in a small breakfast room for an informal meal. Since he was the only male present, he chose to wander the perimeter, submitting gracefully to their teasing while nibbling bite-sized sandwiches and observing.

Mostly, he watched Nora. Someone had shot at her yesterday. All that lovely, dark-eyed composure could be lying dead right now. The notion chilled him to the marrow.

Smiling over clenched teeth, he paced in front of the windows, occasionally checking the drive. Thieves and murderers would not walk up the drive. Instead of riding the estate with a troop of twenty huntsmen, he needed to use his brains and not his mindless brawn to seek less violent, more civilized methods of protection.

"Nick, do sit and tell us what Lady Belden plans for entertainment when she arrives," his sister Diana urged, gesturing toward a chair.

"She has not invited that nodcock Throgbottom," he said, ignoring her invitation. "You shall be bored out of your mind with all the proper guests," he teased.

"Fustian," Diana retorted. "His name is Thornton and I know he is coming, as are any number of his friends and mine. What I wish to know is if I should wear my dancing slippers this evening or save them for the morrow."

His head was full of French spies and assassins, not dancing slippers. He had to remember this was England, not the bloody Caribbean. "You may run up to your room and change should dancing accidentally happen," he said solemnly. "Pipers may pop from the walls at any moment and break into triumphal marches. But you will be prepared for all events."

Curly-haired Georgie flung a bit of bread at him. He caught it and tossed it out the window for the birds. Nora had her head together with Lady Sally over some seating chart and wasn't following the byplay. The luscious widow had the cure for his restlessness.

But he mustn't indulge his animal needs. He didn't even know how he could think of them while surrounded by his virginal sisters and their friends.

"Is there a gun room?" he asked abruptly.

Diana regarded him warily. "There is, but it is not hunting season."

"I would like to practice target shooting." And check the weapons and be certain they were clean and well-oiled, and ammunition handy. Surely, that's what a proper bodyguard would do. Perhaps he could find a balance between civilized London gentleman and murderous renegade.

He thought Nora sent him a wary glance, but at least she did not challenge him to another duel.

"I will show you the direction," Lady Sally said, preparing to rise from the table.

"Just point me to the right door and I'll find my own way," he said, hiding his alarm. He didn't want Quent's little sister setting her cap for him. He'd be leg-shackled in a trice with Lady Bell and Quent both breathing down his neck.

And once they learned of the criminal character debauching an innocent lady, they'd kill him, deservedly so.

"I should like to learn how to load a pistol," the wretched faux princess said with a deceptive air of thoughtfulness. "Since we can do no more here until Lady Belden's baggage wagon arrives with linens, perhaps we should all learn."

Nick wanted to bang his head against the wall as his sisters and Quent's clamored to join them. Who was to guard *his* body if half London's eligible ladies took up shooting each other to entertain royalty?

* * *

"What the devil is Nick doing, setting up a war zone?" Lord Quentin asked.

Riding alongside the open carriage on his black Frisian warhorse, the marquess's son made no pretense of looking like a languid gentleman. Rather than watch the elegant figure he cut on horseback, Lady Bell studied the estate's open fields. She had already seen the figures in the distance and wondered what they were about. War zones hadn't occurred to her, but she suffered a moment's alarm at the notion.

As the caravan of carriages drew closer, feminine pastels could be seen more distinctly as they danced about the grassy field with only Nick's dark blue as contrast. Loud pops could be heard even over this distance. Smoke trailed from...pistol barrels?

"Are they preparing for attack?" she asked tentatively. "Have you sent them a warning and this is Nick's response?"

"I've word to pass on, but pistols aren't the answer. If you'll pardon me..."

His lordship didn't wait to be excused, dratted man. He merely spurred his magnificent horse into motion and galloped ahead.

Isabell admired Lord Quentin's broad back and sound seat and shook her head at her thoughts. Admiring paintings was much safer than admiring virile men, as she well knew.

# Chapter Eighteen

NICK SAW the war horse galloping up the drive and didn't know whether to sigh in relief that reinforcements had arrived or cower behind the shrubbery for fear Quent would take the scene the wrong way. Surrounded by feminine pulchritude wielding smoking pistols, Nick realized there wasn't any right way to take it.

Quent's female relations merely glanced up at the sound of the giant beast's flying hooves and returned to their relentless barrage. They'd decorated the targets Nick had set up with drawings and wielded weapons as fast as he could load them. Nick assumed the sketches represented the men in their lives to whom they were currently ill disposed. Fortunately, neither Quent nor Nick were in that category, because the aims of the Scots ladies were quite good.

"I think I recognized Thornton before she blew his nose off," Quent said nonchalantly as he dismounted and examined the riddled sketches. "Is there a problem here?"

Princess Troublemaker materialized at Nick's side, blowing at the barrel of her smoking pistol. "Good afternoon, Lord Quentin," she said in a lofty tone not replicating the laughing one she'd used all afternoon. "We are preparing to defend ourselves should enemy spies attack. Where are my royal guards?"

Nick bit back a grin at the juxtaposition of guards and shooting spies and let Quent deal with her for a change. His lordship might have a difficult time telling the impecunious widow from the royal maiden if Nora maintained this imperious role.

"Your guards have some idea you are hiding in the baggage wagon with the maids and are extremely displeased," Quent said, making his bow. "If this scene is for their benefit, I doubt it will make them any happier."

"It's a pity then that they are such laggards. It is almost time to dress for dinner. Perhaps we could take pistols with us to our chambers," she suggested, with mischief in her eyes.

"I don't recommend giving my sisters pistols," Nick said. "They've proved themselves very bad shots and will more likely shoot off their own toes or mine. I'll clean up the weapons if you'll chase the lot of them back to the house."

She eyed the old dueling pistol with resignation. "It is too difficult to load in any case. I'll look through the sword collection instead."

Before he could loudly voice his protest, she danced off to lead her little lambs astray. Nick shot Quent a look of misery. "She's an anarchist. We've set an anarchist on Boney's intended throne. You'd best bring word that the real crown has been found."

"If our men have the right female, she's been seen with a man in Brighton. They're looking for transportation to Portsmouth. I've sent a word of warning to Portsmouth. I have men checking all ships before they sail from Brighton, but we can't check all the coaching inns as well."

Nick ran his hand through his hair, smelled the gunpowder, and winced. He would not become involved any more than he already was. "If it's Portsmouth she wants, she's running away to the Americas. You'll have to put out a reward for a murderess and have every man jack on that side of the country hunting for her."

"She won't be treated with much dignity if they think she's a murderess," Quent said dryly. "That's a trifle drastic, isn't it?"

"Not in my book," Nick grumbled. "She's laughing in our faces, leaving her cousin to be shot at by assassins, and placing England in a sorry diplomatic situation if she isn't returned. Not that I care if the French scream bloody murder over her disappearance, but this bodyguard business wreaks havoc with a man's comforts."

"Beds here are hard, are they?" Quent said. "I'll let Montague know your recommendations, but I can't imagine he'll follow them."

"He'll follow them or I'll set Mrs. Adams loose in his menagerie. She wields a mean sword." Disgruntled, Nick began picking up the selection of arms the ladies had chosen to haul to the lawn. At least he knew now that the weaponry was functional.

"Lady Bell is right behind me. She'll restore order, and we'll all enjoy a pleasant garden party for a few days," Quent said with assurance. "By then, we should have some idea where we stand."

"In a peat bog, up to our waists," Nick retorted, unhappy that no one paid attention to his concerns. He wished he understood what the archduchess had meant about tontines and danger. "Or on a powder keg, if one adds Mrs. Adams to the equation. She's plotting, and if she plots like her cousin, we'd all best be wary."

"The widow?" Quent asked in surprise, helping to gather up the rifles and muskets. "She struck me as the meek, demure sort, a bit overwhelmed by all of us."

Nick nearly laughed aloud. "It's a damned good thing you don't have to do business with women, then, or you'd be bankrupt. Perhaps you'd better pull your head out of your ledgers for a while and take a good look around you."

"My ledgers are what attracts the ladies," Quent corrected. "If I had no money, I'd just be another pretty face."

Nick shook his head pityingly. "That's society in general, not the ladies in particular. Really, you need to hire me as your tutor on females. You've been studying the wrong books. Help me survive this escapade, and we'll start a campaign to have you wedded so you'll leave the rest of us happy bachelors alone."

"Did I say I wish a bride?" Quent heaved his collection of weaponry over his shoulder and led his mount back toward the stable.

The open landau rattled up the drive, and both men turned to watch. Head high, ribbons flying, Lady Bell didn't look left or right or notice them, but Lord Quentin's gaze followed her path all the way to the door.

"Oh definitely." Nick whistled as he carried his load toward the house. "You want a bride all right, if only for the sake of your hefty ledgers."

* * *

Lady Belden took charge of her household with the efficiency of a general to battle. As maids and baggage arrived, they were commanded up and down corridors, and Nora and the girls were dispatched to prepare for their dinner guests.

Once bathed and elaborately gowned in ivory crepe over fawn sarcenet, with her hair wound into intricate knots and dangling ivory ribbons, Nora restlessly paced her chamber. Her Mirenzian bodyguards had arrived with the baggage wagon. She'd waved at them from an upper story window as they'd roamed about the stable yard, apparently in hopes she would materialize from a trunk. They'd instantly posted sentries at either end of her corridor.

So now she was back to being a royal prisoner so her cousin could run off wherever she wished. Nick had passed on the information he'd received from Lord Quentin. It seemed very much as if Elena had eloped with a lover, leaving Nora caught in an untenable situation.

Her mother's note about a tontine raised serious doubts about that theory.

As she paced, she composed a note in her head. Now that there were servants about the Hall, surely one could be spared as messenger. If only she could speak to Nick, she was certain he would agree and help her.

Just before the dinner bell rang, she sat down at the plain table that served as desk and scribbled the message: *Sadly, I have lost over a crown in London. If you know where to find more, please let me know. The situation is desperate.*

Viviana would know her daughter didn't gamble and wasn't concerned over a few shillings. Surely, she would understand that Elena was in danger. Or at least that Nora was unhappy with the situation.

Nick arrived promptly as the bell rang. She folded the paper to palm size. When she opened the door, she held out her gloved hand for him to bow over, and in the process, slipped the paper into his palm. Without missing a beat, he slid it into his glove while straightening his cuff and led her past the glaring guards.

"No assignations," he murmured as he escorted her down the stairs to the hall. "We are watched constantly."

She hated to think they'd only ever have those brief moments between them. They deserved more. Which made it more imperative to return Elena. Nick stood so tall and elegant in his gold-embellished waistcoat and dark dinner coat. And now that she knew the man beneath the elegance desired *her*... It was hard to behave.

"You think too highly of yourself," she said stiffly as the assemblage below dipped into curtsies and bows at her appearance on the landing. "I need you to send that message to my mother. She is the only clue we have to Elena's destination. How do I make all those people straighten up and go back to whatever they should be doing?"

"Nod regally and turn to address Lady Belden," he murmured. "And I think highly enough of my head not to wish to lose it."

"And you think I don't have the same concern? If you can't do it, then I will ask someone else." She nodded from the stairs, lifted her trailing skirt, held her escort's arm, and descended to the waiting Lady Belden, amused as all the nobles returned upright.

As promised, the first guests to arrive were the friends and suitors of the ladies who had entertained Nora all afternoon. Once they overcame their awe of royalty, this younger set provided lively conversation, leaving Nora to bury her fears and hope Nick found a way to send her note.

At least they were keeping Napoleon's spies away from whatever it was that Elena was doing. The Mirenzian guards followed her from room to room.

Lady Belden had made certain her protégées and Nick's sisters entertained excellent company. A host of baronets, viscounts, and sons of earls and even the son of a duke separated Nora from Nick at the dinner table. On the whole, they were charming and well-spoken. Even so, Nora idled her time ticking off flaws—weak chin, weak chest, only conversation gossip, didn't know where Mirenze was...

She knew she was being petty. She didn't care. If she wished to settle for a less-than-perfect gentleman, she could settle for Fred Connor, the grocer's son. She knew him as steady and hard-working, and he would never dream of living anywhere else than Hytegate, where she belonged. The gentlemen here were trying to impress a princess, not a seaman's widow. They'd lose interest once they knew she wasn't royalty. So she could be petty all she liked.

Only one man here knew her for who she was and still wanted her. As long as she was content with bedplay—which she most certainly was—then she wanted the best. Which Nick certainly had to be. She couldn't imagine anyone else doing to her what he had done. All the others seemed so young and self-absorbed. Nick had heeded *her* desires.

Well, until she'd asked him to pass a message, then it became about him and his neck. Perhaps Lord Quentin would help her. He was an extremely handsome gentleman. Odd that she had no interest in his bed. Apparently golden hair and lazy grins caused her blood to heat, not intense, dark-haired gentlemen.

After dinner, the ladies retired to the enormous medieval hall while the gentlemen lingered in the dining room with their brandy and cigars. The hall chandeliers had been lit and a fire roared in the grand chimney. In this lighting, the shabbiness of the carpets and upholstery wasn't so easily noticeable. Servants scurried about, setting up gaming tables and tea trays.

Some of the ladies preferred conversation and needlework and chose the settees. Nora wondered what a princess did in the evenings. She paced the length of the stone hall with Lady Ann, who was of a restless nature also. They discussed horses, although Nora knew next to nothing of them except what she'd admired. Lady Ann educated her.

The Mirenzian bodyguards stood stalwartly at all the hall's entrances. Nora wanted to tell them to go to bed, that she couldn't very well escape at midnight on these rural lanes. But she might be tempted to try, if only so she might chase after the real princess.

At last the men returned, still wielding brandy glasses and smelling of smoke. Some were still discussing politics and their latest gambling exploits as if they'd been dragged too soon from the table. Nick was apparently the reason for their earliness. He was the first into the hall, and the look of determination in his eye as he headed straight for her was enough to take Nora's breath away.

What would it be like to have a man looking at her like that all the time? She would no doubt expire of lust.

He bowed to both of them. "Ladies, you light this gloomy hall with your beauty far better than any candlelight. We must share your flames with the others. Lady Ann, I believe Lord Quentin wished to discuss stabling his Frisian mares, and I recommended your expertise."

The duke's daughter positively glowed and departed with barely a word.

Nora narrowed her eyes at her escort. "You certainly know the way to a lady's heart. But I'm not impressed by your flummery. I need that message to reach my mother. I would be far more impressed if you offered to do that."

"It's been done," he said, sounding amused. "Very clever wording. And your mother will understand that you've not been frittering away your shillings on gambling? I would like to meet her someday. We could almost have franked the message and mailed it without a worry."

She glanced at him in puzzlement. "If mailing is faster, why shouldn't we do that?"

"Because, your majesty," he said teasingly, "the Home Office reads almost everything sent by foreign nationals. Or they let it pile up in their office and pretend they're reading it. Lady Belden would have had to send it. But I prefer to be safe. A messenger is on his way south now. I cannot promise his swift return, however. He has instructions to find us in London if he is not quick."

Nora drew in a deep breath of relief and relaxed. "Thank you. I'm terrified Elena will disappear and I'll be the center of an international scandal. I cannot live in the public eye like this much longer. Has there been word of any more assassins aiming at the duke?"

He turned serious. "None. Montague is consulting his own spy network in an effort to discover what might be happening behind the Mirenzian government. It takes time to obtain information from a war zone. We need the real princess."

"Then possibly we should cultivate some of the bodyguards. We know not to question Martine. What do we know about the others?"

"You're enjoying this, aren't you?" he asked with suspicion, drawing her toward Lady Belden.

"I'm enjoying learning to survive out of my element. I'm not enjoying being shot at or having my friends and family endangered. If you must question the bodyguards further, it would be easier after I've retired to my room. I'm sure you know what to do. We apparently need more information than just Elena's direction."

He stopped before the settee. "Lady Belden, I recommend you do not engage in games of chance with her highness. Perhaps it would be safest if you have someone escort the princess to her suite before she robs the company blind."

Lady Belden looked startled, but Nora merely nodded her agreement. It had been a very long day, and she had much to consider.

She wondered if she could discover Nick's chambers and outwit the guards posted outside her door.

# Chapter Nineteen

"IT'S THE PRETENDER," the young guard slurred in Mirenzian. "He would see our princess banished."

Nick leaned his chair back and propped his boots on a kitchen pail. With the duke and his servants out of the way, he had free access to all the guards. He doubted these younger ones knew much, but every piece of information helped.

He sipped the wretched gin the bodyguard preferred and pretended to nod drunkenly. "Men are better at war. Women belong at home." Which was most likely nonsense, but the boy didn't need much encouragement.

"Our princess is a warrior!" The boy hiccuped. "But we are a small country. We cannot fight Napoleon. The Pretender would ruin us."

"Better the devil you know," Nick agreed, doubting he could pry more out of the lonely boy before he fell asleep in his cups, wondering if there was any way he could sneak into Nora's room when it happened.

"*Precisamente,*" the boy muttered in battered English. "The princess is in much danger. We had to take her away until she can be married and Napoleon's army can protect us."

Nick's ears pricked up, but he sipped his drink and poured more into his companion's cup. "Danger? I doubt that," he scoffed. "It's easy enough to give a woman jewels and send her away."

"Not *our* princess," the boy said proudly. "She will fight to the death for us. We all know that, so must the Pretender. We must see her married and on the throne before he can claim it. We guard her with our lives."

More alarmed than he cared to reveal, Nick nodded in muddled agreement. "Then so must we. She will be safe with us."

"If she will only listen and let us take care of her," the boy said morosely. "But she is headstrong."

That was saying it mildly. "She approves of the husband chosen for her?" he asked idly. "Headstrong women like to have their own opinion."

The boy's eyes looked ready to roll back in his head as he

struggled to speak. "She threw a tantrum and swore she would rule alone. But a woman cannot," he concluded with a continental shrug.

"Tell that to Queen Elizabeth," Nick muttered as the boy's head finally hit the table.

Another claimant to the throne willing to assassinate a princess did not sound healthy for anyone's future, Nick mused as he found his way up the kitchen stairs, leaving the young bodyguard to sleep off his excess. Why would anyone care about an insignificant fly speck on the map like Mirenze?

Hot-headed youth was his conclusion. Pride and power hunger. Bad combination. He knew of the existence of Elena's male cousins, but now he needed to know more. Did they think Boney would support their claim to the throne?

Did the tontine involve the male cousins in some way? Did one of the cousins seek to eliminate the others? To what effect?

He located Quent in the study, reading one of the ancient tomes on European history. His lordship's brandy glass was barely touched. The man had a strong Methodist streak in him.

"As we suspected, we have a revolution within a revolution," Nick said tiredly, appropriating Quent's brandy and sipping something smoother than blue ruin. "There's a Pretender to the throne, probably one of the male cousins. The guard seems to think the princess truly is in danger."

"Charming of her to set her English cousin as target," Quent said dryly.

"She probably thought Mrs. Adams would be exposed as a fraud fairly quickly. She didn't count on so intrepid a replacement. She merely hoped to disappear with a head start." Nick frowned, not quite believing this version either.

"Best to see what the lady's mother says," Quent agreed. "If anyone knows what the princess is about, it's the archduchess. Montague says she's quite a character."

"Another day or two here should be safe." Nick abandoned all hope of ever seeing Nora's bed again if this dragged on much longer. "I just fear our widow will take up arms and go looking for her cousin on her own if we don't produce results."

"Surely not," Quent said with amusement, closing his book. "We've provided her with the cream of society for entertainment."

"Have you provided her with fencing duels and sailing classes?"

Nick rose and threw back the rest of the brandy. It would be a long night with no means of slaking the desires the widow had aroused. "Or perhaps a school or two she might teach? She's not likely to sit about discussing needlework."

"Fencing?" Quent asked with interest.

"Fencing. I fear it may be on the morrow's schedule." Nick eyed the decanter but decided he'd need a head on his shoulders come dawn.

First, he had to survive the night knowing he was under the same roof as the most tempting woman of his acquaintance, and he couldn't have her.

He was sadly out of practice at denying himself these days.

\* \* \*

Nora gazed pensively out the French doors overlooking her balcony. She was fairly certain that was one of her guards lurking in the shrubbery below. Another was stationed outside her door. Occasionally, she heard him snoring.

She should be enjoying this brief respite from work and tedium and taking full advantage of the entertainments provided by a generous Lady Belden.

She should. But she wouldn't, not while her family was in danger.

What was that sound?

Nervously, Nora pulled her robe tighter and stepped deeper into the shadows created by the dying embers in the grate. A rattle, as if of boys scuffling in leaves, but louder. Outside, she thought.

Her first hope was that Mr. Atherton had actually dared climb the ivy pillars to the balcony, but that was romantic silliness. Nick was not remotely romantic. He had his family to think of, just as she had hers.

Another disturbance, this one more like *thuds*. Then... scraping? Her heart beat faster, whether in fear or anticipation, she couldn't say. The sound definitely came from outside. She wanted it to be Nick.

She was very afraid that it wasn't. She reached for the small sword she'd propped beside the bed. She'd found a well-balanced one in the weapon room, one that suited her height and grip.

She grabbed a pillow from the bed and flung it at the window. A shot rang out in response, shattering the glass.

*Not Nick.* Nora dashed to the bedchamber door, flung it open, and nearly stumbled over the guard sleeping in front of it as she fled into the hall.

Had she been the only person awake to hear the shot? The girls had housed all the guests in this wing for convenience. Most of the men were on the upper floor, the women on this one. No doors in the long corridor opened—except one.

The shadowy figure stepping into the corridor wore breeches and a flowing shirt and held a sword—not female.

"Nick!" she whispered, dashing in his direction. So, she hadn't been the only one pacing the floors.

Shoving his sword into its ring, he grabbed her by the waist and lifted her bare feet off the floor without saying a word, dragging her back to his room.

"I heard a shot," he murmured, holding her still and listening. She could feel his heart thumping against his chest and almost lost track of his words. "What happened?"

With Nick holding her as if she mattered, Nora tried to be attentive, but the churning in her midsection wasn't entirely due to the shot. "I heard sounds in the shrubbery and threw a pillow at the French door. I feared someone was breaking in." She wrapped her arms around his neck and leaned briefly against his comforting chest. Even though he clasped her tighter, she struggled to be returned to the floor. "We must catch him!"

Nick snorted, pried the hilt of her sword from her fingers, then set her down. "*You,* Lady Boudica, must stay hidden. I'll kick a few guards and fetch Quent. But the shooter is likely to be gone already."

He opened an ancient wardrobe and dropped her inside. "*Stay,* so I know where to find you if we must act quickly."

"Give me my sword back," she demanded, "or I'll do no such thing."

He hefted the blade, apparently approved, and handed it over. "Promise you'll stay?"

"Not long. Hurry!" She tugged the door closed.

* * *

Nick kicked the sleeping guard awake, indicated silence, and slipped into Nora's room. He smelled black powder and felt a draft from the shattered window. The ball had entered high—a lousy shot.

Leaving the guard to wake his fellows, Nick ran to the stairs, glad that he hadn't had the energy to pry off his boots yet. He sent the footman nodding off at the bottom of the stairs to fetch Quent. Before he'd left his room, he'd stashed a loaded pistol in his waistband. Like Nora, he'd kept a sword at hand as well, although he'd chosen a saber that sliced as well as punctured.

He took the terrace door he'd noted earlier, slid along the shadowed wall, and slipped into the shrubbery. He had only to think of that pistol ball grazing Nora's brow to strip off his London façade.

His eyes adjusted quickly to the dark. All his senses were on alert. He smelled the bastard before he saw the denser shadow amid the bushes. Any murdering thief worth his salt knew not to wear *cologne*. Rank amateur.

Slipping silently behind his victim, Nick placed his sword at the man's neck and pushed up his chin with the blade before the shooter knew what hit him. Glancing upward, Nick could see Nora's balcony just above. He pressed his blade harder until his prisoner gurgled and grabbed his wrist.

"Who are you?" he asked in Mirenzian, not in the least fazed by the feeble grasp at his sword arm.

"It is me, Guido," the boy protested.

Cologne and a squeaky voice. With a sigh, Honorable Nick reappeared. "And who the devil is Guido?" he asked, lowering his blade from the boy's neck.

"The princess knows," he said urgently. "I must get a message to her."

"By shooting at her? I think not." This looked to be a damned long night, but he preferred action to pacing floors. "What is the message?"

"You could be one of *them*," the boy protested. "I can only speak to the princess."

"We're in England now. We protect our monarchs. You can rot in a dungeon or you can tell me who you are and what you want. You terrified her just now."

"No, not her highness," Guido argued. "She knows the signal. She knows I would not harm her. Please, take me to her. She's in grave danger."

"From your pistol balls," Nick agreed. "Pistols are damned accurate and a stupid way of sending a warning. I am not impressed."

At a groan from under the hedge, Nick wielded his weapon again.

"The guard," Guido said, spitting his disgust. "I barely hit him and he passed out."

Noting a large shadow creeping along the wall, knowing only one man that massive in the company, Nick held the boy's arms behind his back and shoved him toward the terrace.

"You'll find a guard casting up his accounts in the bushes," he called to Quent. "Sit on him before he does someone harm. I've caught a messenger."

He pushed the boy's empty pistol into his waistband along with his own and wondered what the hell he did next. He certainly couldn't take Guido to Nora—who didn't know to expect pistol carriers for messengers. Their charade would be over in an instant.

"Not a friend of her highness's bodyguards, I take it?" Nick asked the boy while Quent bent over the man in the yard.

"French spies and toadies," Guido admitted. "Her highness hates them. She will want to speak with me if you tell her I bring word from the prince."

"By jingo, the prince, you say," Nick said in his most affected tones. "You speak with princes, too? Didn't think Prinny had it in him to speak Mirenzian."

"Better take him inside before this one comes around," Quent warned, propping up the uniformed guard. "We'll have all the spies out here shortly. I know enough French to know they're not happy that the princess isn't in her room."

"The princess isn't here?" the boy asked in genuine alarm.

"Tell her bodyguards that a poacher missed a shot. Puff-guts there chased him off." Nick indicated the pudgy guard on the ground. "All's well and they can all go back to their tippling."

Nick marched the boy off into the shadows at the rear of the house, finding the kitchen door he'd left unfastened so he could slip in and out. Like any good fox, he preferred more than one escape route. He shoved the boy inside, located the key to the wine cellar where he'd watched the cook hide it, and lit a lantern.

Before guard boots could trample down the stairs and through the kitchen, he marched the shooter into the cellar. The boy was starting to look frightened. Good. Nick still wanted to smack him around for shooting weapons at women. The princess must be a real saint if that was the kind of signal she preferred.

"Where's the princess?" the boy demanded bravely, if foolishly.

"Hidden, and she'll stay there until I say it's safe, so speak quickly. What's your message?"

"I can't tell you! You're English!"

"Fine, then I'll leave you down here until someone finds your bones, while I take the princess somewhere less dangerous." Nick turned to head up the stairs.

"You can't do that! The French know Piotr is in England! They're looking for him. The harbors are all watched."

The southern ports were all minded by Montague's men, who were looking for a runaway princess, not a prince. "Piotr? The son of the Prussian archduchess?" he asked, testing his Mirenzian knowledge.

The boy watched him warily, rightfully so. "You know of Prince Piotr?"

"I know the princess, so I know of Prince Piotr," Nick lied without a qualm. He assumed Piotr must be the Pretender the Mirenzian guard had derided. The princess had a mini civil war on her hands.

"He must be kept safe, at all cost! The princess will know what to do," the boy said frantically.

Ah hah, the princess and her guards weren't on the same page, which might explain why she hated them. Nick suspected the princess was already doing whatever she needed to be doing— although he wouldn't trust her to do anything not in her own interest. Royalty played double games the way others played whist.

Two of the Continental cousins in England, with Nora's archduchess mother playing at intrigue. Nick smelled a plot in the making.

"We have private yachts that will take the prince safely to any port. How do we get a message to him?" Nick asked carefully.

"Through Aldo, the princess will know," the boy said, apparently trying to sound adult and not too eager. "Please, may I speak to her?"

"Who sent you?" Nick demanded.

"Aldo, the prince's personal guard, of course. Only the princess knows how to summon Aldo. I must act as her messenger once she tells me where I must go."

Damned corrupt European royalty with their devious intrigues.

Nick gritted his molars in frustration. "And the princess told you to shoot at her to let her you know you have a message?" he asked, barely hiding his incredulity.

"Yes! It is an old ploy used by our people. In the confusion, we should have time to speak. Besides, if someone shoots at her, she has reason to implore the English king to protect her. Then she will be safe from the French spies who surround her."

"You shot at her in London yesterday, too?" Nick asked, trying to think like royalty and knotting his brain in consequence.

"Someone shot at her besides me?" the boy asked in shock and genuine worry. "That is not right!"

And *he* was the one who had suggested introducing Nora to this nest of vipers.

# Chapter Twenty

NORA BRUSHED off the cobwebs she had accumulated after exploring the wardrobe Nick had stashed her in. The stairway inside the wardrobe explained how he'd arrived on the floor designated for women. The notorious rake was talented—not to mention dangerous— if he'd discovered this passage on his own.

She studied the upper story chamber to which the stairs led, one that must have been assigned to Nick.

In the dark, she could smell his shaving soap and glimpse an open trunk. Male garments were scattered across the narrow bed. Nick hadn't brought a valet, which probably said quite a bit—he either didn't like, couldn't afford, or had no need of anyone taking care of him. Or some combination of the three.

She peered out the narrow window but all was dark below. If her guards were searching the shrubbery for assassins, they were doing so very discreetly. Where was Nick?

She wished she'd discovered the stairs sooner. Perhaps she could have seen what was happening.

She hung his discarded shirt to one side of the hollow wardrobe, folded his breeches and returned them to his trunk. She didn't have an iron with which to press them. They smelled faintly of Nick, and she indulged in a quick sniff that aroused her senses.

The door opened as she was tidying the dresser. She nearly jumped out of her skin until she recognized his scent.

"Nora?" Nick asked in what sounded like amusement, before he carried in a candle to brighten the darkness. "I should have known you would find the stairs."

"Wardrobes are exceedingly boring, and that one was strangely drafty. It begged exploring." She was aware that she was alone with a male whose tension she could sense from a dozen paces. He was operating on the war fever that had driven her father and Billy. She hadn't thought languid city aristocrats possessed that sort of volatile energy. "What did you find?"

"A message boy from *Prince* Piotr who is apparently lurking in England for reasons unknown. Your relations are a scheming lot." He flung his sword in a corner but kept his distance.

She was the one who crossed the room, wrapped her arms around his waist, and laid her head against his strong chest.

He hesitated, but in this, his male nature ruled. He held her against him and rested his chin on the top of her head, and she felt his longing as strongly as her own.

"I've a mind to hide you in a trunk and take you to Scotland and let all the lackwits run about playing spy games on their own," he grumbled.

"Except losing a princess would hurt your family as well as Mr. Montague and the duke and no telling how many others," she reminded him, relishing his strength for however brief a moment she was allowed. She knew herself to be emotionally sturdy, but sometimes, it was just good to share a man's physical strength.

"I'm not qualified to make moral judgments," he said, almost angrily. "I will protect life before anything so feeble as reputation every time. I don't have to like it. It's one of the reasons I didn't wish to take on this task. But they've asked me to guard you, and so I shall."

"But is my life truly in danger?" she asked. "Our assassin seems very—"

"Inept?" he suggested. "That's because this one isn't an assassin. He's a messenger the princess was expecting. Only she's not here to accept it. She obviously had other plans that didn't involve princes and messengers."

"Oh, dear. We really need my mother." Pressed against him as she was, she could feel his arousal. How dangerous would it be to...

As if reading her mind, Nick set her back. "Quent can only hold off your bodyguards for so long. We must return you downstairs where you royally thank them for their duty and return to your chamber."

"Could I not have my things moved to the room with the hidden stairs? That's so much more useful!" Chilled now that she was separated from him, she ran her hands up and down the satin sleeves of her robe.

"You would tempt a condemned man?" he asked wryly. "I need to send messages to Montague and help Quent. Go back down the hidden stairs and as soon as you hear me in the corridor, emerge from the wardrobe chamber as if you'd been there all along. Go."

He shoved her toward the cabinet.

Like any good sailor, she knew how to take orders. She didn't have to like them. And if he did not untangle them from this charade soon, she also knew how to mutiny.

Using her sword to cut through any lingering cobwebs, she worked her way back down the narrow stairs to the ladies' floor and waited beside the door of the empty chamber until she heard Nick. Then she emerged from the dark room in her nightrobe, and nodded regally at the overexcited guards waking up the household. Walking past their stunned reactions, she returned to her assigned chamber without explaining a word. Royalty didn't have to.

She was starting to appreciate Elena's penchant for mischief.

If the guards could have nailed the door shut from the outside, she thought they might. She listened to Nick jolly them along with laughter and backslapping and probably the offer of a bottle of rum.

She slept late the next morning, as apparently did everyone else awakened by midnight searches. Groggy, she lingered over the breakfast table, wondering how long it would take her message to reach her mother and return—or if she should even wait.

Lady Ann led a contingent of the company to the limited stables. Lord Quentin, Lady Belden, and Nick weren't to be seen. Nora sipped her tea and contemplated her next act.

What if she disguised herself as a maid and slipped out to take a coach home? Her hands were rough enough to pass inspection. She had heard dialect all her life and could speak like an uneducated servant without too much difficulty. Thanks to Lady Belden, she had plenty of coins in her purse.

The ramifications were too many. She didn't wish to hurt her hostess or any of her friends. She didn't wish to set Mirenzian guards scouring all England and perhaps discovering Elena.

She pushed an egg around, nibbled some toast, and read a newssheet someone had left on the table. The remaining ladies talked of fashion and gossip, of which Nora knew little. She was relieved when Lady Belden arrived and spirited her away with excuses.

"Mr. Montague is most alarmed with this latest development," Lady Bell whispered as the Mirenzian guards followed them to the conservatory added to one of the newer wings.

Lord Quentin and Mr. Atherton appeared from behind trellises of dead vines to frown at the guards and force them to stay outside the conservatory, where they could only see Nora but not hear the conversation.

"We fear an elopement between Princess Elena and Prince Piotr," Lady Bell continued. "They are first cousins, as are you, but such matches are not unusual for royalty."

Mr. Atherton had returned to his casual elegance in the latest fashion of dark green riding coat, fawn breeches, and high-topped boots with crisp linen elaborately knotted over his embroidered waistcoat. It was hard to imagine this fop sailing a yacht and wielding a small sword, but he was a man of mystery, Nora now knew. Normal gentleman did not transform from fop to spy in the blink of an eyelash.

"If Elena and Piotr meant to join forces, then they would not be skulking about trying to reach Portsmouth," she protested. "They'd marry and announce it to the world as a *fait accompli*."

"That's what Jocelyn said." Lady Bell sent the men a look of triumph. "If the princess has found a man to help her rule, she'd thumb her noses at the French."

"But Montague's mind is more devious than any woman's," Nick said heavily. "He thinks Piotr doesn't know where the princess is, or still thinks you are Elena. Montague believes that Elena has run off with her lover, and she has left you to claim the throne with the prince."

Nora had never sputtered in her life, but she came close now. Finally, she managed, "That's ridiculous," and began pacing the aisle between tables. But the more she thought about it, the less ridiculous it became. A marriage between royal first cousins cemented power in the family's hands. She still had difficulty thinking of herself as royalty, though. "So what do we do, invite the prince here and say 'Look, no princess, go home'?"

"And invite male hysterics?" Nick asked dryly. "If the prince has his father's support—which includes an army valuable to both Boney and England—I don't think we'd enjoy the results."

"We need to produce the real princess, force her to state her intentions, then help her to carry them out," Lord Quentin insisted. "These ridiculous games aid nothing."

"These games are what Mirenzian royalty do for entertainment," Nora said. "It is in the blood. My mother indulges in chicanery for the sheer pleasure of it, now that there is no danger to family. She has garbed herself as a Gypsy and appeared at our door to sell us our own pots, then laughed when we did not recognize her. I hadn't realized she was teaching me to deal with her family should they come looking for me, but she is wise and has taught me well. We could quite likely hold the princess at gunpoint in the Tower of London, and she would lie without blinking if it suited her purpose."

Nick raised a mocking eyebrow at her. "And we are to believe you after you tell us this?"

Nora shrugged. "My father was a good English Navy captain. He taught me honesty. I have the ability of both my parents to deceive or be direct. But last night I remembered my mother's story of the prince who was raised by wolves."

Three elegant aristocrats swung about to stare at her, enrapt. Nora hoped she remembered the fable properly.

"There were four princesses, but only one could be queen. They made an agreement to each share the burden of the crown as needed. The eldest fell in love with a bear and was carried off to live in the forest, leaving the others to choose who would be queen. Each of the others had their own story. I thought they were fairy tales, but..." She hesitated, trying to remember details. "The princess who lived in the forest with the bear had a prince cub who was raised by wolves. He was strong and brave like his brother wolves, but he had to live in the wild. He could not live in a palace. As a child, I thought he was a sad excuse for a prince."

She watched Nick's expression and smiled the moment he caught on. His mind was as devious as her mother's, even though he leaned against a table and toyed with a half-dead rose as if her tale was a giant bore.

She took a deep breath and continued. "But the wolf could lead an enormous pack and rescue princesses. And so, one day, he arrived at the palace to save his little cousin from an ogre, and they lived happily ever after with the prince guarding the palace with his brother wolves."

"The Prussian archduchess is the eldest of the four instead of Elena's mother?" Nick instantly asked.

"It would seem so," Nora agreed.

"And she raised her son in the safety of the Prussian courts, prepared to lead an army if the need arose," he concluded. "Which it always does among the many fractious factions of European monarchy. The original princess chose a powerful ally for her small country rather than be queen."

Lord Quentin frowned. "Wouldn't a male be the more logical ruler? Why is her son not already next in line instead of Princess Elena?"

"Politics." Nick shrugged. "The princess chose not to be queen, so her next eldest sister apparently took the throne. Princess Elena is the eldest daughter of the late queen and their government has apparently appointed her next in line. The devil they know and all that."

"One wouldn't want Prussian wolves on the throne," Lady Belden agreed.

"And Napoleon certainly doesn't want the Prussians on his doorstep," Lord Quentin said with a heavy sigh.

"But England might," Nora said quietly. "My father might have been only the younger son of a younger son, but he was the grandson of a *marquess*. My mother married into English aristocracy so Mirenze might have another powerful ally."

"And..." she paused to straighten out the crooked thread of her mother's tale..."If the four archduchesses had a pact to share their power, might that pact include their children? A tontine, as it were, in sharing the crown equally?"

* * *

Viviana's message didn't arrive via the messengers who had been sent to deliver Nora's plea. It arrived in the hands of a fisherman's boy who tagged along as his father delivered fish to the kitchen. Most normal princesses would have ignored a maid who passed a message from the kitchen that someone wished to see her. Nora, however, half expected her mother to be down there, except Viviana's arthritis made travel difficult.

Pretending to take a stroll in the kitchen garden to admire the herbs, Nora recognized Johnny from the village. With her bodyguard watching with an avuncular expression, she greeted the boy running up to her with a question about the fish she liked. Surreptitiously she palmed his message, slipped him a shilling, and sent him skipping off to rejoin his father. She leisurely continued admiring the garden.

Not until she returned to the ladies' parlor and picked up a book was she able to unfold the message. Viviana's shaky penmanship and poor grasp of English spelling was as difficult to decipher as ever. So was her coded message.

*Ta wolf is et ta door. Ve canot aford ta bote. Can tu com?*

Anyone intercepting the note would think it the work of an ignorant peasant. Even if they translated *bote* as *boat,* they would think it had to do with fishing, especially with a fisherman carrying it.

Nora translated it to mean that the prince—the wolf— had contacted Viviana about finding a ship, and they needed Nora for some reason.

She was rather glad that she'd never been inflicted with her mother's insane family in the past. Mirenzian royalty wreaking havoc with lives endangered their normally staid existence.

At the same time, the tales of such activities were all too familiar. Her father had told her of the exploits of English agents who carried secret messages to foreign shores. Her mother had filled her head with court intrigue and treachery. She'd never thought to use those lessons in her quiet life as schoolteacher and seaman's wife, but she knew her duty.

If Prince Piotr needed help to protect her mother's country, Nora was obligated to do all in her power to aid him—if it aided England.

She closed the message inside her book and pondered. If she were true royalty, she would have no qualms about using her friends for her own purposes. But her parents hadn't raised her that way. They'd given her the information she needed to make her own decisions and taught her to respect others.

Carriages and baggage wagons were already pulling up to the doors with guests invited for the evening's ball. The corridors were a bustle of activity upstairs and down. Exiting the parlor, Nora led her retinue of guards through the masses, greeting familiar faces with a nod, intent on seeking the privacy of her own chambers.

She and Mr. Atherton had no understanding other than mutual lust. She disliked disappointing him, but he needed to do what was best for his sisters, and aid his dying father, just as she must see to her mother's request. Perhaps after she did what she had to do, he'd come looking for her.

She doubted it, but time would tell. Maybe she'd learned to be brash enough to look for him.

# Chapter Twenty-one

STANDING IN the shadows of the massive medieval fireplace, leaning his shoulder against the timber mantel, Nick sipped his brandy from a crystal goblet and studied the elegant crowd garbed in rich silks and satins. The rural musicians were playing a fast-paced *contre danse* and London's aristocrats were behaving like rural squires, kicking up their toes and prancing about the ancient hall under the iron-wheel chandeliers.

Someone had suggested that everyone be masked as they entered, so masks had been hastily ordered from the city and passed out to every guest beforehand. Not that anyone was truly disguised. Nick knew to avoid the redhead who had wanted to drag him to Brighton. Quent loomed above most of the gentlemen, as did his sisters in most cases. Petite Lady Bell was hurrying about, commanding the musicians, the servants, and tardy guests, so her ever-present chestnut coiffure was obvious.

Nora's gold-streaked brunette and unassuming figure easily blended with all the other young ladies, except she was wearing the silk woven with gold thread that he'd chosen, and not white muslin. And her bronze coloring was far richer than her English rose companions. Nick counted her royal guards scattered about the perimeter, keeping track of them as well.

His one concern was that Guido had escaped the wine cellar where he'd hidden him. The boy had been well fed and provided a cot and pillow and warned of the danger of the royal guards. The brat had apparently not listened. Nick feared he lurked somewhere about, hunting for the princess.

Instead of looking for a suitable partner for his bed tonight, as was his usual wont, Nick scoured the crowd watching for assassins and Nora. She had been behaving with unusual complacence, not even demanding a fencing lesson or archery contest.

Nora was ignoring him, and that made him crazy. She behaved just as she ought, and that worried him beyond measure.

He watched as she danced in the same set with his sisters. They were all laughing over some misstep or jest, just as any young women should be. Trouble was definitely afoot.

Quent plowed a path through the guests, handing Nick another drink while laconically studying the crowd as if only observing his female relations. "Nothing from the mother yet?"

"Not that I'm aware of." Another tiny gnat niggling at him. "We'll have to return the party to London in the morning. Any word from Montague?"

"He doesn't have enough men to hunt both a prince *and* princess. He's ready to inform His Grace of events and tender his resignation. Says life's too short for this."

Nick snorted. "That means Jocelyn is polishing pistols and threatening to shoot royalty. Blake doesn't like her near his firearms after she shot him in the foot."

"Can't say I blame him, but I hate for a good man to take the fall for a wayward princess. England needs his fine mind. He's giving thought to having our faux princess ask for asylum to see if that will lure the true one from hiding."

"It will certainly make London exciting for a few days. And longer than that if the Imperial Guard decides to shoot her," Nick said morosely.

"The offer to take them all to Scotland still stands," Quent said with what passed for joviality in him.

"Only if you take up my duty as bodyguard. I'm not made for northern climes." Nick shuddered as if he already felt the chill.

"I doubt your princess is either, if she's fled to the south coast. We'll find her. Montague is considering warning the duke that a Prussian prince is loose in the countryside and asking for reinforcements for our search. We may have to call in the Horse Guards."

"Call in the Navy, the bloated bumbling idiots," Nick said gloomily. "That should create an international incident to eclipse all others."

"You speak from experience?" Quentin asked, raising a dark eyebrow.

Unwilling to answer that, Nick set his glass aside and left his friend behind as the music ended and the dancers scattered. He needed to claim a dance with Nora before he exploded all over the well-dressed crowd. Assuming the gaggle of young women gathering in the corner hid the object of his interest, he discreetly elbowed his way toward them, wishing Quent's sisters were less tall or the widow of better height so she didn't disappear so conveniently. He caught a glimpse of the gold gown and strode faster. But when he arrived at the gaggle of maidens...

Nora wasn't there.

Biting back a *Merde!* he strode for the stairs. No more disappearing princesses, faux or otherwise.

\* \* \*

Garbed in a maid's old muslin and a wool cloak, Nora nursed a mug of grog and studied the nearly empty tavern. No one appeared to be raising an alarm yet, and even the presence of the regal Lady Ann hadn't truly raised eyebrows. The inn was the only one on this small harbor; they had no private parlors, and it was raining.

"You have no idea how much I appreciate this," Nora said. "I suppose I really should learn to ride—sometime when I have a stable at my disposal."

"Mirenze is small. It is understandable that you would not need to ride often." Lady Ann dismissed the protest with a wave of her hand. "I am happy to place my carriage at your disposal. I'm not often called on for aid. People think I'm arrogant, I believe."

"They are worried His Grace will chop off their heads," Nora said with a smile. "But dukes cannot chop off the head of a princess, and he will not chop off yours, so I do not hesitate to ask your aid. You've been a true friend, and I hope I may assist you someday. It is a pity the rain has delayed our escape, though. I'm afraid we may have to turn back."

"Nonsense. Ships sail in all types of weather. They are merely waiting for the tide to turn. You are sure you will be safe until your prince boards? Your escort is scarcely reassuring." Lady Ann glanced at young Guido standing stalwartly at the door, watching over them.

"The prince's men are everywhere," Nora lied, gesturing to indicate the weathered sailors lounging about the tables. "I did not wish to endanger anyone with French spies all around me. Tell your father to have my guards thrown from the country. I will be safe now. He has done a good deed through you. England will have the support of the prince's men in this terrible war."

"He would rather hear that from the prince," Lady Ann said. "Could you not persuade him to London?"

"Possibly. But assassins are everywhere, as you have seen. I will leave that choice to Prince Piotr. I am just relieved that he was able to find his way here without harm."

"I wish I could meet him," Lady Ann said almost wistfully. "Is he very handsome?"

Nora shrugged. "He is Prussian. What can I say?" Since she'd never seen the man in her life, she couldn't say anything. It would be lovely to introduce the duke's lonely horse-mad daughter to a genuine prince, but for all she knew, he was a filthy pig.

An urgent clatter of horses tearing up the street outside warned her guards had discovered her absence. Nora had hoped for more time. With a nod, she directed Guido to depart. "It is time I slipped out to the ship, my lady. I thank you—"

The tavern door slammed open and Nick swaggered in. *Swaggered.* Still garbed in his fashionable black evening attire, his linen still a gleaming white, he flung back his cloak with a dashing gesture and hailed the barkeep. "Ale for the gents behind me, good sir! Good English ale for all around!"

He glanced at the tavern's occupants and added, "And for the ladies, of course. Good evening adorable ones! This must be my lucky night. May I join you?"

As if he'd be put off if they said no. Nora scowled at him. "We were just leaving, sir. My lady has a carriage waiting."

"What, go out in this beastly night? I forbid it! Sit still. Have a warm toddy. Your driver will appreciate it." Spreading his cloak by leaning his hand on the booth back, he shielded them from the audience he'd created. "Or I will wring your bloody necks," he whispered as boots clattered through the doorway.

"My prince is waiting," Nora whispered maliciously. "Lady Ann will explain to the duke. Just chase away the menaces you have led here!"

His normally blue eyes flashed an icy gray. "You are not going anywhere with only a boy as escort. You are waiting for me."

"Mr. Atherton!" the duke's daughter exclaimed in horror. "You are speaking to a reigning monarch."

"I am speaking to a spoiled hoyden, monarch or not." He glanced over his shoulder as two of the Mirenzian bodyguards entered in damp uniforms and gold braid. "Ahoy there, good fellows! Bloody miserable night out, ain't it?"

Nora watched him swirl to pound the soldiers on the backs and steer them toward the barkeep. She knew fishermen and was accustomed to traveling about on her own. She had not wanted to lead the guards to her mother, and she had hoped to protect all her new friends by departing quietly. And she might have done it, too, had the rain not slowed them down.

"I can still slip out through the kitchen if Mr. Atherton keeps them distracted," Nora whispered to her companion. "This is even better because he can see you safely home."

"Atherton?" Lady Ann asked incredulously. "I'd be safer taking myself."

And to the casual observer, so it would seem. Nick was quaffing ale and teaching the Mirenzians a naughty sea chanty. Nora's insides warmed with fondness just watching him, knowing precisely what he was doing. She was sorry Lady Ann couldn't see it.

"He's a good man," she said, "with a dying father who would be hurt should his son disgrace him. Be sure to tell His Grace that Mr. Atherton behaved in all ways honorable. If you'll rise and swing your cloak about as he did, I'll slip out back, unnoticed."

Lady Ann wasn't very good at dramatic gestures, but Guido darted out from the shadows and made a production of helping the lady with her garment. At the front of the room, Nick again raised loud protests about ladies and rain. Under cover of the distraction, Nora in her maid's disguise slipped behind the booth and through the door to the kitchen.

The weary woman stirring the pot over the fire glanced up but said nothing as Nora pulled her hood over her head and stepped into the drizzle. The downpour had lessened.

In seconds, Guido joined her to take her to the ship he had arranged.

* * *

Nick raged internally as he caught the motion near the booth from the corner of his eye and turned to block the women from sight of the bodyguards. He was taller and broader than the two soldiers who'd followed him into town. They'd have to physically lift him out of the way to see around him.

Damn the woman! Could she not stay put for two seconds? Or trust him to take her safely wherever she wished to go? Of course not! What bloody woman paid a bit of attention to common sense?

And devil take it, now he had a duke's daughter on his hands. As Lady Ann progressed through the tavern, looking neither to left or right, Nick pounded the closest guard on the back, forcing ale up the bloke's nose until he spluttered.

"The lady needs an escort, gentlemen. Looks like I'll have to be it. Enjoy your evening." He threw a guinea across the counter at the dour barkeep, who bit the gold coin to test its veracity.

Sweeping out as if he hadn't another concern in the world, Nick wasn't surprised when the two guards stumbled after him. He didn't know why they followed him except that they knew they couldn't trust the princess, and they thought he was in collusion with her. Her dressing one of the maids in the gold gown and hiding the wench behind a mask hadn't fooled Nick for an instant, but it had bamboozled the idiot guards long enough to give him time to search Nora's room and discover she'd cleared out.

She hadn't left him any choice. He'd known precisely what she was doing, and he simply couldn't let the fool woman do it alone.

Two could play her game. Shouting sea chanties at the top of his lungs, Nick entered the stable where he'd left his horse. Dropping his high-crowned hat and cloak on the tall stable lad, he handed him a coin and pointed him in the direction of the carriage maneuvering out of the yard. The rain was letting up and the duke's daughter was a blazing good handler. She'd be fine. He just needed to divert the bloody spies.

The stable lad eagerly accepted coin, horse, and disguise, trotting out after the carriage and swaying drunkenly.

"Good lad," Nick muttered, grabbing up the valise he'd left in the stall. He wasn't about to cavort about the countryside in satin breeches. The sword was starting to feel much too comfortable at his hip.

He hurried down the path to the harbor, not doubting in the least where his runaway was headed. Guido had said he'd sailed up from Sussex. Fishermen from Hytegate had delivered fish to the kitchens. The damned woman was too comfortable with seamen.

The harbor was small. The fishing trawler setting sail was easily identifiable. Without a hitch in his stride, Nick dropped his valise into a bobbing row boat. He leapt down and rowed himself out, hailing the trawler.

Fishermen stared from the bow at a gentleman in flapping cloak and knee breeches, but Nick knew their language. He asked for permission to come aboard. They dropped a line. Roping his valise over his shoulder, he climbed hand over hand to the deck.

He met stares of astonishment with a shrug. "Admiral Nicholas Atherton, late of his majesty's Navy, at the lady's service. Proceed as usual."

They stared, but they'd already given berth to a lady and her foreign guard. Their passage had been paid, and no one had told them to guard a princess with their lives. They accepted the gentleman at his word.

Still in his evening satin, Nick swaggered to the hatch and climbed down as if he truly did rule a navy. He had more honest knowledge of how to do so than most of the figureheads in the admiralty office and suffered no qualms at his pretense.

Guido guarded the captain's door. Nick approached the stern wearing his most menacing frown. Guido nervously crossed his arms over his skinny chest.

"I can break your jaw or you can let me by. Your choice," Nick threatened.

"Let him in, Guido," Nora called in Mirenzian from the other side of the door. "Go find something to eat and get some sleep."

Guido glared. "You will respect my princess."

"As well as she respects me," Nick promised sarcastically.

"I heard that," Nora said in English as he shoved open the door.

She had discarded the wet cloak and was drying her hair in front of the coal stove. It fell to her waist in golden-brown waves that captured and held the firelight. Nick caught his breath and nearly stumbled in weary appreciation.

"I'll not thank you for nearly aging me a decade," he said, shutting the door on Guido and struggling to remove his soggy dress coat. "I'm charging the damned duke for this Weston I've ruined running after you."

Still brushing her hair, she tilted her head and boldly watched him strip. "You could have gone home with your sisters and washed your hands of the whole affair without a moment's dishonor," she informed him. "As far as the world knows, I escaped French spies and assassins in the company of a duke's daughter and the prince's men. I could send a message thanking you for delivering me safely from harm."

"Thought it all out, have you? All those sailors out there are known to you? You know precisely where to go to meet your prince? Planning on sacrificing yourself on the royal altar?"

"If necessary," she admitted, answering the last question first. "Mostly, I wished to relieve everyone of my presence and meet my cousins. Wouldn't you be curious if you were me? My mother says the prince is a bit desperate."

Nick knew how far he'd crossed the line when he debated throttling her or heaving her across the bed and having his way with her. A proper gentleman would have simply walked away.

"All of Europe and half England is desperate!" He tried to keep his voice to a low roar. "You cannot go about rescuing everyone!"

She studied him with curiosity and—he hoped—mischief, given her next words.

"As a princess, I very well might," she suggested. "Guido thinks I'm real."

"Guido thinks anything in skirts should be worshipped. If you sacrifice yourself on the royal altar, I'll never speak to you again," he asserted insanely, unable to tear his gaze from her half-opened bodice.

"Well, then, we should quit speaking and start doing now, before I decide." She set her brush aside and dropped the bodice.

# Chapter Twenty-two

NORA HAD never learned to be shy about her body. Robbie had shown a healthy enjoyment of what she had to offer. She knew men watched her, even if she was nondescript in comparison to the elegant feathers of society. Nick had made no secret of his male appreciation.

His hesitation now as she untied the strings of her skirt caused a moment's trepidation, however. His hand had frozen at his damp neckcloth as if she'd done something totally reprehensible instead of acting on the desires she'd thought they both experienced.

"I know I'm no longer as slender as I once was," she said, not completing her task. "Perhaps I am too plump for your tastes?"

"Plump?" He nearly strangled himself before he finished untying his complicated knot. "I enjoy *women*. I want experience, not skinny sixteen-year-old virgins who have to be taught to enjoy my attentions."

He stepped closer, his gaze now fully focused on her breasts. She had been unable to resist wearing the gauzy chemise under the coarse cotton. In her haste, she'd kept her own corset, and it pushed her flesh upward to fill the gown she'd been wearing earlier. Nick's gaze brought her nipples to rigid peaks pressing against the thin fabric.

"A connoisseur," she said faintly as her blood heated. She was already wet and ready for him just from the caress of his words.

She ought to be concerned about making babies, but she wanted children, and she could support one on her own now. Children were the least of her concerns.

"But if I take you now..." he said, casting aside his neckcloth and nearly ripping his linen over his head. He scarcely took his gaze from her as he did so. "It will be a rough rogering and no lengthy bedplay. I've reached the end of my tether, Mrs. Adams."

Beneath the civilized elegance of frock coat and waistcoat and linen, Nicholas Atherton was all male animal, with rippling muscles under a golden-bronze sprinkle of hair. His nipples were hard. His biceps bulged. Nora's gaze dropped lower. He was large all over.

"Yes," was the only senseless reply she could make as she

dropped her skirt to the floor.

Without any more warning, he lifted her from the puddle of fabric and carried her the two steps to the bed. His heavy weight crushed her into the thin pallet—just the way Nora wanted him, needed him. She spread her legs and reveled in the hardness pressing into her there through the fine chemise. What he'd done for her the last time was still fresh in her mind. She didn't need more foreplay. She longed for completion.

"Inside me, now, please," she demanded, or tried to demand, but her voice sounded weak and thready. She grabbed a hank of his hair and steered his mouth to hers.

His kiss was fierce and hard and nearly consumed her. This fiery hot-blooded creature was the man beneath the shallow frippery, the intense man who lurked in the depths of his eyes. Finally, at last, she was about to meet him.

His rough hands pushed up her breasts and his mouth took her there, suckling so hard she cried out with the pleasure and pain of it. The urgency building inside her demanded release. She wrapped her legs around his hips and rocked against him.

They wrestled for control, while wrestling with the sheets and their clothing. Tugging and pulling at strings and buttons, they occasionally stopped to savor the brush of flesh against flesh, and fence with tongues when their bodies could not join fast enough. Nora scarcely noticed the chill when Nick divested her of her last fragment of fine silk. Surrounded by his steel-hard nakedness, she could only cry out with gratitude and grab his hair again, covering his jaw with fervent kisses.

He'd already shoved her bare legs apart. Nora had only a moment to take a breath before Nick drove into her slick passage, plunging deep and true, filling her so thoroughly all the blood rushed from her head and the room spun.

The ship lurched against a wave, heaving them closer, and Nora cried out with the joy of it. Nick propped one arm on the side of the bed to hold his place. Hovering over her, holding her pinned with his weight and male equipage, he met her eyes, and his mouth thinned in determination.

"No royal altar while you are mine," he declared.

He gave her no chance to reply to his insensible declaration. He covered her mouth with his and drank her cries as he did as promised—royally rogered her.

Nora smothered her cries of release by biting his massive shoulder. Still shuddering with the aftershock, she clung to muscled arms as Nick drove deeper, higher, and brought her to ecstasy a second time with the powerful waves of his own climax.

"Yes, that is even better than I thought it could be," she murmured from the moist cocoon his great body wrapped around her. He cradled her closer and she fell asleep to the rocking of the ship as it took to sea.

She woke to damp, dark cold and Nick fondling her breasts to readiness again. It had been a very, very long time since she had come close to satiation, and her hunger was as strong as his. They rocked the ship as surely as the waves did with the strength of their need.

In the morning, with dawn spilling through the stern window, she woke to an empty bed.

* * *

With the crew convinced they harbored royalty, and possibly an admiral, Nick was free to confiscate the captain's rough clothing as well as his cabin. The trawler was a good size and made rapid headway to the southern port it called home.

Nick paced the deck, debating the insanity that had him aboard a ship again, no doubt sailing into in international imbroglio. He was trying hard not to think about the generous woman lying sprawled in the bed below. The old possessiveness returned every time he did, and that was one passion too many for his life now.

Guido joined him at the rail, giving him better occupation for his mind.

"I was told to ask for Her Highness's aid, sir, not her presence. The prince will be displeased." The boy's overlong black hair blew in the brisk breeze.

"Pleasing royalty is about as fruitless as pissing in the wind," Nick said callously. "Find a pretty girl, settle down in a quiet village, and forget royalty."

"I have no family or coin other than the king's," the boy said with a shrug. "I go where I am told."

"The king, you say? I thought he'd abdicated in favor of his daughter and Boney's cretinous relations." Hands behind his back,

Nick gauged their course, reckoning they had traveled past Dover over night and were not too far from Brighton. *Brighton.* He could just spit.

He ought to simply return to the beautiful, receptive creature he'd left spread between the sheets and forget royal messengers. Nora was so much more luscious than he'd imagined that he'd almost been afraid to leave her bed. Which was why he had to do so. Self-control was the secret to comfort and family, and he'd honed it to a fine art.

"His Majesty still worries about his daughter and his people," Guido said with all the solemnity of the young.

"Right. Prince is rich, is he? Brings a nice dowry?"

"The Prussian court is not poor," Guido agreed. "Our country is poor. Revolution has bankrupted France. We would fare better with a wealthy monarch."

Nick snorted. "So you're not entirely stupid, just naïve. Fair enough. You have no way of shooting at the prince as you did the princess to pass a message?"

"Of course not," the boy said, outraged. "His Highness is a foreigner. He does not understand Mirenzian ways."

"Unless his mother is long dead, he understands all right. Why is the prince in England?"

"To speak with the Home Office and to escort the princess home."

Nick suspected that last part was the reason the princess wasn't to be found. He ground his molars at the very real possibility that Nora could step into her cousin's shoes. If the prince had never met Elena, he wouldn't know the difference between them. A Mirenzian court could do little if one cousin ran away and another stepped in, not if the prince accepted the exchange.

It shouldn't be any of Nick's concern if Nora chose the life of royalty over being a poor seaman's widow. She was quite right. With power, she'd have the ability to make changes for the better. He simply intended to make certain she wasn't coerced into the role.

The object of his thoughts arrived before he could quiz the boy further.

She'd apparently packed the simpler garments of her new wardrobe, but even in a high-necked muslin day dress and a concealing cloak, Nora looked like a princess. It was in the way she held her stubbornly round chin, the richness of her exotic complexion, the flash of dark eyes. Even the way she carried herself as she crossed the deck—shoulders back, head high, her gait confident—radiated aristocracy. No wonder she'd had no difficulty fooling all society. A few unsophisticated seamen would see what they'd been told to see.

"We are not sailing up the Thames," she said with sarcasm and no indication that they'd spent the night together.

There had been moments when Nick had considered redirecting the ship to London. He could have taken the wheel, if necessary. But he'd stayed in the lady's bed instead. He hoped they both wouldn't live to regret it. "I am brushing up my Mirenzian in anticipation of meeting a prince," he said in that language, for the boy's sake.

"I see." She turned to the worshipful lad who had dipped to his knees. "Do we have time to break our fast before we land?"

"Yes, your highness. I will see it done." He raced off.

"Weevily biscuits," Nick said morosely. "I'd rather go hungry. Have you any notion of how to find a prince?"

"Ask," she said with a shrug. "If I can send word to my mother, she will aid us."

"And then what?" Nick braced himself on the rail, refusing to look at what he couldn't have. But she must have brought her rose-scented soap. He could smell her. She aroused his cock without him even looking at her. She could probably whisper in his ear, and he'd have her up against the bulwark.

"I assume we ask your friend Mr. Montague to find the prince a ship," she continued. "I do not know what Elena promised."

"A throne," he said promptly. "It's always about power and riches."

"Sometime, I'd like to hear your story," she said. "Your cynicism exceeds your circumstances."

"You don't want to know my story. This is who I am now, a man with doting family and no responsibilities, and I like it that way."

"No, you don't, or you wouldn't be here with me now. I gave you a rabbit hole to escape through, and you didn't take it. We may lie to others, but it is pointless to lie to each other."

She was probably right, but he'd been lying for so long, he didn't think any truth existed. "Your body doesn't lie when I'm inside it," he said crudely. "That's all the honesty I need."

"You're still lying. I'll see you below. Strangely, I've worked up an appetite for weevily biscuits."

Damnation, he couldn't even insult the woman. The wife and daughter of sailors wouldn't affect airs. She knew vulgarities as well as he did.

A tiny futile flame of hope rose that maybe he'd finally met the one woman with whom he could be himself.

He doused that flame as the coast rose into sight. She'd sail off into the sunset to a future ripe with promise. A retired reprobate with no ambition would have little appeal to a young, idealistic woman of Nora's nature.

\* \* \*

"I am known here," Nora murmured as they stood at the railing, watching the trawler ease into the harbor on the tide, after a breakfast that had *not* included weevily biscuits. "We need to send Guido away so the 'princess' can disappear and I can be myself. You can be an old friend of Robbie's or perhaps son of one of my father's friends."

"An interesting switch of positions," he said without rancor. "You're known and I'm not, until we meet one of Montague's men."

He'd been humoring her these past hours, giving no sign that they'd lost themselves in each other's arms last night. Nora understood that men didn't like revealing vulnerability, and neither of them dared display affection as long as she played a princess. Or even if she became herself. But the ease with which he distanced himself hurt, just a little.

"The fewer people who know of my relation to Elena, the safer my mother will be. Perhaps my return will draw the princess out of hiding."

"Or send her eloping to Scotland," he scoffed. "Let us address immediate concerns. You know a respectable inn?"

"The Whaler's Arms is the most respectable but not one I could normally afford. Perhaps the King's Inn. Plain but clean and quite respectable. If people recognize me there, they won't be surprised." Nora wasn't entirely certain how she felt about returning home. She would have liked to have seen more of London, but there were aspects of traveling with Nick she wouldn't exchange for entire cities.

"You're an heiress now," Nick protested. "Won't they be

expecting you to live like one?"

She sent him an amused look. "Everyone who knows me would be shocked. Leave my mother in a drafty cottage while I cavort with the wealthy? No, I'm much more likely to be starting a school and perhaps interviewing one of your sisters as a teacher."

He didn't look particularly pleased to hear that. But then, aristocrats were shocked that people actually had to work for a living. She hadn't thought Nick easily disgusted, but then, what did she know about him, after all? "What name shall I call you by?" she asked, to see if he was ready to play in her world.

"Bartholomew," he said gloomily. "Just call me Bad Bart."

She laughed. "Will you wear an eye patch and a parrot on your shoulder?"

"I might," he threatened, gazing out to sea. "Don't trust Bad Bart for a minute."

"Well, Mr. Bartholomew, if we're to start a school for sailor's children together, you really must behave with civilized decency. You'll simply have to reform Bad Bart."

"Would that I could, my lady, but he's a notorious scoundrel." Losing his morose tone, he turned a gleaming eye in her direction. "Your reputation will be in tatters. Perhaps we should say we are betrothed. Bart has no intention of letting you sleep alone."

"I have an understanding with someone from my home," she reminded him, although she thrilled at the heated look he bestowed on her. She hadn't forgotten so soon what all that male power and desire could do to her. "Bart will simply have to behave with circumspection."

"You still intend to let your butcher have your inheritance?" he asked, his lustful look replaced with horror. "Are you mad?"

"He's a well-respected grocer, and I'm certain he'll agree to a settlement that allows me control of half my funds. I doubt he's seen such wealth and wouldn't know what to do with it. How many aristocrats of your acquaintance could say the same?" she asked with a degree of hauteur at his reaction.

"We'd all waste it on brandy and linen," he agreed stiffly, returning his gaze to the waves. "I'm sure your grocer is the better man."

Nora tried to reassure herself of that as well. A *better* man, not a more exciting one. Steadfast. Reliable. Not a warrior like Robbie who would never be home when she needed him. Not a man like Nick who would always be in another woman's bed.

She was perfectly content with that decision—after this little adventure was over.

# Chapter Twenty-three

ISABELL SIGHED in resignation as a flood of lovely, very young, blond ladies tracked her to her private parlor and besieged her with questions the day after the princess and Mr. Atherton disappeared. She'd feared this. She wasn't certain she was prepared.

She didn't know what the usually practical Mrs. Adams and the irresponsible rake could be thinking to create this sort of scandal. And she had no idea what to say to Nick's devastated sisters.

"Nick wouldn't do what they're saying!" Georgiana declared without preamble.

"He would never ruin a princess!" Diana insisted.

Nick had a great many sisters. They all spoke as one.

"You must tell the old biddies that Nick is doing his duty and protecting the princess," Abigail insisted with more dignity than the others. "We have said it and said it, but the gossip is too titillating and they do not listen."

"It will *kill* our papa!" Bertrice cried, truly near tears. "Nick would never ever disgrace us like this."

Lord Quentin scratched politely at the open door, and Isabell glanced up to him with relief. "You have heard from them?"

The Atherton sisters turned in expectation, twittering unfounded phrases of excitement and relief.

Quent looked as if he'd back away under the deluge, but he bravely raised his hand for silence. "Your brother is on a diplomatic mission. There's no more anyone can tell you. Just smile and look mysterious and invoke His Majesty's name upon occasion if anyone dares speak gossip to you."

Isabell added her reassurances and suggestions and shooed the earl's progeny off with grave regret. She shook her head as Quent closed the door after them. "They are too young to understand. Atherton is breaking their hearts. I don't suppose he's done anything sensible such as deliver Mrs. Adams to safety and joined Montague in his search?"

"They commandeered a trawler to Sussex with the royal messenger. The Mirenzians will figure that out soon enough and be on their trail. The Imperial Guard has already taken his horse back to town. I've sent one of the stable lads to follow him."

Isabell narrowed her eyes and paced the floor. "If Atherton is coerced into marrying my protégée, our wager is off. I wished Mrs. Adams to have *choices*. This charade has ruined everything."

"I doubt that those two can be coerced into anything," Quent said mildly. "What we must concern ourselves with is who *they* will coerce and into what. I have a feeling our rake is a wolf in sheep's clothing and has fooled us all."

Isabell halted her pacing to stare. "Atherton? He does nothing but charm women and has done so for years. The two are no doubt holed up in an inn somewhere, enjoying themselves while we walk the floors."

Quent looked amused and handed her a note he produced from his pocket. "Nick spent his youth in the Navy until the crew mutinied in the Caribbean. At the age of twenty, he was already leading a pack of pirates. It seems most of London has underestimated him."

\* \* \*

With Guido carrying a message to Fitz Wyckerly, the Earl of Danecroft, Nick took two rooms at the King's Arms for Mrs. Adams and Mr. Bartholomew.

Nora knew half the town, it seemed. She stopped to speak with nearly every man she met, forcing Nick to fight his primitive possessive instinct.

He'd avoided Brighton all these years for good reason. Being thrown back to seaports and creaking inns and a milieu he hadn't encountered in well over a decade cracked his carefully-constructed façade. He kept his hand on his hilt, his back to the wall, and his gaze all about him as he escorted Nora up the narrow stairs to their rooms.

With keys to both chambers in his hands, he opened the first door, shoved Nora in, and threw in the baggage. Without bothering to look at the second room, he joined her, shutting the door and locking it behind him. He *needed* to release this pressure to keep up his pretense of civility.

Nora was the civilizing effect he needed most.

She arched her lovely eyebrows in surprise as he flung the captain's rough woolen cloak to a chair and ripped at his neckcloth.

"Don't. Say. *Anything*," he grumbled, reaching for her prim bodice and practically pulling off the buttons.

Her eyes lit with laughter as she grabbed his rough cotton shirt and tugged it from his breeches. He loved an obedient woman.

The tension seeped out of him once he had the golden globes of her breasts in his hands. Her sighs of pleasure were music to his ears. Her kisses grew bolder, and he was laughing with her by the time they tumbled to the bed.

"Not a princess," he declared as he kissed her ear and ruched up her skirts.

"Just a wench," she agreed, unfastening his trousers.

Wenches were more likely to swing grappling hooks than shoes, but Nick preferred good, honest lust to seductive persuasion. Simple, mindless, and pleasurable plowing, gratification of basic human needs with no strings attached, that's all he asked.

And that's all Nora gave, with much enthusiasm and the wonder of a healthy young woman long denied. While she bucked beneath him, he didn't have to think about the gossip no doubt raging through Whitehall by now. He didn't have to worry about alienating his sisters or his stepmother or infuriating his irascible father or suffer the fear of being disowned again. He didn't need to watch his back. He need only give and take pleasure.

It was only later, when they'd washed and Nora began hooking her bodice over her generous breasts, and he must button his placket, that the desperation returned.

"We need to rescue royalty quickly," he said, shrugging on his coat. "How will you send a message to your mother and find the prince?"

She studied him with curiosity as she fastened a hook. "As myself, of course. A lovely letter excitedly explaining about Mr. Bartholomew's investment in our school and the teachers we will hire. I'll ask her to send my royal blue gown to this address."

*Royal blue gown.* Damn, but she was good. He admired her far more than was healthy.

It was easier just to think of bedding her. A woman who could choose between a prince and a grocer had more facets than a diamond.

"I don't suppose there's any chance that your mother knows how to find the princess and will tell us?" he asked, buckling on the damned sword.

"If it was not for the note about the tontine, I would believe Elena to be long gone, with no intention of looking back. But there may be more to come," Nora said, pinning up her hair. "I don't know if my mother can manage to write a message that would discreetly convey her discussion with Elena. I really need to return to Hytegate to speak with her."

"All London will believe I've run off with a princess, so we must be quick about this." He'd donned his oldest clothes this morning. He glanced with regret at the valise containing his good linen. "Perhaps I ought to find an eye patch."

She crossed the room to kiss his unshaven jaw. "Your beard will suffice, Sir Bart. Drink rum and eat with your fingers. Come along, I'm starved, and I need writing implements."

Nick was aware she was leading him around by his prick and he didn't care. The head on his shoulders had proved useless in preventing the insanity they'd embarked upon, so he might as well think with the little head in his trousers.

* * *

That evening, after sending the note to her mother, Nora nervously nibbled her dry pen nib as the first big stranger walked up to the bar and ordered ale in a guttural English with a distinctly foreign accent. Had her message reached her mother already?

The scratch on her palm tingled while she pretended to scan the notes she was writing and surreptitiously checked to see what Nick was doing. They'd decided to be seen in public so any messenger from her mother or elsewhere wouldn't have to search for them. The massive stranger made this decision questionable. The second stranger taking a table at the window was even more worrisome. His goatee was very foreign.

Nick was idly whittling at a stick at another window table. He looked even more glorious in rumpled stock and stubble than he had in silks and lace. His hair was a bit too neat, the angle of his jaw too crisp, and his gaze too sharp to pass as a common seaman idling his time, but he would do as a wealthy country squire willing to invest in her school.

It was a pity he was neither seaman nor squire. He excited her as no man had since her husband. And if she was perfectly truthful with herself, he excited her far more than Robbie had. Her husband had been young and would no doubt have grown into an exciting man, but Nick... Nick surpassed anything Robbie could have become.

But she was a practical woman and knew their days together were numbered. She would just enjoy the intensity of Nick's desire for as long as it lasted. She suspected it would burn off now that the pampered London gentleman had been reduced to rough linen sheets and no servants. But while it lasted...

She still tingled every time she thought of what they'd done. And there was so much more that they hadn't had time to do.

She watched as Nick took his empty mug back to the bar and said something to the large stranger. It was almost the dinner hour. How could her note have had time to reach her mother and be forwarded to a prince?

Viviana must have had Prussians camping in the attic, if they'd appeared so promptly. It would have been easy for Mr. Montague's men to have missed them if her mother had chosen to hide them.

It certainly wasn't easy to miss them now.

Nick turned to lean his back against the bar and gesture with his mug. The bear of a man beside him did the same, pulling out his watch and checking it. He glanced at her, back to the watch, and muttered a guttural approval.

They were speaking Prussian! She was almost certain it was Prussian. And broken English. Neither man was fluent in the other's language. But Prussian! How had Nick learned any such thing?

He fascinated her far more than he should. Had she been foolish in thinking she could simply enjoy the pleasures of the flesh without involving her heart? She didn't think herself so silly. She had a mother and a home she'd be happy to return to. As soon as this was done, at least.

The Prussians left and Nick sauntered over to her table, holding out his hand. "A little stroll before dinner, perhaps? The sun has almost come out."

She eyed the gray day through the window with skepticism but knew he wished to speak without anyone hearing. She packed away her writing material and accepted the cloak he threw around her shoulders.

Under cover of the cloak, he squeezed her hand, and she felt the gesture all the way to her toes. This was it, then. They were headed out to meet a Prussian prince. Or archduke. Or whomever. She still thought Nick's strong hand more exciting.

But she had to release his hand to respectably hold his arm as they strolled into the evening gloom. Her skirt brushed his trousers, increasing her awareness of his tall presence beside her. She could feel his tension.

"What was that all about?" she murmured, although she doubted if anyone passing would care what they said. It was a relief not to be followed about for a change.

"We have agreed to meet in private. Apparently your likeness to the princess passes his inspection. He keeps her image in his watch."

Nora winced. "I cannot imagine how I must look as a painted princess. Where are we going?"

"To the Whaler's Arms, of course," he said wryly. "Did you think royalty would accept anything less?"

"He's not staying with Prinny at the Pavilion?" she asked in mock horror.

"In the new stables?" Nick asked in the same tone. "The Pavilion is terribly outdated unless one wishes to stable horses. I'm sure your prince has better accommodations than a horse stall."

"Not in Brighton," she concluded in her usual voice. "Although, I suppose as royal palaces go, the Pavilion is probably better than an inn. Perhaps Prussian royalty would be impressed."

"One assumes he is traveling incognito. I doubt your prince has introduced himself to the fabled corridors of the Pavilion. I simply want the war-mongering Prussian on his way home and the princess found so I may return to my life," he stated flatly.

And there it was, the rift between them. He wished to return to idle frippery. She wanted to be useful, to aid England as her father had, or aid a prince, if that was what it took. She was *enjoying* herself.

Oddly, she'd thought Nick was enjoying this break from polite society, but apparently she was wrong. She pointed out the sign for the inn they sought. Instead of immediately entering, he stopped to adjust her bonnet and scan the street around them, as skillfully as if he pursued secrecy all the time. Well, so he must, if he indulged in frequent clandestine relations.

It was her own fault that her heart beat a little faster with his gentle caretaking.

"No Frenchman in sight," he said cheerfully, leading her into the elegant inn paneled in rich woods and lighted with brass chandeliers.

The smaller, elegant foreigner who had departed earlier from the table by the inn window nodded discreetly in their direction and led them down a carpeted hall. Nora barely had time to admire the paintings on the wall or wonder what lay beyond the thick paneled doors before the Prussian opened one and gestured them inside. He, too, scanned their surroundings to be certain no one followed.

The chamber was a small parlor, complete with mahogany dining table, high-backed chairs, and a fire crackling in the grate. More paintings adorned the wall, mostly images of horses and hunters.

"His Highness will be with us shortly," the older man said in accented English. "It is a most anticipated pleasure to finally be in the presence of Your Highness."

Nora darted Nick a quick look. He hadn't told them Elena was missing yet?

Nick performed a formal bow as if he were wearing court dress. Straightening, he made the introductions. "My lady, Aldo Berezin, the prince's second in command. Lord Berezin, may I present the Archduchess Viviana's daughter, Lady Elena Marone Ballwin Adams."

The narrow shoulders of the other man stiffened. Before he could speak, a door to the rear of the chamber opened, and an aristocratically tall, uniformed bear of a man entered.

"Ah, my little cousin, at last we meet!" He crossed the parlor, grabbed Nora by the waist in a hug, and lifted her from her feet.

When he bussed her on both cheeks, Nick pulled his sword.

# Chapter Twenty-four

LORD BEREZIN yanked his sword from his ornate scabbard before Nick realized what he'd done. Gritting his molars, he shoved his weapon back where it belonged—only because Nora placed her gloved palms on the prince's shoulders and shoved him away.

So much for diplomacy.

"Prince Piotr, I presume?" she asked with dry delicacy. Once returned to the carpet, she made a show of dusting the wrinkles from her skirt.

Nick took a deep breath to calm his racing blood and tried to deduce what had just happened here. He'd almost caused a diplomatic *faux pas* of international proportions because a prince had greeted his cousin?

Or because another man had touched Nick's woman? He'd *never* fought over a woman. They came and went far too easily. It would be like fighting over china dishes. But Nora was different... somehow.

Apparently only a little flustered, Nora held out her hand to the prince. Having donned sash and gold braid and medals, the prince clanked as he bent over to kiss the back of her hand. Nick's blood heated all over again. He'd have to behead royalty if the prince mauled her one more time.

The Prussian smiled as he straightened, wielding sharp cheekbones and formidably square chin in a manner that probably had ladies swooning. His cropped hair was the same brunette as Nora's, without the gold streaks.

"Perhaps some tea while we talk?" Nora suggested, seemingly oblivious to Prussian dimples. She gestured at the table already set with good English china.

"This is not the princess!" Lord Berezin protested. "She is an impostor!"

"She is the Archduchess Viviana's daughter," the prince corrected. "Her Grace feared it might be so."

The fierce-looking Prussian gently assisted Nora to a chair near the fire. Nick continued to grind his teeth but resisted pulling a weapon. So far, no one had offered them any threat. It was time they had a few questions answered.

"I am sorry I cannot be Elena, your highness," Nora said, accepting the cup and saucer the furious Berezin handed her. "She seems to have run away, leaving me in her place. We hoped you might know where she has gone. And why."

Nick stood at the table near Nora and served himself for fear the prince's steward would poison him. If looks could kill, he would be dead already. In retaliation, Nick insouciantly sipped his tea, smiling over the brim as if he'd planned this charming little tête-à-tête between a disappointed, power-hungry prince and a seaman's honest widow.

The prince doctored his tea with the contents of a flask and offered the flask to Nick, who knew better than to accept it. Vodka was deadly to a man who must think on his feet.

"It is goot," the prince insisted. "You will like."

"My duty is to the lady," Nick said agreeably, leaning his shoulder against the mantel in a position that allowed him full view of the room. "I will wait."

Berezin scowled. The prince nodded and swallowed the contents of his cup before responding.

"Elena is opposed to the French," the prince announced in his accented English. "She vants war. Mirenze cannot hope to fight Napoleon, even with all my soldiers. I told her I vould marry her and help her rule wisely, but I will not ruin my men for her. She was not happy."

Nick focused on Nora's reactions rather than crush the fragile cup he held. She seemed to listen with interest and nothing more. Did she understand that the Prussian was *not* volunteering to ally England against Boney?

"You do not know where she is, then?" Nora asked, ignoring the political for what mattered most to her...and to Nick.

Prince Piotr waved a big hand. "With Arturo, no doubt. She prefer that boy to a man like me."

"Arturo?" Nora prodded gently.

Surprisingly, Berezin responded. "The Austrian cousin," he said with a sneer. "He claims to be a man of science. Now that Austria has fallen to Bonaparte's military prowess, he is running for his life. He won't help her against the French either. So, they flee."

Nick resisted squeezing the bridge of his nose to prevent his head from exploding. "The princess has run off with the son of the

Austrian archduchess, leaving Mirenze and Napoleon in the lurch? No wonder she has the Imperial Guard on her heels."

"*Exactemente*," the prince said in satisfaction, resting his heavy boots on the andirons. "And that is why I am here. The throne of Mirenze needs a Marone. Two Marones would be even better. Archduchess Viviana agrees and has given me permission to court Lady Eleanora." He nodded cheerfully at Nora.

Nick waited for his lover to spew tea across the room, but she seemed remarkably complacent. She had, after all, predicted this state of affairs. He was the one stupid enough to think he could disentangle royalty and send them all home.

"I will make no promises until I have seen Elena," she said with confidence. "I wish to hear her desires and not by way of gossip."

By George, the lady had a head on her shoulders! Montague might be saved yet. Nick hid his admiration by sipping his tea and wishing he'd accepted the vodka.

"If I knew where Elena was, I wouldn't have bothered your so-charming mother," the prince said with a deep sigh. "I fear we have endangered the archduchess as it is. It is best if the French do not know all our people here."

Nick grabbed the teapot and leaned over Nora to refill her cup, forcing her to stay seated. Otherwise, she'd leap up and hare off to throw herself as shield in front of her mother. "The Earl of Danecroft is whisking Her Grace off to his estate as we speak. She is safe."

"The Earl of Danecroft?" Nora asked faintly.

"Fitz. We sent Guido to him this morning. There should have been ample time for Fitz to spirit your mother to his estate, where even the most intrepid of Frenchmen would get lost and fall into a swamp before he found the front gate. At which point, a dozen tiny ruffians would beat him up, bury him in the mud, and trample over him with elephants."

Nick smiled at the mental daggers she shot with her eyes. So, he hadn't told her all his secrets. Or any of them, for all that mattered. He had difficulty trusting anyone.

"A goot man to have on our side, yah?" the prince asked affably. "So, must we speak with your king to ask for your hand? Or your guardian?"

"You don't need either," Nick said while Nora tried to recover from a fit of the sputters. "You only need the tontine, as I understand it." He didn't understand it, but he bluffed and waited for their reaction.

Interestingly, Berezin scowled and the prince looked surprised.

"What is this *tontine*?" the prince demanded.

"The archduchess did not tell you?" Nick asked, fisting his fingers and trying to keep them from his sword. This was worse than negotiating safe harbor for a pirate ship.

"It is of no moment," Berezin insisted, pouring more tea for his prince. "Marriage will ensure the succession."

Recovering, Nora applied her wiles to the confused prince. "My mother did not explain? Perhaps you should go back to her and ask. But I believe all four of us need to meet before any decision can be made about the future of Mirenze."

Nick shrugged and needled the scowling Lord Berezin. "These things cannot be rushed."

"They must be," the older man insisted. "The Imperial Guard has hired assassins to stop the prince from claiming the throne. His Highness must be returned to the custody of his retinue on the Continent before the French find us."

"Then you will have to return without Lady Eleanora," Nick said firmly. His hand went to the hilt at his hip as the bear of a prince shoved himself from his chair.

"That is for the lady to say," the bear growled. "We came here to take the princess back to Mirenze with us. But now that we have found Lady Eleanora, she will suit. She will be *queen*."

"The lady wishes to speak with *all* her cousins before she does anything," Nora said sweetly, handing her cup to Nick, forcing him to release his sword. "We will continue searching for the missing princess. And our Austrian cousin, if you say he is here. We will give you word when a ship is available to sail you safely home, if that is your preference. Or you can wait to join us after we find Elena."

She rose and gestured for her cloak as if she were the missing princess—or already a queen. And accustomed to obeying, Berezin provided.

Nick hid his smirk as he escorted her from under the noses of the two silent Prussians. He could feel their frustration—foiled by what must seem to them to be a hank of hair and a bit of lace. They couldn't very well attack a lady on foreign grounds and expect to escape with their lives.

"We had best find new lodgings," his inamorata whispered when they reached the streets. "In mama's tales, the wolf's family is prone to kidnapping."

* * *

Energized by the verbal fencing with a *prince*, Nora was prepared for almost anything when they returned to the King's Inn. Even though she'd been mentally braced for the prince's preposterous proposal—she thought the alliteration appropriate to her sputtering reaction—she hadn't been ready for his physical presence.

The prince was gorgeous. *Strong.* And behaved with an admirable loyalty to the Mirenzian throne. Prince Piotr was true royalty, of the kind one read about in storybooks. He was a wise monarch who protected his men while attempting to protect his people. *Elena's* people. Nora approved—up to a point.

She had a strong suspicion that people in power thought that what they wanted was best for everyone. Combine arrogance with power, and one had dangerous men willing to use any means necessary to obtain what they wanted.

The tall man gripping her elbow as they traversed the darkening street oozed tension, glaring at poor merchants as if they were treacherous pirates, tensing at every small sound. She probably should not have mentioned kidnapping until they were back at the inn. She had not thought the insouciant rake would take her speculation so seriously.

Bad Bart did. She wished to know this other side of her companion better. Perhaps, in bed tonight... She hurried a little faster at the prospect of sharing a bed again.

"We'll have to find another inn," he murmured as they approached the well-lit tavern. "That will delay any kidnapping plans for a day or so. I'm not certain we can bring all four of you together before we run out of hiding places."

"Surely they will not come after us tonight," she protested, not wishing to give up the lovely room awaiting them.

"I would, if it were me. The element of surprise works in his favor." He shoved open the tavern door, keeping Nora behind him until he'd scanned the occupants. Some of the tension seeped from his taut shoulders, and he caught her waist as he pulled her inside.

"We have company."

Nora didn't want company. She wanted a bedchamber so they needn't waste any of their short time together. She glanced almost resentfully at the scattering of customers at the tables, looking for someone she might recognize.

She saw no one. A gentleman wearing an expensively tailored dress coat in a style from a previous year was the only person who looked vaguely out of place. The coat's sleeves had been neatly re-hemmed and trimmed in a manner Nora had used to remedy the fraying of Robbie's coats. But he was trim and elegant and bore the same aristocratic air as Nick and all London society as he expertly flipped cards at several local businessmen. He seemed to be winning the card game if the coins in front of him were any indication.

A lady pouring his tea was shorter, rounder, and quiet in a knowing way that spoke of intelligence, but not necessarily of the first society. She would make a good squire's wife, so perhaps the aristocratic man was a local man Nora did not recognize. But Nick did?

The lady looked up, saw Nick, and smiled but did not interrupt the card player until the hand was played out. Then she tapped his shoulder and nodded as Nick approached. Nora hung back, uncertain of how she would be greeted, uncertain of who she was anymore.

"Ah, there you are old fellow. Thought you meant to stand us up. If you'll excuse us, gentlemen..." The auburn-haired gentleman turned in his cards and rose from the table, shaking Nick's hand and pounding him on the shoulder at the same time. "Come along, we've taken a parlor. This school of yours sounds just the thing."

Nora raised her eyebrows at the lack of introduction, but she assumed they were playing the role of acquaintances for anyone watching. She released Nick's arm and let him greet his friend, while she turned to the quiet lady with the pleasant smile.

"Do you ever have the feeling we are of no more importance than the cloth around their necks?" Nora murmured, smiling and following the two handsome men catching up on gossip ahead of them.

"The cloth with which we can hang them?" the seemingly cherubic lady asked. "They know we're here, no doubt, and they are showing off like a complicated knot they are pretending they didn't just spend three days learning."

Nora laughed. Both men turned to glance in their direction. She beamed innocence back.

"Plotting," Nick said in a resigned voice. He bowed and gestured them to proceed through the doorway the other gentleman had opened.

Once inside, with the door closed, Nick hastily made the introductions. "Fitz and Abigail, Lord and Lady Danecroft, this is the intrepid Mrs. Eleanora Adams, currently princess presumptive of Mirenze."

"Princess presumptive?" the gentleman asked with amusement. "Or princess apparent since our other candidate has gone truant?"

"Neither," Nora said firmly. "I am a schoolteacher, nothing more. Pleased to meet both of you, my lord, my lady." She did her best not to reveal her reaction to the earl and countess of Danecroft. They could easily be a squire and his wife. Really, she needed to get past her awe of aristocracy—especially if she was actually heir to a throne!

"Abby," the countess encouraged. "I was a farmer's daughter far too long to be anything else. We left your mother entertaining the children with tall tales. She's a charming woman, and we'd be delighted if you would join her and stay with us a while."

Nora squeezed Nick's hand and turned a worried glance up to him. She didn't want to go anywhere he didn't. She knew that was silly of her, but these people were strangers. As much as she wished to see her mother, they had spent a lifetime together—and she'd only had a few days with Nick.

Right now, she wanted to find a princess. And sleep with Nick. She wasn't entirely certain which was uppermost in her thoughts—pleasure or duty.

Nick caught her eye, quirked one corner of his mouth as if reading her mind, and turned back to his friends. "What we really need to do is find the princess, who is apparently absconding or plotting with her Austrian cousin. Your offer of a roof for our heads is thoughtful, and we may take you up on it later, but we've just talked with the Prussian prince. We need to send a message back to Montague and be on our way—if he has directions for us."

"Mrs. Ballwin said you'd say that—something about all of you must meet to discuss some document. But I don't think she understands that all London thinks you've made off with a princess." Lord Danecroft removed a sealed message from his coat. "Quent and Lady Bell are doing their best to squelch rumors, but you know the gossip mill. If you or the lady don't return soon, they'll have His Grace and the Horse Guards after you."

"My mother understands that it would be far better if the real princess returns," Nora explained. "Or at least verify that Elena has fled to safety."

Nick slit the seal with a knife and quickly perused the document. "The French spy has left London and is heading this way. Montague has men following him but that's no guarantee of safety. The rest of the Mirenzian bodyguards are throwing fits and protesting to His Grace. We need to find Elena quickly. And keep the duke from killing us, at the very least."

"There's more," Lord Danecroft said. "We could not trust it to paper, which is why I'm here. Your crown has been sighted in Portsmouth. Quent has made his yacht available. It should be in the harbor by now."

The prince would not be pleased if both his queens ran away, Nora knew.

One yacht. Two princes. One princess. Possibly three, no four, potential candidates for the throne. And an Imperial spy. It was simply too much like her mother's fairy tales. Nora snickered.

Everyone turned to her with astonishment.

"We'll need a Navy man-o'war, maybe two, to contain that much royalty in one place," she explained, barely containing her hysteria as the complications mounted. "You'll have to meet the prince to understand."

"We could dangle both prince and princess overboard until they came to terms," Nick suggested, grinning. "How many seamen will it take to tie a Prussian bear?"

"A wolf!" Nora protested. "My mother calls him a wolf!"

The earl and countess looked on as if they were crazed, but the spectacle could only be imagined by those knowing all the parties involved. After a day such as this one, Nick's grin stirred Nora's giggles, which made him grin broader.

"The Prince and the Runaway," he suggested.

"The Princess and the Wolf," she countered.

"Two Frigates, Four Royals, and a Spy!"

Shaking his head at their antics, the Earl of Danecroft poured himself some brandy and lifted it in toast to his puzzled wife. "We've never driven men mad before, my dear. Let us drink to this new era of fun and games! Do you think it will pay better than cards?"

"I think we'd fare better to send the children with them. They're more likely to understand the jest," the countess replied.

"Children, yes!" Nick shouted in glee. "Can they tie up bear princes and transport them to the yacht, please? Perhaps I could send for my sisters to see if they'll drum up some frigates."

"Should we live to tell it, my mother will love this tale! By all means, let us summon the yacht," Nora poured a round of brandy for all.

Because she suspected no good would come of telling royalty what they did not want to hear, and if they must storm Portsmouth, the warships would be English and very real.

# Chapter Twenty-five

AFTER MORE rational discussion, Nick and Nora repaired to their bedchamber to pack their bags. Once the door closed behind them, Nick grabbed Nora, pressing all those luscious curves against him. She might think the task ahead funny, but French spies were no such thing.

He had not liked that the prince knew nothing of a tontine, but his steward did. Of course, he hadn't liked anything about the Prussians, including their offer to spirit Nora off, so he could be biased. He hadn't wanted to offer them Portsmouth or the princess either, but in the end he had, against his better judgment. He'd sent word to Piotr about both yacht and princess.

"Go with Fitz," he murmured in her ear. "They will provide you with excellent company until this is all over. You might even train their gaggle of miscreants to behave."

She pressed kisses to his unshaven jaw while wiggling out of his grasp. "No. I'm responsible for unleashing Elena on the world. If my mother thinks it's best that all of us meet, then I cannot abdicate just yet. They are my relations, not yours."

"You have no notion what you are asking," he said, unable to contain his anger when she began heaving her few unpacked items into her bag. "It wasn't Guido shooting warning shots at you in London!"

"Someone may have simply shot at the duke's carriage," she countered. "Where is Guido now?"

"If he's smart, he's sweeping floors in a tavern, but he's loyal to the prince." Frustrated, Nick paced the floor. "You know Martine does not act alone, don't you? And that the prince doesn't mean to leave England empty-handed? These games are larger than both of us. This is *war*, Nora."

And again, he had no control of his fate. He curled his fingers into fists. *This* was why he'd chosen to return to his family and a life of ease. Yes, he preferred his comforts and didn't wish to shame his family. But mostly, he didn't like the killer he had become.

"Yes, and I've lost both husband and father to war, I understand." Nora calmly cleared off the dresser as if discussing a ballroom scene.

"If you wish to withdraw and return to London, I'll not blame you. Your family would be much happier."

"This isn't about me!" How the devil had he got himself so far embedded in this ridiculousness? He was merely supposed to be seeing to her safety, not volunteering to hunt royalty. He should be heaving her in a carriage and heading straight for home. And still, he didn't shut up. "I can damned well take care of myself, but I don't wish to do it while endangering you! Let me deal with our stubborn royals."

Instead of appreciating his insane gallantry, she flung his brush at him and continued folding clothes into her valise. "Oh, yes, an indolent aristocrat should do fine if the Navy is called in to catch an escaping spy or guard an endangered prince. I'm sure you can do it all single-handed and over a teacup, if need be."

"I can and I have." Damn the woman, what did he have to say to convince her that he was a bloodthirsty wretch concealed in sheep's clothing? He planted his feet akimbo, folded his arms, and glared at her. "You do not know everything, your royal majesty."

If he told her all, she would flee into the night, which was what he wanted, wasn't it? Send her to safety. Nick's insides roiled at the thought of bringing up his past. He didn't want to lose her just yet. And she could destroy him and his family if he gave her such a weapon. Women in a rage were unpredictable.

He waited in trepidation as she straightened and regarded him warily.

"You have caught spies and guarded princes?" she asked.

"I wouldn't call them princes and spies, but close enough, yes. Believe as you will, but I started out as a Navy man." He'd scarcely been one step above middie when his career ended in flames, but that was beside the point. "I can walk the prince and his henchman onto Quent's yacht at sword point, if need be, then sail the blasted thing to Portsmouth on my own." He repeated her mockery. "*You* would only be in the way."

"I see." She sat down on the bed's edge and studied her hands in her lap. "I have become a burden instead of a help. That is rather humbling."

He smacked his hand to his forehead. Why must she twist every damned word from his mouth? He was telling her *he* was a blackguard, and she was hearing that *she* was a nuisance. "Devil take it, Nora, don't go all Friday-faced on me. I'm no better than a pirate, a scoundrel who has captured ships and slaughtered men and done my fair share of kidnapping. I *know* how these things are done. They are not for women."

*Now*, his notorious past got her attention. She regarded him with wary interest. "I don't think we'll have need of kidnapping or capturing ships," she said. "We'll just be eluding a spy or three and hiding royalty. It's not quite the same as piracy."

Perspicacious, she might be, but her naiveté in these matters could only hurt. He wasn't accustomed to arguing. This was the point at which he generally walked away. But he couldn't walk away this time, not and leave the lovely widow at the mercy of the bullies and mercenaries of the world.

"Nora, believe me when I say these things happen without planning," he said earnestly, practically pleading with her. "There is no polite society at sea on a ship full of men carrying arms. We don't know your princely cousin and his men. If he is set on ruling Mirenze, then he's capable of almost anything, up to and including hijacking Quent's yacht and stealing you. You admitted that yourself. And we already know what havoc Elena can wreak. Add French spies, and it's a recipe for disaster."

"If only men are involved, possibly," she said with a trace of acerbity. "But I have observed that men tend to behave with a little more civilization if women are about."

Nick contemplated bashing his head against the wall. What other argument could he offer to a contrary female who didn't care if he'd captured ships and slaughtered men! He couldn't believe she'd sailed right past his dastardly deeds and hidden shame, on to the next adventure.

She simply wanted her own way. Nick ran his hand through his hair and studied her with incredulity. "Do you understand nothing I say? I am a *killer*. I have *killed* men. Unpleasantly. I may have to kill Martine or, for all I know, Lord Berezin, since I can't trust him. I must be prepared for anything if I'm to see two royals and their cousins to safety."

"War happens," she said quietly. "I know my husband and father killed men. They didn't like talking about it. I don't like thinking about it. But if Napoleon's spies are willing to shoot at us, we have to be willing to shoot back. I am no hand at pistols or cannon. I don't want to be in your way. But I'm tired of being left behind. If nothing else, I might cause distraction or confusion to the French. There is no reason why only men can go to war, and women should only be pawns."

"You are mad!" Nick tried not to shout but he was fairly certain he was beyond polite converse.

"Perhaps," she agreed, snapping her bag closed. "I was young when my father died and not much older when I lost Robbie. I felt helpless. Do you have any idea what it is like to watch your world crash around you and be able to do *nothing*?" She sent him a look of both desolation and determination.

And it was that look that defeated him. It contained all her fears and tears and the power of a fighter unable to fight. He knew that look. He'd spent these last years of his life trying to escape it every time he glimpsed a mirror.

Helplessness was a perishing abscess to be lanced.

He dumped the rest of his clothing into his valise and latched it. "I do. And I never want to go there again." He took both bags and opened the door, gesturing with his head for her to proceed him. "Onward to Portsmouth, my lady. And we won't be traveling in Quent's yacht with the prince."

\* \* \*

The fishing boat had no beds, only hammocks. Nora glared in disgruntlement at the smelly cabin below decks. The captain hadn't offered his bunk.

"You wanted adventure, you get adventure," Notorious Nick said, looking over her shoulder. "You didn't really expect me to take the yacht and leave the prince to find his own way to Portsmouth, did you?"

"No, of course not." He was perfectly correct in pointing out the flaws in her noble plans. "If this is all my father's men could find for us, then this it must be. I only hope we will reach Portsmouth before the festivities are over."

She flung her valise into her hammock and wondered how one slept on canvas.

"Since I'm certain our Prussian wolf is capable of kidnapping any available princess, I won't be sorry to miss any war between your charming cousins. I just hope I won't owe Quent a yacht when all is said and done." Nick threw his bag up to join hers. "With weather moving in, it could be tomorrow before this bucket has any hope of approaching Portsmouth, so you may as well get some sleep."

"That's easy for you to say." She reluctantly removed her bonnet and cloak. The stench of fish and...urine?...permeated the sleeping quarters. "Where will the men sleep if we take their hammocks?"

"On deck, if they have time. But they've been in port long enough to be well rested. Our coins will pay them better than any fish they're not catching. Here..." He took her cloak and spread it across the canvas. "I'm sorry I can't offer you a pillow."

"And you really slept like this?" she asked dubiously. She didn't want to pry too far into his past. He seemed to be ashamed of it. And she must admit, it was very hard to imagine the elegant aristocrat actually *killing* anyone, even in a duel. Blood would be involved. It would stain his lace. But she'd seen the tense man beneath the mask. He existed on some level.

"I've slept in worse, I assure you," he said. "So did your Robbie if he was with the Navy. Here, let me help you."

He lifted her feet and Nora grabbed the hammock's edge to steady herself as he swung her in. The whole thing rocked unsteadily, and she froze, afraid she'd be thrown onto the filthy floor.

"I cannot imagine worse," she said through clenched teeth. "Men would wallow in mud if left to themselves."

Nick chuckled as he stripped off his coat, rolled it up, and tucked it under her head. "Aye, and you have the right of that. Should I join you, mud baby?"

"How?" She was grateful he was willing to wrinkle his coat for her, but no matter how much she longed for him to join her, she could not imagine his large frame in this lurching structure.

He didn't waste time explaining but fell in beside her, swinging the hammock with his weight but easily staying balanced within the cocoon of canvas. "Like that. Let my shoulder be your pillow."

They were touching from head to toe, pressed together like pages of a book. Once she let herself relax just a little, it was quite cozy. He wrapped his arm around her and she laid her head against his shoulder and they swung to the rough rhythm of a ship sailing out to heavy waters.

He seemed to unwind a little as well. "That's better. Had I had you when last I sailed, it all might have turned out differently."

"How did it turn out?" she asked, her words buried in his shirt sleeve. "Tell me a story."

"It's not a pleasant bedtime story. I went to sea as a cheerful boy and came home a cynical but wealthier man. Let it rest there. Tell me what you hope to do if you become Queen of Mirenze."

His voice sounded distant, so she did not press. If only she could have his broad shoulder every night, the musky male scent of him near, then perhaps they could talk of dreams. But that wasn't happening, as he was making clear.

"I don't wish to be any such thing," she reminded him, just in case he misunderstood. "Power comes at too high a cost."

"Then tell me what you will do with your inheritance once you return to your sleepy little village. Give me a bedtime tale."

And so she did, until they both relaxed and nodded off.

* * *

They woke to pitching waves and howling winds. The hammock careened wildly, nearly spilling them from their snug nest.

Nick hit the floor, boots first, and reached for his coat. He only caught himself when Nora stretched and yawned and grabbed the hammock to keep from falling out. He sighed, realizing his duty was here. The ship was not his problem. Reassuring ladies was far more his style, even if occasionally just as dangerous.

"Breakfast may be delayed," he said wryly.

"With weather like ours, whyever did England form a navy?" she grumbled. "We only need build up barriers on the bones of wrecked ships and wait until the weather destroys any fleet trying to sail around the reef."

He pressed a quick kiss to her brow. "All our enemies drown, add to the barrier, and we go on our merry way?" he asked in amusement. Amusement. They were pitching and rolling like a drunk after a night of blue ruin, and he was laughing. The woman had infected his brain.

Or the situation had. He recognized the thrill of action, the racing of his blood as he approached battle. He'd be shouting bloodthirsty curses and slashing throats in no time.

But right this instant, all he wanted was this woman.

"Something like that." She held out her hand for him to haul her out of the filthy canvas they'd slept in.

She'd slept in a hammock. With him. Without complaint. His admiration grew, when he ought to be irritated beyond measure at her for dragging him into this catastrophe in the making.

But when she stood up and the rocking ship threw her against him, he wrapped her in his embrace and soaked up the joy of holding a lush, sleepy, rose-scented woman. Even in this hell of noxious fumes, she perfumed his world.

"What time do you think it is?" she asked without stirring from his embrace. "And what must I use for a chamber pot in this place?"

"It's nearly dawn, and this is where the term *pissing into the wind* has meaning," he said with a laugh. He wasn't even trying to be the polite gentleman. Nora didn't seem to require artificial niceties. "Otherwise, you must use the head. You won't appreciate the simplicity or lack of privacy. I'll stand guard."

The look she sent him was a little crankier than earlier, but she accepted the accommodations when the hole in a bench was pointed out to her.

He turned his back and whistled until she was done, then grabbed her arm when she tried to stand and fell into him.

"We must be near Portsmouth. The sea will calm as we pass Wight and we should sail safely into harbor," he told her.

"Someday, you will tell me your whole story," she said grumpily. "And then explain to me why all London believes you no more than an unambitious rake."

"I am merely upholding the family honor," he said blithely. "You have met my flock of sisters. It takes an entire family to launch them, stair-step as they are."

"Well, surely no one is stupid enough to believe that a rake would kidnap a princess. What would be the point when you have all the ladies of London at your feet?" She sighed at her crumpled gown and folded her cloak tighter.

"Those who truly know me will be concerned," he warned. "Let us hope they keep those thoughts to themselves. You do not want to go above just yet. Let me see what I can find to eat, if you think you can keep down some bread and cheese."

She looked undecided but finally settled on a bench that did not pitch as much as the hammocks and let him go.

Nick made his way into the howling wind, looked up and

approved repairs apparently hastily made to the rigging, checked the coast, and knew precisely where they were. His naval training had begun here in Portsmouth. Those had been days of avid excitement and insane dreams of an action-filled future. Boys had no brains.

Disgruntled that he'd been such a sapskull, he located the mate. "Any sight of the yacht?"

"It'll be lying up snug in harbor," he admitted. "We snapped a mast, had to fish it, and lost sight of land."

Nick had hoped Quent's crew would stay within sight of the fishing boat, but Quent's drunken captain no doubt held resentment for Nick commandeering the yacht earlier. He could delight in the vision of the prince and his men making the captain's life a living hell.

"There'll be vittles below deck," the mate said. "We'll be to harbor shortly."

Not shortly unless a wave tossed them there, but Nick didn't bother correcting the genial fellow who was simply humoring him. He touched his hat brim and made his way back through the wind to the cabin.

Maybe he could lie to Nora and tell her all was well and they could have a holiday on the beach. She could gut him later when she discovered the truth.

# Chapter Twenty-six

PORTSMOUTH was crowded with imprisoned Russian invalid ships and Navy vessels. Maneuvering into the harbor in the stormy wind with an injured and exhausted crew required finesse. Nick's knowledge of the waters secured a snug berth.

His gut still churned at the proximity of the military vessels littering the landscape, but the Navy no longer had power over him. Once upon a time there had been those who knew what he was, but those days were past and most of those people were gone. The Navy had a real war to wage now.

The water was rough, but the rain had stopped. He deemed it safe enough to row ashore. The sight of Quent's yacht safely moored at the dock made it imperative that he go hunting a prince and princess before a diplomatic incident ensued that would reflect badly on Montague.

But the trawler was small and the intrepid Mrs. Adams wouldn't allow him to escape without her so easily. She had her bag on deck and was ready to leave before he could slip away.

"Dammit, woman, why can't you let me take care of you for just once?" he muttered as she wrapped her skirts around her in preparation for descending into the rowboat.

"A woman on her own learns to do for herself," she retorted. "I see no reason to depend on men at this late date."

Nick blinked, trying to absorb that anomaly. A woman who didn't want to be taken care of? Impossible. Incongruous, at least. "Ridiculous," was all he muttered as he clambered down first to assist her. "Women are not meant for climbing ladders or rowing boats."

"Most gentlemen aren't either," she reminded him. "It takes practice, is all."

She'd spent the night in his arms, small and deliciously soft and warm. When he hadn't been tortured by his straining cock, he'd been absorbing the oddity of her sweet breath in his ear and her utter trust in his embrace.

He could come to enjoy Nora's confidence, if only he trusted himself. He had too much evidence of his unworthiness to do so.

Whatever other experiences he might like to repeat with Nora, he was quite certain waiting for her to plunge into the pounding waves as the ship rocked and the rowboat bobbed wasn't one of them. He nearly had seven failures of the heart before he had her safely in his hands.

Once she was seated, Nick held onto her while the frail shell rocked and wallowed against the tide. He'd rather lose the damned princess than Nora. When had that happened? He'd take Nora over his best friend?

Unaware that Nick's careful façade was fracturing, Nora pragmatically asked, "Where are a prince and princess likely to stay in Portsmouth? Brighton is the only town I know outside Hytegate."

"The Crown Inn, no doubt," he said, once they were on shore.

Outside the Customs House and other official buildings built along the quay, he flagged down a wagon. "At least, we'll stay there while we set up a search. Montague should have his men about."

The Crown was a coaching inn of three stories and elegant bay windows, suitable for royalty. Given his hope that they wouldn't stay long, Nick took a single suite and asked for a tub and hot water to be carried up. The grateful look Nora bestowed on him was worth any cost.

Of course, if she thought he'd leave her to bathe in peace, she didn't know the limits of a desperate man. He saw the maids out, bolted the door, and swung to regard Nora and the tub of steaming water. To his delight, her smile widened, and she reached for the bodice buttons of her modest morning gown.

That's when he realized why Lady Ann and the other modest maidens he was expected to pursue would never, ever suit. If he must marry, his wife needed to be sensual and bold. He still didn't think leg shackles a very good idea for a man of his nature.

"We needn't rush out to look for Mr. Montague's men or the prince?" Nora asked with an enticing tilt of her generous mouth.

"If Montague's men are as good as I think they are, they were standing in the Customs House watching our arrival and will send someone to our doorstep shortly. We should greet them properly bathed and attired, don't you agree?" Nick already had his neckcloth flung across the wide bed and was prying his shoulders out of his wrinkled coat.

"Oh, most certainly." She glanced down at the tub. "But it is a trifle small, I fear."

"We'll manage." He tugged his linen over his head. When he emerged, she had her bodice undone and was wriggling out of her wrinkled skirt. She still wore the sheer silk chemise that clung like gossamer to her high, firm breasts. He could see the rosy crests through the filmy fabric, and he sighed with ecstasy.

"This is why God made men and women," he murmured, lifting her against him to ravish her moist lips and feel the glory of her curves against his skin.

She wrapped her arms around his neck and boldly returned his kisses. "I was so afraid that you would send me home before we could do this again. You must think me a wanton."

"I love a wanton woman," he said with complete sincerity. "I love that I don't have to seduce or plead, that you welcome me as much I want you. I might even learn to love honesty if this is what it entails."

Her laughter rang like rich chimes as he finished undressing both of them. She had her legs wrapped around his hips as he stepped into the bath. Nick let her indulge in soapy caresses and returned the foreplay, but after his long-suffering night, he didn't intend to be interrupted before he had his desires met.

Suckling her glorious breast, he lifted her over him and brought her down where he needed her most. Nora cried out in delight and surprise and quickly caught on to the power the position offered her. With glee, she teased and toyed and sought her own pleasure. But as soon as she cried out with her release, Nick grabbed her hips and pushed as deeply as her open body allowed. Within seconds, he lost himself in her, pumping his seed without care of the result. For the first time in his life, he lost his famed command of his surroundings, and he reveled in the moment.

He refused to regret his carelessness later as they toweled each other off and dressed. He wasn't without funds. Neither was she. Neither of them were bound to another. They'd find a means of dealing together, whatever happened. For now, he simply enjoyed the freedom singing through his blood. For the better part of his life, he'd felt the weight of his world rested on his shoulders. Nora lifted that burden every time she laughed.

He would dispense with a few puny royals, and soon, he'd have Nora to himself.

* * *

Nora still tingled with excitement from their watery explorations when the knock on their door warned their idyll had ended. Nick was so much more than a pretty face and a strong arm! And broad shoulders and muscled chest, she added with a mental lick of her lips.

Had they time, she would have been quite willing to learn more about the new positions Nick had taught her, except he had been right about the efficiency of Mr. Montague's spies. Wearing her least wrinkled London gown, she was still pinning up her hair when Mr. Penrose intruded.

Nick closed the door to their bedchamber where she was arranging her clothes, and welcomed their visitor into the parlor of their suite, but she could hear their discussion as she hastily finished tying her ribbons over her still aching breasts.

"We've found the princess," Mr. Penrose was saying. "Your suggestion that all four of the cousins talk is a good one. They need to know what they face ahead."

"Just be aware that Boney's Imperial Guard is tracking the royals, and that Lord Berezin may not be what he seems. I have reason to believe one of them shot at the princess when she escaped the oversight of her bodyguards in London. We'll need men at all the doors and safe passage prepared to the docks so the royals may escape swiftly and discreetly once they decide what they wish to do," Nick warned.

"We've our eye on a few Frenchies passing themselves as Mirenzians," Penrose agreed. "The Navy is on alert for unknown vessels. We can't do much more. Do you need more weapons?"

"I've my own, but with luck, the discussion will be civil."

Nora heard the dryness in Nick's voice and didn't know whether to wince or smile. He was no fool. The four cousins in the same room for the first time could be an explosive reunion.

Wrapping in the elegant gold-and-bronze kashmir shawl she admired more than any of her other purchases, Nora checked the small mirror one more time. Without maid or hair dresser, she could accomplish no more than a knot of hair with a few loose curls about her ears. She'd chosen an afternoon gown with an open but modest bodice adorned with a lace fichu.

Now that she wasn't playing a princess, she'd abandoned white. The terracotta muslin with gold ribbons she'd recently bought seemed elegant to her. She dared say it was nothing to royalty.

But the admiration in Nick's eyes was all the praise she needed as she joined him in the parlor. Despite the arm he wore in a sling, Mr. Penrose bowed deeply. She still didn't know how to act when someone did that.

"Where is the prince's suite and how did you find him so quickly?" she asked, hoping that would put them back on a more equal footing.

Penrose straightened. "His Highness made no secret of his arrival. He sailed up in Quent's yacht, his men ordered the best conveyance to the best hotel, and he appropriated the entire top floor of this inn. He has four staircases for a hasty exit and men stationed in all of them. Perhaps he means to impress the princess with his wealth and power. She's his key to claiming Mirenze."

"We can hope it works, and that it's not a trap." Nora took Nick's arm. "When do we meet? I must admit I'm excited to have such a family reunion. I regret that we may never have this opportunity again."

"Consider England's royal family. They're not close," Nick said, covering her hand with his. "Do not go spinning fairy tales of happy families."

Her head already spun with impossible fairy tales. Her mother's fault, she supposed. The beautiful princess was supposed to win the handsome prince, except the man Nora wanted wasn't a prince but possibly a pirate. Oh well. She shrugged and let her shawl fall off her shoulders so she would make Nick look at her again. Which he did. Silly of her, but her feminine soul thrilled at knowing that she had his attention no matter how important the discussion.

"I have my men delivering a royal repast upstairs as we speak. I want the suite in our control." Limping, Penrose opened the door and gestured them into the carpeted corridor. "If you are ready, I'll lead the way."

"It would be lovely to always travel in such style," Nora said wistfully, admiring the gilded frames of the portraits in the corridors they traversed.

"It's too expensive and dangerous to travel this way," Nick pointed out with a trace of irritation

Not understanding his irritation, she merely nodded. "Royals often lack freedom, I know. But who else has such wealth?"

From in front of them, Mr. Penrose snorted. "Not royals. They spend *our* money."

"A revolutionary," Nick said in a stage whisper. "Be wary."

Unable to grasp her companions' ill humors, giddy with anticipation, Nora scarcely noted the guards stationed stiffly at every turn. She had little fear that the French would intervene here, in a good English hostelry. She was a little more wary of the prince, but with Nick at her side, she wasn't afraid. She'd seen him tuck a pistol underneath his waistcoat at his back and a dagger in his boot. He wore his deadly saber in a sling, and a rapier on his belt.

Had he worn such preposterous attire earlier, she might have recognized the pirate in him.

Lord Berezin greeted them at the door, frowning at Mr. Penrose but gesturing Nick and Nora inside. "The discussion should be private," he said disapprovingly.

"You're here," Nora pointed out to the steward, breezing past as if she were truly the princess. She was starting to enjoy this level of poise. "We should be able to have our own men. It's the French spies you want to keep out."

Accepting defeat, Berezin gestured them into an elegant chamber twice the size of the suite Nick had taken. Crystal chandeliers, woven carpets, and velvet draperies warmed the parlor as much as the fire. The innkeeper's finest dishes littered a long mahogany table.

Famished, Nora sauntered along the buffet, deciding what she wished to eat first. By refusing serving maids, they were left to forage for themselves.

Nick, on the other hand, took a position at the gable window overlooking the harbor. With his bandaged arm, Penrose was unable to take a proper military position like the good soldier he'd obviously been, but he stationed himself at the door into the main corridor. They had said there were four exits, so Nora assumed the others were through the bedchambers and to servant's stairs.

Mystery and intrigue and royalty, just as her mother had depicted. Nora picked up a dish, filled it with a few selections, and offered it to Lord Berezin, who looked uncomfortable in his stiffly embroidered tunic. Unable to decline a gift from a possible future princess, he accepted the plate. She watched from the corner of her eye to be certain he sampled her selections before she filled more plates. Italy, after all, had the dubious history of poison to overcome.

"More of the beef," Nick said with amusement as she prepared a plate for him. "And bread. A man never knows when he'll have his next meal."

Unlike Berezin, he was enjoying being served by a possible princess. She raised an eyebrow but finished filling plates for Penrose and Nick, serving them as she would have served Robbie. Food seemed so civilized at times like this.

"Here comes the brat," Nick said a while later, with his plate still half full. "She has a maid with her. Two guards. I don't see Arturo."

"How do you know one of the guards isn't Arturo?" Nora was too excited to eat much. She had sampled a little of everything on her plate but her stomach was too knotted for more.

"Lord Arturo is tall, like His Highness," Berezin said gruffly. "He has been told to use the rear entrance."

"And His Highness will greet him alone in the bedchamber?" Nora asked, realizing why the prince hadn't arrived to welcome them. "I don't think that's in our best interest. Penrose?"

He nodded. "Lord Berezin, if you will, we should greet Lord Arturo with His Highness. Let the ladies meet in here, where we will join them shortly. Atherton?" He raised a questioning eyebrow.

"Mr. Atherton stays," Nora said dismissively, as if she'd commanded troops all her life. "I'll try to keep him from throwing the princess out the window."

After the others departed, Nick saluted her with a chicken bone. "The queen could take lessons from you. You were born to command."

"It serves me well in the schoolroom," she said wryly, setting her plate down and slipping on her gloves. "I doubt that I'll fare well against Elena."

He set aside his plate, crossed the room, and leaned over to kiss her. Nora slid her hands over his strong jaw and into his hair, fearing it might be the last time.

"I'm at your command," he whispered against her mouth. "You need no more."

Arrogant and wrong as that was, Nora loved hearing the words anyway. She needed someone at her side in the confrontation that would decide her future and possibly the fate of her mother's country.

# Chapter Twenty-seven

NICK OPENED the door for Princess Elena and her entourage. Finally, he had the chit where he could strangle her, and he could do no more than stand aside and pretend to be part of the wallpaper.

Nora looked golden and lovely illumined in the sun's light. She graciously acknowledged her royal cousin's precedence by waiting for her to speak first. Elena's maid took her concealing cloak. The princess still looked frumpy in gray muslin with only a silver chain for adornment. Her two guards—or Arturo's men—stupidly stationed themselves outside the door to the suite.

Not until she was prepared did the princess greet the cousin she'd endangered. "I am happy we meet once more," Elena said stiffly.

Nick folded his arms and leaned a shoulder against the wall. Apparently he had succeeded in becoming no more than wall décor. As before, the princess didn't even glance his way. He began to suspect the princess didn't like men.

"Arturo and Piotr will be here shortly," Nora warned. "I need to know your preferences before they storm in and start making demands. Do you not want to return to Mirenze?"

Nick watched the princess's reaction with interest.

As if she might almost be human, the princess briefly deflated. Her eyes glittered with unshed tears, and she slumped wearily. He almost felt sympathy for a young girl torn from her family by war.

And then the proud princess returned. She straightened her shoulders and proceeded to the table, where she grazed among the dishes just as Nora had. Nick thought it a great pity these two hadn't the chance to grow up together.

"I cannot return to Mirenze," Elena said indifferently, masking her true feelings. "My father has abdicated. The French are in control. I will not marry a French swine or I'd be beheaded within a week after I poisoned his swill. You understand, do you not?"

"No," Nora said simply. "You have Prince Piotr in the other room willing to marry you and defend your people to any extent available. He's not swine. You are abandoning your home and family, for what?"

"I do not abandon them," Elena said angrily, finally facing her.

"Our mothers agreed that we should share responsibility." She gestured toward one of her guards, who produced a document bound in blue ribbon. "They understood that not all of us are able to protect our people. I will be only a puppet to the French swine. Another must take my place."

Nick wanted his hands on that document. He had a strong suspicion many others did as well. The guard held it as if it were a ceremonial sword.

"Is that the tontine my mother was hiding?" Nora asked with interest. Nick approved of the way she skipped right to the crux of the problem.

"My mother spoke of it, but I did not know it was real until your mother showed it to me," Elena said stiffly. "Our mothers understood better than any that times change and so must our leadership. I would leave as Aunt Viviana did."

"I am sure you think you have no choice except to run away," Nora said with an unnatural reserve. "You are young and should not have the fate of a country resting on your shoulders. I comprehend. But we are here now. You have help and support. Do you really wish to throw everything you know and love away?"

"All I loved is lost," Elena cried, her formal reticence dissolving. "The people, they embrace the French swine! My mother is gone. My father has a new playmate. And my Donato, he is dead, fighting Napoleon's armies! There is nothing there for me, *nothing*."

Prince Piotr, Lord Arturo, and their retinues chose that moment to enter. Nick thought he should have guarded that door instead of the hall, but holding royalty at sword point was probably bad *ton*.

The women both donned fake smiles, curtsied, held out their hands, and pretended all they did was exchange formalities. Even though Nick wanted to rip out the princess's hair, he had to admire her pluck in refusing to bow to the whims of others. He knew how difficult such rebellion was—at least the princess's mutiny had not led to acts of piracy.

Arturo was a tall, slender man wearing wire-rimmed glasses and a retiring smile. Like the princess, he apparently disdained fashion in favor of comfort, although he'd made some attempt to look business-like for this meeting. His coat and waistcoat, while loose and otherwise unadorned, were fastened with silver buttons, and he wore a conspicuous watch on a chain across his chest.

Piotr, of course, wore all his gold-encrusted elegance. Half a head taller and considerably broader, he was the royal presence the others were not. Nick gritted his teeth and tried not to growl when Nora smiled a greeting.

Nick knew, deep in his gut, that Piotr was the princely, well-intentioned hero that Nora deserved.

* * *

Nora's heart swelled with the emotion of seeing all her proud cousins in the same room. She wished she could assuage Elena's despair, but she'd known despair, and understood it needed time and work to dispel. She could not help Elena, except to show her that life had many facets.

Elena might have been raised to rule, but she had never been given a chance to be herself. Nora could sympathize.

Giving Elena time to recover, Nora daringly kissed Piotr and Arturo's cheeks, making them blush. As if she were the one in charge here, she ushered all of them into comfortable chairs beside the fire.

"I wish I had known all of you when we were young!" Nora exclaimed with the excitement the others didn't express. She poured tea, then settled in a chair at the end of the semi-circle of cousins. She knew Nick was smothering irritation and impatience, but she was thrilled at the chance to have this reunion. "You have no idea what it means to me to have family!"

"It is not always so goot to have," Arturo said stiffly. "It is much a pleasure to meet so charming a cousin as yourself, but it is not the same as family at home."

"My family is good to me," Prince Piotr objected. "They are strong and approve of what I do."

"That's because you're doing what they want," Elena said dismissively. "Not all of us are meant to lead armies."

"One does what one must for the goot of all," the prince argued. "You are spoiled."

"No name calling." Nora intervened. She thought the prince might be older than her. Arturo was possibly of a similar age. Elena, younger. That put her on an equal enough basis to stand her ground. "We cannot all be the same. I simply wished to see if we can support each other. That's what families *should* do."

That momentarily silenced them. They looked to each other, then at her, as if she were speaking a foreign language. Well, to them, English was foreign, but Nora didn't think that was the problem. The web of court deceit was the problem.

"How do I support anyone?" Elena asked. "I have no money of my own."

"You are a princess!" Piotr objected. "That is enough. Your name, your royal heritage, that is everything."

"No, it is not," quiet Arturo argued. "Not on a continent torn by war, where titles are traded like prize cows. You simply vant Elena so you can have Mirenze. She doesn't vant you or the pathetic rock that is Mirenze."

"It is her *duty* to protect her people!" the prince shouted. "Now that she is found, I will take her home so she may stand as queen."

"I believe our mothers meant for us to aid each other when they signed that document." Nora interrupted the tirade and gestured at the beribboned parchment. "May I see it, please?"

Silence reigned as every set of eyes in the room focused on the beribboned document that had been stored in her mother's attic for decades—a document that could create a king or queen and be worth killing to possess.

As the servant lay the parchment on the table in front of them, she noticed Nick wrapping his hand around his sword hilt. Surreptitiously, she followed his gaze. Lord Berezin was eyeing the document as if it were gold and jewels. Odd. He wasn't royalty.

"The French will not care about our mothers' wishes," Arturo was saying dismissively as Nora examined the parchment. "Their spies will be here any moment to hold Elena prisoner and take her back. The rest, it does not matter to them."

Nick appeared at Nora's side, helping her unroll the parchment. It was written in Mirenzian, of course. Nora admired the signatures at the bottom while Nick whispered the translation in her ear, along with commentary about being a recipe for an assassin to wipe out the entire royal family.

Nora ignored his cynicism. "Have all of you seen this?" She gazed in admiration at the long-ago idealism of her aunts and her mother, signing as daughters of a king, swearing that they would support each other and their offspring in choosing the holder of the crown. Her mother, the daughter of a king. She had royal aunts.

Piotr waved a dismissive hand. "It is meaningless. I will marry

Elena, and the French can do nothing."

"Elena has shown it to me," Arturo said. "It appears genuine. We are to share equally in the responsibilities of the crown. Elena does not have to assume the throne."

"Very original," Nick said aloud. "I daresay no other monarchy in the world would allow a gaggle of women to decide on the next ruler."

"That is why a man should sit the throne," Berezin declared, attempting to take the tontine from the table where Nora held it open.

Nick placed his hand flat against the parchment, allowing the steward to merely read but not touch it.

"Mirenze is and has always been run by women," Elena declared. "This is why I cannot allow a French swine to believe he may be king by marrying me. I will go to America until the French are defeated, if I must. But one of us must sit the throne until then."

"That's ridiculous," Piotr sputtered. "I take it the tontine does not say only the *daughters* rule. It is the French who would destroy this agreement and place you on the throne. If we marry, then they cannot part us."

"Arrogant idiot," Arturo said. "The French can—"

Nora clattered her tea cup against her saucer and stepped in again. "We don't have time for arguing. I simply wished to have a few moments' honesty between us before the French spies turn up and start shooting. This document gives the princess freedom to make her own choices."

"I can force the child to behave as she must," Piotr grumbled, eyeing the company as if he'd command a unit of soldiers to take over.

"No, you cannot. This is England, and we do not allow slavery," Nora said tartly. "Arturo, what is it you wish to do?"

"I will sit the throne until Elena can return," he said gravely.

"No!" shouted Piotr. "You are a weakling. They will give you one of Bonaparte's fat cousins for wife and your children will become the next generation of rulers. This cannot be allowed!"

"Argument will get us nowhere!" Nora insisted as voices raised in objection. "Our mothers had the advantage of growing up together and knowing they could count on each other. We will have to work harder at it. I have only just come in to a little money, but I know people. I will do what I must to help any of you."

"You will marry me and be my queen and we will rule together," Prince Piotr declared, changing direction again. "When Napoleon is defeated, then we maybe let the runaway come home."

"Or you could marry me, and we could set up schools all over the Continent after Napoleon is defeated," Nora retorted. "I have no interest in ruling anyone."

"I hate to interrupt a good family squabble," Nick said from the window. "But the wind just blew in a ship flying a Dutch flag, accompanied by a couple of British men-of-war. I do not think it coincidental."

The prince stood and shouted abrupt commands. Arturo and Elena looked alarmed. Nora glanced quizzically at Nick.

"The king of Holland is another of Napoleon's relations. Holland is essentially a French province," he explained. "Martine has summoned cohorts would be my surmise. This inn is the first place they will visit. It's time to break up the party."

Elena bundled up the document, hesitated, and handed it to Nora. "I must hide from them until it is decided what I must do. You have done such an excellent job of being me that the French do not know of you. Return to being yourself and slip away. Take this back to Aunt Vivi."

At the prince's shouts, his staff came running. Penrose appeared along with them. A quick conference confirmed Nick's warning, and the prince's retinue hurriedly gathered baggage.

While Nick and Penrose consulted, Nora hugged Elena and wrapped the kashmir shawl around her as a parting gift. Elena impulsively hugged her in return.

"Piotr is a good man," Elena whispered. "You could do worse."

Unable to think of king and country at a moment that demanded love and family, Nora grabbed her hand. "Promise you will stay in touch?"

"I will call you the sister I never had," she vowed.

With tears in her eyes, Nora watched Arturo and Elena hurry off under the guidance of Penrose. An English escort should keep them safe.

Nick took the tontine, and surreptitiously tucked it inside his coat while holding out Elena's cloak for Nora. "Much as I detest admitting it, the princess is right. We need to end the masquerade here. Penrose will escort her back to the duke on Quent's yacht now that she's had a chance to speak with all of you. We'll let the diplomats decide the next step. What is your wish?"

"I have so very many wishes," Nora said without thinking, while tears threatened to spill. "I suppose I had best go back to my mother. She will want to know what happened." She shook her head in puzzlement. "All this, and *nothing* happened."

"Be very glad," he said dryly. "The potential for disaster still looms. Let's get you out of here before the prince chooses kidnapping."

She glanced over her shoulder at the men ruthlessly taking apart the elegant room. "The wolf is supposed to save the princess," she said sadly.

"Fairy tales are just that. Your mother and her sisters could hope their children would act for the best, they could even plan for the future. That doesn't mean their children or the future will turn out as planned." He pressed her toward the door.

"And you?" she asked cautiously. "What will you do now that the princess is found?"

"Return to the family graces, attend Georgie's ball, but for now... I think we need to keep you and that blasted document away from the prince."

"Shouldn't all the royals go to London and the duke?" Nora whispered, slipping into the hall with Nick all but pushing her out. "Nothing has been decided!"

"I will remind you that you are one of those royals and you're not going to London. Unless you wish to marry Boney's cousin in Elena's place, then it's no matter to us what the others choose to do." He glanced at her curiously. "Do you wish to sit the throne? I can take you back to London if you have changed your mind."

"No," Nora sighed. "I think I am just disappointed that the adventure has ended."

"We don't have to hurry back," he said suggestively as they took the back stairs to their room. "Once your cousins are on their way, we can hire a carriage and take a leisurely journey home."

"You tempt me," she admitted.

But she couldn't shed the vague niggle of dissatisfaction. The fate of a throne had passed into the hands of others with more experience and authority. A rural mouse could have no place in the wider world her cousins traversed. She was English, through and through, and not meant to rule a country where she could scarcely speak the language. But surely... shouldn't there be something more?

"You hesitate," Nick said as she closed up their valises in their room and he kept watch on the corridor. "Perhaps you're not ready to give up London yet?"

She could hear the hope in his voice, and her spirits lifted a little more. He took the bags from her and hurried her toward the back stairs. "I would see more of London, yes," she said tentatively. "But I cannot abandon my mother."

"But you could come to London more frequently," Nick said with assurance as they clattered down to the rear alley, his hand at her waist preventing her from stepping out just yet. "I could find a little nest for us."

There it was, the source of her dissatisfaction. "No," Nora said decisively, stepping out of his embrace and walking toward the stable. "I want a home and babies and a normal life with someone who wishes to be with me for a lifetime."

That was the final word she shared with Nick.

Pistol-wielding swordsmen leapt from the stable. While one held a barrel to her temple and dragged her backward, the others rushed at Nick with swords drawn.

\* \* \*

Nora!

Frantic, Nick dashed down the alley after her. Swordsmen blocked his path. He sliced two wrists, permanently disabling two attackers, before the shot ringing past his head warned him that blades couldn't win over pistols.

Racing after Nora and her kidnappers, he drew his own pistol and took aim, but all he could see was Nora's terror as she struggled with the men heaving her into a cart. He could shoot one, but the man at the reins was already sending the horses careening down the alley. He couldn't shoot four men.

The cart disappeared around the corner, leaving Nick sick with terror.

He dashed back into the hotel and out the front entrance to the busy street in hopes of seeing where the cart went. It was nowhere in sight.

He knew Portsmouth better than any foreigner. From his viewpoint in the garret window, he had marked precisely on which corners suspicious shadows lurked, which was why he'd taken Nora out the back. He had assumed the spies were Martine's henchmen.

Martine did not know of Nora's existence.

Martine would have followed the elegant shawl the spy had seen Nora buy in London—the one Elena had been wearing as she'd walked out to her carriage.

Nick had made certain that Nora had blended into the crowd with Elena's old cloak. Only the Prussians had known Nora wore that cloak.

Breathe. Don't panic. They couldn't get far without a ship, surely.

Seeing one of the lurkers he'd noted preparing to climb onto a saddled horse, Nick whistled sharply. The horse whinnied and reared in alarm.

The horseman whirled, sword drawn—

Martine! Nick didn't know whether his luck was finally with him or still against him, but he needed that horse.

The Imperial spy pulled his sword. "Where is the real princess?" Martine cried. "You cannot fool me with this false one you have sent to the dock."

"Now is not the time to figure out which princess is which, you lackwit," Nick told him, producing both saber and rapier. "Not while *my* princess is being stolen!"

That startled the Frenchman sufficiently to give Nick an advantage. The clash of steel against steel rang out. He didn't have time to be polite. Wielding both weapons, Nick had the Frenchman pinned to the ground by the time one of Penrose's men came running.

"Imperial spy," Nick told the soldier. "Hold all the foreigners. Someone has stolen Mrs. Adams."

"Where is my princess?" Martine cried in French. "She must be kept safe from the thieving Prussians!"

"She's on a yacht with at least one of her cousins, although I'm wondering if that's as good an idea as we thought," Nick replied, as much to himself as anyone else.

"There's fighting on the dock," the ex-soldier warned. "I was told to fetch you."

"Bad idea all around," Nick muttered. Nora came first and foremost. King, country, and all royalty be damned.

He saluted, grabbed the horse Martine had been about to steal, and gained the saddle. Nick feared his last image of Nora and her terror might be permanently imprinted on his brain.

He'd been careless. He'd been thinking of seduction and not safety. The Honorable Nick was a right useless prick.

Riding hell-bent for the dock, he spotted the cart that had carried Nora away. They'd left it in an alley not far from the pier. The cart was empty. Dismounting, Nick stalked down the alley on foot, keeping his eyes open.

There! A single gold slipper where the alley intersected with a lane behind a warehouse. They'd taken Nora this way. He didn't doubt for an instant that his intrepid Nora had toed that slipper off as a signal just for him. He tucked the shoe in his pocket and ran down the lane...

...to arrive in a scene from Bedlam. Piotr's black-coated Prussians dueled with the Mirenzian blue-coated bodyguards. The English Navy and Quent's crew clashed with both, guarding Elena and Arturo as sailors hastily rowed two of the royal cousins to the yacht. Nick thought there might even be an invalided Russian seaman or two engaged in the melee, just for the hell of it.

Where was Nora? And Piotr?

The lane he'd run down had led to an area of the dock not easily observed from the section where the others fought. Nora's kidnappers could have carried her through here without notice—if bystanders were distracted by the brawl.

*Merde!*

* * *

Nora's kidnappers wrapped her in her cloak, bound her with rope, and shoved a rag in her mouth when she screamed. They carried her like a seaman's bag from the cart into a skiff. They held her in the bottom of the boat with their boots while she struggled to untangle herself. The boat stank. Their boots smelled worse. She gagged on her gag.

From their speech, she knew the scoundrels to be English, but the shouts from the ship they rowed her to were foreign. Coins were exchanged. She was dropped on the bobbing deck of a much larger vessel. Sails flapped overhead. They were preparing to sail!

Frantically, she struggled with the ropes, finally loosening them sufficiently to move her hands. She tugged the knots around to where she could work them while men argued in foreign and familiar accents further down the deck.

Someone leaned over to remove her gag. Her gaze focused entirely on the hilt of his sword. She didn't care who the devil this was. He was about to die.

"Just give us the document, and we will send you ashore," Berezin promised, standing over her.

The document? The *tontine*.

"Why?" she demanded, biding her time until she could free her arms.

"You and the others are expendable fools," Berezin said with a shrug. "With that document, Piotr need only sail into Mirenze and declare himself ruler and the Mirenzians will flock to him without need of any of you."

"You were the one who shot at me!" she exclaimed, fighting with the painful rope.

"I shot at Elena," he said in disgust. "If she'd simply agreed to the marriage instead of running away, we would have all been saved a great deal of trouble."

"Piotr would never marry an unwilling woman!"

"True, he is an honorable idiot," Berezin agreed without regret. "But there are many willing women who will suit once we have the throne."

He meant to kill her. She was on a ship filled with the enemy and she couldn't swim. Could she row? The rail was right behind her.

"Where is Piotr?" Nora demanded, hiding her fear. Almost... She stretched her freed fingers beneath the hampering cloak, working the blood back into them.

"Below, of course, waiting to be taken to Mirenze, where he will heroically marry one of Bonaparte's cousins, and we will rule as we ought once he learns of the tragic death of his cousins. Just give me the tontine so we can prove he has that right." Berezin leaned over to remove her cloak.

Nora grabbed his sword hilt and yanked it from the scabbard. "I don't think so, your elegance."

\* \* \*

A woman's war cry shriveled Nick's spine. Sword in hand, he spun around on the pier, searching for the source.

In the harbor, the Dutch freighter raised her sails.

Silver glinted on the deck. Nick grabbed a spyglass from a bystander, focused, and gasped.

Nora! *Fencing with Berezin.*

She didn't have a chance in hell. Even if she killed the bastard, she was surrounded by men and water.

He couldn't row fast enough. He needed cannon to stop this travesty of justice.

He shouted at his comrades, but the melee was escalating. One of the damned Prussians shot at the rowboat heading for Quent's yacht. Elena screamed. Nick didn't care.

"Keep him busy, love," he muttered under his breath as he ran for the nearest man-o'war. If that freighter sailed out, the Prussians would escape. Why the devil wasn't the Navy brig preparing sail?

Because as far as they knew, the freighter wasn't doing anything illegal.

If he never had to set foot on another Navy ship, he'd die happy, but he had little choice.

Hailing the brig loading supplies on the dock, Nick shouted up at the mate, not as the reckless boy he'd once been, but as a self-confident aristocrat, welcome in the homes of the most powerful men in the country. Admittedly, his attire was a little worse for wear, and his weaponry was a trifle unsuitable for a normal citizen, but he spoke with the authority he'd not possessed the last time he was here.

"I need to speak with your commanding officer," Nick shouted up at the brig's mate. "It's a matter of national urgency."

"The captain don't like his lunch disturbed," the mate said, apparently more afraid of his superior than anyone not in uniform. And therein lay the problem of ultimate authority, Nick furiously observed.

"Pity." Without waiting for permission, Nick grabbed a rope and began climbing up, hand over fist.

Officers ran up, weapons in hand. Nick didn't have time for this. He held them at bay with his sword and pistol, and shouted, "The freighter carries Prussian soldiers who have stolen an English lady. Just look! She's fighting the bastards."

One man wielded a spyglass. The others seemed more interested in murdering him.

"We cannot shoot at a friendly trader in a civilian port. Bring us the orders from the Admiralty, and we'll do as told," one of the lieutenants said.

That was the mentality Nick had once rebelled against—bureaucracy over common sense and a little actual *thought*. "In this case, *I* am the authority," he shouted at the wretch. "Do you think His Grace writes orders commanding me to intercept spies? It's what all good-thinking Englishmen would do without need to question!"

Nick knew he was yelling. Roaring at a Navy officer was as useless as shouting at a buzzing bee. They merely lifted their eyebrows and drew their weapons to escort him off.

Nick straightened his coat, gripped his hilt, and said more politely, "Fine, if that's your final word, I give you leave to go hump yourself." He wielded his blade, backed up to the cannon, and gestured for a sailor to load the ammunition while the officers consulted.

The Dutch freighter was about to weigh anchor. He couldn't let it sail with Nora on it. Nick's heart lodged in his throat as he held off the Navy and mentally urged the sailor to hurry. He whacked the side of the cannon when the man attempted to dawdle.

To Nick's horror, while he watched, Nora's cloak flew over the side of the freighter.

The vision of Nora floundering in the icy waters of the Channel hammered the final nail in his coffin. With the filthy experience of his pirate past, he'd already laid out a plan in the back of his mind. He'd tried hard not to revert to the old ways, but stiff-necked authority raised all his rebellious fury. He'd never been good with that chain of command thing.

Years of indolence hadn't quenched his inner devils, he acknowledged.

Even knowing that he'd shame his family and be banned forever from polite society, Nick didn't hesitate. He'd burned his bridges before in defense of a maltreated crew. He'd do far worse for Nora.

He grabbed the cannon and swung it in the direction of the freighter's bow. Lighting the fuse, he shot the officer rushing to stop him—just like in the bad old days.

# Chapter Twenty-eight

NORA DIDN'T politely riposte and parry. Her stolen saber was nearly as large as she was, and her arm would never hold up. Instead, she slashed at anyone who came close, sending Berezin's rapier flying. But she was surrounded and couldn't hold them off forever. She edged toward the rail and her only chance of escape. The cloak interfered with her arm, and she let the wind carry it overboard.

The deck shook with the force of cannon shot. Nora stifled a scream and used the momentum to grab the rail and swing over the side, into the rowboat she'd been retreating toward.

While sailors screamed to set sail and bring their cannon around, she hurriedly unslipped the knots tethering the small craft to the side. Above her, Berezin shouted for a pistol.

She didn't have the strength for hauling the craft down properly. Praying she would stay upright, she let the rope go and held on as the boat crashed into the water.

Above her, men shouted in several languages. Once the rowboat splashed into the icy water, she grabbed the oars and did her best to row away. This was where men excelled—in strength she didn't possess.

Pistol balls splashed around her, but their accuracy was limited at this distance. She made herself very small and pulled with all her strength. Her progress was almost infinitesimal.

Berezin jumped overboard and swam toward her. With a sigh of regret, Nora lifted an oar out of the water and swung the instant he grabbed the side of her craft.

* * *

That was Nora in that fragile skiff! By herself—with pistols balls shooting all around her. Nick flung off his coat and ran for the rail.

With the freighter listing and sailors on both ships running to man their weapons, Nick took a flying leap into the icy harbor. He felt the familiar slam of a pistol ball to his shoulder. His luck was always bad.

He had no intention of doing away with himself, although his heavy boots nearly accomplished that without his will.

His only goal was to reach Nora. He spewed filthy water and grabbed a floating log after he kicked his way up. Ahead, he watched as Nora swung an oar and knocked her assailant backward. He wanted to shout in triumph and relief, but he could barely breathe.

He struck out, holding the log with his injured limb to keep from sinking in his heavy clothing. He made about as much progress as Nora did in her tiny boat.

He prayed the Navy figured out how to signal the freighter that it wasn't under attack so all-out war didn't break over their heads. This far below the towering ships, he and Nora were mere flotsam.

To his relief, she must have spotted him. The boat corrected its course in his direction. In what seemed like eternity, he was grasping the side.

"No time to talk," he gasped, wiping his hair off his face and drinking in Nora's beauty one last time. She seemed unharmed, and his lungs worked better at the knowledge. He gulped air and wrestled the leather-wrapped tontine from his waistcoat. "Make the Navy take you home. Penrose will help. Tell my family that I love them, and I died honorably. Lie."

"You're bleeding! Get in this boat now," Nora insisted in alarm, dropping the document in the bottom of the boat as if people weren't killing for it. "I'm not letting you die!"

"Only symbolically, fair lady," he said, summoning a smile for her sake. "I'd die for real should Georgie get her hands on me after this." He tried to jest, but just speaking his family's name nearly broke him. He'd tried so very hard to be what they needed....

But it was patently obvious that he couldn't.

"Don't be ridiculous. We need you. You can't leave me like this!"

"There is a better way to leave a pirate?" he asked in mockery. "Have a good life. Don't marry anyone you don't love."

He released the boat and disappeared under the dark water as the first rowboat from the man-o'war hit the waves, sailors raising muskets ready for firing.

\* \* \*

Safe aboard a hired yacht some time later, Nora tugged a seaman's cloak around her and studied the harbor, as she had been doing ever since Nick had vanished. The wind was brisk as the crew prepared to sail, but her thoughts were icier than the wind and water.

Guido hovered anxiously beside her. She'd found him abandoned by all the royals and taken him with her.

"Monsieur Atherton is gone, too, my lady?" Guido asked.

"It seems so," she said, hugging her elbow as if she'd never be warm again. But she couldn't accept that Nick's golden smile was lost forever to the world. Her heart wouldn't allow it.

*Symbolically*, he had said. He would only die symbolically. But he'd been bleeding and winded and the Navy wanted his head.

"I have watched," Guido said sadly, lowering his spyglass. "I have not seen him."

*He'd said good-bye.* She had to accept that meant she wouldn't see him again.

He'd also said not to marry anyone she didn't love. Odd. Had he been telling her not to marry one of her cousins to save Mirenze?

As if echoing her thoughts, Guido continued. "Will you marry Arturo, then? He is not so strong as the prince."

"I don't think it wise for cousins to fight," she murmured.

Besides, she'd been married before. She knew it was the little things in how a man and woman treated each other that made a big difference in their relationship. She'd always wanted Robbie near her when he was in port. She wouldn't want either of the foreign princes around so often.

For all that mattered, she wouldn't want deferential grocer Fred about so much, either. She'd rather envisioned their lives meeting only in the bedchamber, but she knew that wasn't so. What on earth would they discuss over meals?

She and Nick had never run out of topics. Or arguments. And there were so many more things she might never discuss with him...

Tears flooded her eyes as the yacht set sail.

"Will you go to London?" Guido asked.

"On my own?" She thought about it, if only to distract from the pain. She didn't think she could bear it without Nick. "I don't think so."

"Maybe the prince goes to London?" Guido asked with hope. "Perhaps I could go there."

"You might find Elena and Arturo there," she replied, understanding he felt lost, and trying to reassure him. "I don't think

Piotr is heading for London, though. The freighter will be sailing for the Continent."

Without Berezin, she hoped. She ought to feel guilty for leaving a man floundering in the icy harbor, but she didn't. She rather viciously hoped the man had drowned.

"Will we sail directly to London?" the boy asked hopefully.

"To Brighton, to see my mother first," she corrected. "It's only a few hours away."

Which meant time was running out if she meant to decide her future. But she still felt attached to Nick while she could see the town where she'd seen him last. Foolish of her, but she would indulge the sentiment for just a little bit, just long enough to realize how empty sentiment was.

She was a practical person who must make practical decisions. She could be carrying a child. She couldn't, however, allow the sentiment over a child that did not yet exist to influence her now. As the yacht sailed further and no familiar golden head appeared, she clutched the rail and wept.

Guido handed her a grimy handkerchief.

Stupid, foolish time to realize what she should have known earlier. She was incapable of having an affair without offering her heart.

\* \* \*

By the time the yacht reached Brighton, Nora had made some decisions. She let poor Guido sail on to London to find his princess, but she had no intention of giving up on Nick. She had to know that he was alive.

Wrapping the cloak tightly around her, protecting the blasted tontine hidden inside, she hired a coach.

A few hours later, it rattled up a rutted lane, past untamed hedges and ill-trimmed lawn. On the horizon, a colonnaded portico rose above newly shorn yews. Palladian design, Nora assumed, admiring Wyckerly's home. Despite the unpolished landscape, the earl's residence was appropriately impressive.

Had she not already met the earl and his wife, she'd have had grave doubts about descending upon them without invitation, but this was where her mother stayed, and she didn't think the charming Lady Wyckerly would throw her out.

She was praying Nick had sent word to his friends. So she rolled up to an earl's estate as if she were a welcome guest.

A cadre of children spilled out of the overgrown shrubbery into the evening's twilight. One galloped up, whooping, on a pony. The wide double doors at the top of the high steps creaked open, and a nanny shouted and clapped her hands, demanding proper behavior. It seemed unexpected guests weren't entirely unexpected.

Nora climbed down and politely nodded as the children introduced themselves and made their curtsies and bows. She'd guess from their stocky build that the twins and the carrot-haired boy on the pony were relations to Lady Wyckerly, and the slim girl with the laughing green eyes was the earl's progeny. She'd heard tales, but they'd been hard to credit. The earl and his countess apparently did not believe in strict nurseries or boarding schools for their rambunctious charges.

Should she ever be so blessed, perhaps she'd take a lesson from them.

She took the hand of one of the younger children and marched up the stairs, feeling far more at home than she'd thought possible.

A servant of sorts—he was old and doddering and wore no uniform she recognized—led Nora up to the countess's suite. The children swirled about her, running in to relate excited tales and dodge out again. She let the tide ebb and flow as the countess winked at her, listened to childish stories, and shooed them away.

"Thank you for your patience," Lady Wyckerly said once the parlor emptied of piping voices. "They really do know better, and had you been a stranger, I might have had them rounded up and locked away before you stepped from your carriage. But after meeting you and seeing how much you are like your mother, I thought you might prefer a friendlier greeting."

Nora bobbed a curtsy and settled on the chair indicated. "They are lovely children and shouldn't be locked away and forced to be little martinets. Is my mother well?"

"She is, and I have sent for her. Gossip is flying so fast and furious, I'm hoping you've brought good news."

Nora's hopes plummeted. "I'd hoped you had news for me."

Viviana—the *archduchess*—entered in a swirl of scarves and shawls, looking more animated than Nora had seen her in years. "Has Mr. Atherton returned the princess to London? Or has she gone with her prince?" Vivi demanded, at the same time reaching to hug Nora. "How are you? Did you enjoy your adventure?"

Nora tenderly embraced her mother's slight frame, attempting not to hurt her aching joints. "I cannot say *enjoy* is the word I would use." She produced the rolled document from her cloak pocket and handed it to her mother, who merely set it aside with disinterest and waited for the story.

"One prince and the princess have sailed to London to fuss and fight," she explained without her mother's story-telling abilities. "I suspect Piotr has persuaded the Dutch to take him to Mirenze if their ship has been repaired. And I have come here hoping to hear what has become of Mr. Atherton."

She settled her mother into a chair by the fire and poked the embers into flames.

The countess was the one to respond. "Nick and Fitz are fast friends, and I fear Fitz will do something reckless if he hears one more wild account of Nick's behavior. You must tell us all so we know what to do."

Under the countess's friendly persuasion, and with her mother clucking excitedly, Nora related the entire tale. Almost. She didn't explain how she'd foolishly surrendered her bed and her heart to a notorious rake.

In conclusion, Nora added, "I don't know what happened after I left Portsmouth. The Navy boarded the Dutch trader and was searching the waters for Nick. They were beside themselves with fury that he'd nearly started a war."

She did not tell them that he meant to *symbolically* die, not when he might have done so in certainty.

Her mother applauded with a gentle tap of fingers to palm. "My sisters would be most proud dat you work together for Mirenze. But your poor Mr. Aterton! We must help him after all he has done for us."

"If only I knew what happened!" Nora cried, giving away some of her fear. "I was hoping if word came, you'd be among the first to hear it."

The countess glanced at a mantel clock. "It will be dark soon. I doubt that we'll hear from anyone this late. Have you had any supper? Let me have someone bring up a small repast. You'll stay, of course, until we hear word."

"I cannot impose—"

"Don't be silly, child," Viviana said as Lady Wyckerly waved away the protest. "You must go to London to quiet ta gossip and help his family."

The countess added, "It's easier to reach the city from here than from the coast. We'll send a messenger to Lady Belden. There is no sense in leaving until we know what to do next."

Going to London hadn't been Nora's first thought. What she really wanted to do was take the first coach to Portsmouth and find Nick. She would far rather he did the explaining in person.

Giving Nick's doting family his farewells would be distressingly difficult. From all reports, he'd single-handedly commandeered a British man-o'war and fired on a foreign national. The Navy would want him hanged. His family would be in tears.

And all she could do was pray that he'd somehow managed to swim to safety with a wounded shoulder and that he now hid from a thousand angry soldiers until he could escape to...where?

"You see now, you are meant for more tan ta grocer's son!" Viviana said as she kissed Nora's hair in preparation for returning to her chamber. "Experience is good."

Experience might be good, but as the evening wore on without word of Nick, it didn't mend Nora's breaking heart. She might eventually —in time—accept she'd never steal blissful moments with him again, never smell his shaving soap or see his unabashed grin, as long as she knew he was somewhere happy and safe.

And so she prayed as the evening wore on without any word.

She had to repeat more of her tale in the privacy of the earl's study when he returned. She sipped sherry with the countess while the earl paced the floor, bombarding her with perceptive queries.

"Society will simply not believe Atherton capable of protecting a princess," Lord Wyckerly kept saying. "They'll think the worst until proven otherwise. His sisters are practically in mourning. Lady Belden is trying to help, but..." He shrugged eloquently. "As Nick says, his sisters twitter. And his stepmother is devoted to the old earl. She's afraid to leave his side for fear he'll have an apoplexy. The Home Office will launch an investigation shortly."

Nora clenched her hands in her lap. "Elena and Arturo were already sailing off when Nick rescued me. Without his desperate shot, I would have been captured and would even now be dead or sailing off to the Continent. But besides me, we have no witnesses except the Navy. If you can provide introductions, I'll happily explain to his family. Really, Mr. Atherton has been brilliant. I cannot fault a decision he has made. I'm the one to blame, if anyone."

Galloping hooves outside the mullioned windows drew their attention. It was dark, well past the time anyone should be out and about.

"The children are abed?" the earl asked of his lady.

The countess nodded. "I left a footman at the door."

Amazed that aristocrats in a sprawling mansion could live almost as simply as she and her mother, Nora merely waited as they did, praying.

A few minutes later, a young servant led Mr. Penrose in. One look at his face, and Nora bit back a wail of grief.

"It's Nick," Penrose said without preamble. "He commandeered a Navy warship, bombarded a foreign trader, and escaped. We don't know if he's hurt or drowned or where he is."

"Berezin," Nora said vehemently. "He shot the freighter to stop Berezin from hurting me."

Penrose looked apologetic. "Berezin is dead. They found his body floating in the harbor with his throat cut."

Nora stifled a gasp. She'd *hit* Berezin. She hadn't cut him. Had Nick been well enough to do so? Did she dare hope so? Bloodthirsty of her, but the man had intended to kill all of them, she was fairly certain.

"Martine, the princess's bodyguard, was shot on the pier during the melee. We need not worry about him following the princess. The Dutch trader registered a formal complaint while it's being repaired, but Piotr is no longer aboard. I'm on my way to Montague. The Navy is brandishing epithets like swords, dragging up horrifying tales of Nick's past, crying mutiny and piracy, and I don't know what to believe. His family needs to be warned."

Both Lord and Lady Wyckerly turned to Nora. She feared she had gone white as snow, but she tried not to stutter and shake, thinking of that brave gentleman boarding a Navy ship... *Commandeering* it. Single-handed, as he'd said he could. To save her life.

"Nick was shot, by our own Navy, while trying to save *me*," she warned, keeping her voice low and clenching her chair arm.

"We thought so, but we can't find him," Penrose said. "After the wild tales we're hearing of his pirate days, there are those who figure he swam to safety as he might have in his youth. I'd hoped that was so, but there is no evidence of it."

Nora's heart plummeted to her shoes, and she shook her head, trying desperately to hide her fear and despair. "Please, have your men keep searching for him. He's not a pirate. He's a man who does what needs to be done. I'll go to his family."

"We'll go with you," the earl said.

Nora managed a smile at Wyckerly's loyalty to his friend and shook her head. "No, if there's to be gossip, let it be about me. I have nothing left to lose."

# Chapter Twenty-nine

LORD AND LADY Wyckerly took Nora to Lady Belden's London home the next day. There, Nora changed into one of the stylish gowns she'd left behind and consulted with her hostess.

"The princess and the archduke Arturo are staying with His Grace," Lady Bell explained. "The Mirenzian bodyguards are in much confusion since the Imperial Guard, Martine, was shot. And Prince Piotr appears to have disappeared."

"I think the prince is resourceful enough to be on his way to Mirenze by now," Nora said. "We may never know the plot, but Martine was a danger to Elena, and Lord Berezin was a danger to the prince. If Piotr had to abandon the Dutch freighter, he may have shot Martine if the spy tried to interfere. Now that I know that Elena and Arturo are safe, they don't concern me. It's Nick's family I must speak with."

Lady Bell frowned anxiously. "The malicious gossip escalates. There are broadsheets posted showing Nick kidnapping princesses and pirating a Navy ship. His family is practically in mourning. There are reports his father is at death's door."

It broke Nora's heart to hear Nick's brave name maligned. She clasped and unclasped her hands, not knowing if she was hiding her fear or praying.

"Somehow I must tell them that the tales are false and Nick is a hero." Nora didn't say *was* a hero. Her heart had been hollow for so long, that death knells tolled too loudly, even when unspoken.

"Is there any chance his father will believe me over the Admiralty?" Nora asked. The news from the Admiralty was black indeed.

With a husband well-connected to events at Whitehall, Jocelyn Montague had joined them with the latest news. She raised a satirical blond eyebrow at Nora's question. "The Admiralty is covering its fat posteriors to excuse the fact that one man pirated an entire warship."

"Nick will never live that down, if he lives," Lady Wyckerly said with a sigh, not understanding how her words pierced Nora's soul. "They'll prosecute him for impersonating an officer or piracy, even if he *is* a hero."

"If he once mutinied from the Navy and actually commanded a pirate ship in the Caribbean, as they're saying, then they may have the right of it," Lady Belden corrected. "I just can't believe it of him. He's such a charming beau."

"He's a hero," Nora said firmly. "He saved me and possibly even Prince Piotr and Mirenze from Berezin's intentions. I will make his family understand that. I can't change society, but his family should be proud of him."

"His cousin Thurlow has already come to town. They say he expects to provide the heir to Atherton that Nick's brother won't," Lady Bell said worriedly. "He'll be importuning the earl for support."

"He'd better make certain Mr. Atherton is dead then," Nora retorted, "or Mr. Thurlow is likely to end up overboard."

The ladies tried to smile at this small jest, but their hearts weren't in it. Nick had never harmed a soul within their knowledge. Nora knew better than that. Heroes weren't polite gentlemen. Heroes killed bad people to save the lives of good ones. Heroes sometimes died trying to protect others. Her heart cried that it wished Nick wasn't so much of a hero. But she was being selfish when she had no right to be. She knew her duty.

She tied her bonnet and picked up her reticule and headed for the stairs.

"I'll come with you," Lady Bell said.

Mrs. Montague and Lady Wyckerly echoed her.

Nora shook her head. "No, I wish to speak to the earl, not the ladies. He's the one who needs to know the truth. From what I understand, he isn't well enough to entertain any but family. I'll have to be very persistent. It may be unpleasant."

"We will distract the ladies of the house, then," Mrs. Montague insisted. "They'll guard him better than any servant."

"But the ladies think I am a princess," Nora objected.

"That's how we'll distract them," Lady Belden said. "They haven't seen the real Elena, only elegant you. Elena is still confined with His Grace, talking to diplomats. We'll disguise you by changing your hair to look dowdy, pin a cap on it, and tell them you're an older cousin of the princess—which you are, you will note."

Nora considered, then reluctantly agreed. She was so nervous she might have agreed that the moon was blue. A fortnight ago she had been too timid to write to Lady Bell, if her mother hadn't encouraged her. She'd challenged dukes and royalty since then, but confronting a dying earl... That took the confidence Nick had taught her.

That was the only reason she was putting herself through this— Nick had helped her and her family when they needed it. And now he couldn't speak for himself, so someone had to. Had she been the one lost, she'd want someone to tell her mother the true story.

Besides, if she was staying busy, she didn't have to worry about all that joyous life and vitality at the bottom of the sea, being nibbled by fishes. She'd had enough death in her short time on earth and refused to believe in Nick's. He was too hardheaded to die.

They found the Atherton ladies at home, weeping and debating mourning clothes and loyally raging against the biddies who whispered against Nick. The countess and her daughters fell into sympathetic arms without hesitation. After exclaiming over Nora's likeness to the princess, they descended into wails again, not interested in the wonder of Nora's appearance. Or how she fitted into the story at all.

Their love for Nick was heartbreaking. Nora wished she'd never dragged him into Elena's foolery.

The worst awkwardness was when Nora attempted to elude the ladies, and Georgiana broke into an inconsolable spiel about Nick promising to be there for her debut. Georgie swore he'd be home, just as he promised, so he couldn't be dead. Even Nora wept at the girl's devoted certainty.

Murmuring about fetching a servant, Nora finally slipped out while Mrs. Montague broke into loud tears and began listing every good thing Nick had ever done for her husband. Nora had a suspicion Jocelyn was making it all up, but she didn't linger to hear.

They'd been taken to a private parlor on the family floor, so she shouldn't have far to go. The quiet corner suite at the rear of the town house was most likely the master chamber. No one stood guard.

She tiptoed the last few feet of carpet, listening for sounds behind the door. She heard a thud, as if of a book or other object hitting a wall. A voice murmured soothingly. Nora darted behind the draperies of a window at the thump of footsteps just inside the earl's chamber door. The latch tumbled, and an irascible grumble followed whoever opened the door into the corridor.

She held her breath as a gentleman in black tail coat departed the earl's room and hurried down the corridor with a hand full of documents. An assistant or solicitor, perhaps? There could still be a footman or other servant inside. She had to take a chance that they wouldn't dare throw her out.

Defiantly entering a gentleman's bedchamber, an earl's at that, would have been beyond the humble seaman's widow she'd been a few short weeks ago. These days, she simply didn't care about gossip. Nick did, for fair reason. The weeping ladies in the other chamber were proof enough. He wanted their love and approval, and society would deny that, if it could.

She opened the door so quietly that the man in the bed didn't seem to hear her. He had his eyes closed and looked weary sitting against his pillows. He must have once had a full head of silver hair, but it straggled lankly from beneath his bedcap now. He had Nick's strong jaw with that little cleft in it, she noted with a smile. His shoulders were still wide, although the muscles appeared wasted.

She poured water from a pitcher into a glass and approached the bed. He opened his eyes and peered out at her.

"Poisoning me won't solve anything," he said irritably.

"Might make Cousin Thurlow happy from what I hear," she said with a modicum of cheer.

He narrowed his eyes. "Who are you and what do you want?"

"I'm Eleanora Adams, impersonator of Princess Elena, apparently the daughter of a Mirenzian archduchess, and I've come to tell you the truth about your son."

He took the glass of water she offered and gestured for pills on the table beside the bed. "Why should I believe you?"

She handed him the pills. "Because I love him dearly and think he's the strongest, bravest, most intelligent gentleman I've ever met. And because he doesn't deserve whatever gossip says about him."

"Oh, he deserves it, all right," the earl said with a feeble wave of his hand. "Nick's not what he seems. I've always known that. I'd hoped he'd grow out of it, but he's a notorious hothead with a disturbing penchant for thinking for himself. When he's at his worst, men hate him. Ladies revile him. The Admiralty wants to hang him. Can't blame any of them. I know my son better than he thinks."

The way he said that gave Nora just the tiniest shred of hope that the earl understood his son's depths and didn't entirely disapprove. "Then you know how hard he has worked these last years to be what you and the countess wish him to be. You know he wasn't meant to be confined to society's restrictions."

He choked a little on the water and handed it back to her. "In Mirenze, they admire blackguards?"

Nora shrugged. "I've never been to Mirenze. My mother taught me to admire men who act in the best interest of others. Do you want to hear the story or not?"

"I want to hear the truth. And then I want witnesses."

"Fair enough." She took a chair and began at the beginning, with the runaway princess and her impersonation, naming Montague and his wife and Lord Quentin and Lady Belden as witnesses.

Listening avidly, the earl waved away his manservant, and then his assistant when he returned.

Once Nora was done, the earl collapsed against his pillow. Nora hastily jumped up to call for help, but he waved her back.

"Even the duke doesn't know?" he asked with what might have been a chuckle.

"Most certainly not. He'd have to tell the king and Whitehall and there would have been a dreadful uproar. I don't know how one goes about telling him that the princess ran away and Nick brought her back."

"Let me handle that," the Earl of Atherton said in a voice of authority, weakened by a hint of glee. "I want you to find my son and tell him I have an offer to make."

Nora cast a worried glance to the assistant working on the far side of the chamber. Was the earl slightly mad? The black-coated man continued scribbling at his documents, apparently not listening. Or not concerned.

"Did you hear me when I told you he said good-bye?" she asked cautiously. "He was badly wounded."

Atherton waved away her concern and removed a scrap of paper from beneath his pillow. "He's done that before and come back when we asked it of him. I hadn't decided what to do about this. Now I know."

Puzzled, Nora unfolded the scrap and her heart nearly stopped beating. Nick's bold scrawl covered the page. Once her heart resumed pounding, she focused on the incredible words.

*I'm alive, should you need me. For the sake of the girls, you may call me dead. I'll remove myself from England so they need not live with my scandals. If that's not enough to satisfy the gossips, write Prince Piotr once he reaches Mirenze. I helped him escape the damned French spy and the Dutch and put him on a ship that should deliver him safely. I don't know if that's enough to reclaim my honor, but I can no longer pretend to be what I'm not. I'm sorry.*

*Nora is the only woman I could marry, so if she's bearing my child, send word. Otherwise, I'd see her happy with a more steady sort. I fear you must marry off the girls to wealthy men who will thrash Thurlow if he denies them their home. I'm aboard the* Sea Folly, *but will be sailing shortly. Respectfully and apologetically...*

He'd signed it just *NA*. Nicholas Atherton.

Crying, Nora held the scrap to her heart, rocking back and forth in grief and relief. He was alive! He needed to be swatted about the head, but he was alive and recovering! She wanted to rush out and cry her joy to the world.

She would only get Nick arrested.

"The *Sea Folly*?" she inquired, unable to speak her heart.

The earl regarded her with admiration. "The two of you should do well together. No twittering and sentimental gushing, right to the point. His schooner. I thought he'd sold it. I should have known better. Nick only *hides* his wildness."

"For the sake of his family," she agreed. "You knew he was a pirate?"

The earl lifted a dismissive hand. "He shipped out to the Caribbean under the wrong damned officers. The whole crew mutinied once they reached safe waters. He was a lad of fifteen. What else could he do but join the more experienced crew against officers who starved and beat them?"

"And to survive, they became pirates," she said, knowing her sailing history. "Does Nick know you know this?"

"I traded favors at the Admiralty, had it all filed away. The officers were cashiered without Nick's crew as witnesses. That was about the time I got sick. He came home a wealthy man, not a boy, and everyone believed he was what he pretended to be. There was no reason I shouldn't pretend the same. But he spent five years on a privateer's brig and ended up as the captain as a lad of twenty."

Nora nodded. "He's a natural-born leader who doesn't tolerate fools. He couldn't abandon men to whom he owed loyalty. So he saved them from starvation by doing what they all knew best. I trust he only attacked the French," she added dryly.

"A privateer without letter of marque and reprisal is a pirate," the earl countered. "But yes, that's how I saw it, too. But that's not the life he wants. He despised it." He eyed her thoughtfully. "I still have a few favors I can call in."

She reluctantly returned the scrap of paper to him. "He shouldn't be forced into a life of privation because he did what was necessary to protect me."

"Then you'd be willing to help?" he asked, with what she could swear was a twinkle in his eye.

"As much as I am able," she agreed.

"You will need to be very intrepid," he warned, "but if you love my son as you claim, then you are not without courage."

"Or stupidity," she corrected. "Loving your son is an example of naught else."

He chuckled. "I like intelligence in a woman. So will Nick, once he grows accustomed to it."

The plan he related was so outrageous, that Nora was free to question her own intelligence in agreeing to it.

# Chapter Thirty

NICK STARED at the cabin's wooden ceiling, noticed the sway of his ship as his crew disembarked for a final night of carousing, and ignored the painful twinge in his shoulder. It was the mysterious ache in his chest—where he hadn't been shot—that he couldn't disregard.

The parrot some joker had brought aboard squawked. Nick glared at the filthy creature. Blake would laugh himself silly should he ever learn he now shared a bunk with a stupid bird.

"I have no interest in my crew's dock dollies, so shut up," he told the foul fowl. "I've become more discriminating with old age, that's all. One doesn't find females as captivating and luscious as Nora on docks. Princesses don't come scattered about in the sand, you know."

The fishing crew that had hauled Nora from her rowboat had gleefully gabbed up and down the coast, telling the tale of the seaman's widow disarming a Prussian lord with only a short sword, an oar, and her sharp tongue. Nick had lapped up every word his men had carried back.

The Dutch crew had added their own tale of a prince roaring too late to the deck, only to slit his steward's throat and fling him back overboard when Berezin had returned from nearly killing Nora. Even though the prince had been aided in disposing of Berezin, Nick was happy that his involvement in that bloody bit hadn't been included in the stories sweeping the coast. The tales were the only news capable of making him smile these days.

Once Berezin was eliminated, Piotr had gladly accepted Nick's offer of better transportation than the foundering freighter. Encountering Boney's Imperial spy in the process had been a bonding moment. Nick still didn't know which of them had shot the fatal ball. Didn't need to know. He still hated killing. Let the prince be the hero.

*Roger the bird!* squawked his bedraggled companion. *Take sail, matey!*

"Take sail is all I can do, Roger Bird," Nick said, stuffing one hand beneath his hard pillow. "Maybe I can find a Tahitian maiden to nurse me while I waste away beneath a tropical sun. I've grown soft, preferring brandy and my friends, but beggars can't be choosers."

He was no doubt beggaring himself by the simple act of hiring crew, but he wasn't in any shape to sail on his own. And even Tahitian maidens didn't entice him when he envisioned his brave Nora with sword in hand.

He wanted to go to her, but even if he had access to his investments, he had less to offer than the grocer these days. She wanted a steady man and children and a home, not a wayfaring sailor.

*Navy shits!* Roger squawked. *"'Ware Navy!"*

The Admiralty would no doubt hang him without trial if they discovered him lazing about in their harbor. Nick tried smiling at his ability to hide right beneath their noses, but he hurt too much.

"I'm just waiting on the cook I hired," he told Roger. "Don't fret. We'll slip out from under the Navy's noses once the last of the supplies are aboard, with none the wiser. You better like fish food," he warned.

If he was destined to abandon all hope, he'd do it with as many creature comforts as he could afford, but he shuddered at the thought of a steady diet lacking good English beef.

He could hear one of the crew's light skirts chatting with the guards on the dock. No other type of female dared approach the harbor at this hour. She'd have to wait until the men returned. He wasn't interested. He assumed once he recovered from blood loss, his lust would return, but not this minute.

The physician had said he must rest to heal, but he was growing damned bored just lying here, talking to a bird and trying to doze off. As the high-pitched voice became more argumentative, he contemplated going on deck to watch the entertainment. He kept a pair of thugs employed while the ship was anchored, just in case anyone realized the *Folly* was his. Quent had seen it registered under a legal business name. It would take digging through barrels of paper to discover it.

As far as he could tell, the Admiralty hadn't even searched for his drowned carcass. According to reports from his men, the officers had simply spent all their time screaming about his offenses to cover up their own. Typical.

Male shouts. Interesting. Thugs generally didn't bother shouting at strumpets. There were far better things to do with them. Perhaps he should investigate.

That his blood had actually started to race a little said he was foolishly anticipating the impossible. Just because the reports said Nora hadn't sailed after her cousins didn't mean she knew how to find a dead man. Still, there was some very slim chance that his father might have sent a messenger—although not a female one.

Bored, he swung out of bed and tucked his shirt into his breeches. He didn't bother donning coat or waistcoat. Bandages ruined the line of the tailoring. Besides, it hurt to tug on clothes. He'd go to hell with his boots on.

The elegant teakwood companionway was short and easily navigated by a man with one arm in a sling. Nick sauntered out on deck in the evening dusk. Figuring the fog rolling in would disguise him sufficiently, he stood in the shadows to lean over the rail.

A petite female held a sword and parasol on his hired thugs.

Nick didn't know whether to laugh or weigh anchor.

He didn't need to do either. Gowned in a fashionable bonnet, wearing a shawl draped over her lacy sleeves, Nora forced his guards into a rowboat.

Moments later, she was climbing to the deck, jabbing her weapons at his hired thugs if they came too close. Had she looked like a lightskirt, or spoken in accents any less than a lady's, they'd have thrown her overboard. As it was, they were too flabbergasted by a lady with a sword to act at all.

"You found me," he said with amusement, stepping from the shadows to disarm her and help her over the rail. "I don't know whether to admire your pluck or heave you into the drink."

"Admire, please. I was prepared to hire a yacht and sail after you. You made it far too easy." Nora sounded quite disappointed as she released his hand and set the parasol under her arm.

"You always were an intrepid little shrew," he said with admiration. "Why are you here?"

"Your father called me intrepid, too. The two of you are much alike, you know." She stepped back to study him, her gaze as probing as any damned doctor's. "Only the shoulder wound?" she asked with a little more concern.

His *father*? Nick would have liked to have seen that occasion!

How had she got past the gorgons? Warily, he replied, "Sorry to disappoint. If you had some notion of nursing me to life, you may return to the city, reassured. Or have you bought your cottage by the sea?" He didn't invite her to his cabin. Didn't dare.

"A cottage by the sea would be pleasant, but I doubt I'd have time to stay there much. Perhaps you should invite me somewhere more private?" She lifted dusky eyebrows and her voice lowered to a seductive octave.

"That's not a good idea, Nora," he said cautiously. "We're sailing with the tide. My crew will be returning shortly." Another thought jolted him from his self-pity. "You cannot possibly have discovered you're with child yet, can you?"

"The contrary, actually. We might discuss children some other time, but we must overcome other hurdles first. I did not wish to confront them out here where anyone can eavesdrop, but if that's your wish..."

*Discuss children?*

She sauntered closer, and her rose scent enveloped him, trapping him more surely than any rope. Nick had feared he would never enjoy that scent again. She barely reached past his shoulder, but he didn't underestimate her. He'd found a lady who knew how to wield a *sword*. Verbally as well as literally, it seemed.

He wanted to reach out and tip her bonnet back, but he still clung to a shred or two of honor. He gestured toward the companionway, giving no indication that his heart was in his throat. "My home is yours."

"That was my hope," she purred, following his lead.

The blasted woman left his empty head spinning. "You are not living aboard ship," he warned. "My crew would rightly mutiny."

"I doubt it, not if they are good, loyal men. But that wasn't my intent." She gazed around her, taking in the fine teak and narrow quarters. She made no further comment until he opened the door to his private cabin. "Cozy," was all she said as she took a seat on his rumpled bed.

*Roger the bird!* the parrot shrieked gleefully.

Nora studied the foul fowl with interest. Nick covered its cage, then turned his desk chair around and straddled it. With Nora sitting there looking as desirable as a *petit four*, he wanted to do far, far more, but he was leaving England. He wouldn't do her the disservice of tumbling her and leaving her with child when he'd not be back again.

"My father sent you here for a reason?" he asked, trying to understand the chain of events that could possibly have led to such an improbability.

"Yes. He has an offer. But first, I'm to remind you that Georgiana fully expects you to return for her debut." She waited expectantly.

Nick thought the pain in his chest would kill him. He wanted to tumble to the floor and just die and be done. But Nora was here. As long as she was here and still speaking to him, he'd live another day. Which was an insane thought, but he'd apparently abandoned sanity the moment she'd entered his life.

"And you and my father know why that's impossible. Surely he hasn't told her I'm still alive," he replied angrily.

"Georgie has faith in you, as does your father and many others. As we speak, the officers of the ship you commandeered are being severely reprimanded. His Grace is furiously calling the Admiralty to task for not aiding you in rescuing royalty from both French and Prussian spies."

She played with her parasol and didn't give him time to interrupt. "Princess Elena and Prince Arturo have demanded that the king recognize your heroism and knight you accordingly. And with the help of a few friends, the tale of your rescuing the next king of Mirenze is merrily being whispered about ballrooms. The warrants for your arrest have been rescinded. The countess is still fretting about donning mourning, though. Georgie refuses to allow it."

Nick heard a hint of disapproval in these clipped statements. Stubbornly, he met her gaze. He'd had days to consider how his life had gone so far off course, to suffer all the regrets, but he'd learned a thing or three about himself lately. "I cannot go back to what I was, Nora. I am sorry. Send my regrets. Tell Georgie I love her. Do whatever you must. They're better off without me."

*Awwkkk!* the parrot muttered in sleepy protest.

"Without the Notorious Atherton, you mean," she said with a curving smile. "That's what they're calling you. Georgie's debut will be quite spectacular if you'll simply put in a brief appearance—the black sling is a nice touch. But your father and His Grace have more important tasks in mind for a man who can deal with wayward princesses and French spies and Prussian princes."

She stripped off her gloves. "Oh, and in addition, Piotr sent a message to the duke. You are invited to visit Mirenze at any time. He also sent for Guido, but he prefers acting as my footman. I don't think anyone can silence Guido. The servants are ready to worship at your feet."

Nick kept his grip on the chair back rather than shake her until she told him *all*. Touching her would be disastrous. He simply had to stay the course he'd decided on. Nora had a right to enjoy the prosperous life she so deserved. A footman!

"If I never meet another wayward princess again, I will die a happy man," he asserted fervently.

"Well, that could be a problem, but let's not leap that hurdle yet." She studied him expectantly. "Your father would like us to accept the invitation to Mirenze and carry the tontine with us. He hopes to arrange for us to travel on the Continent as diplomats, helping to maintain our relationships with countries not yet under Bonaparte's rule."

"He wants spies," Nick translated, not wholly appalled by the suggestion except for the part where she said "us." But even that gave him pause, because he wanted there to be an "us." He simply didn't want to endanger Nora in the process, which was why he had to leave, wasn't it?

"Not precisely," Nora said, unknowingly answering more than one question. "Diplomats sometimes carry secret papers, yes, but we're aristocrats, your father says. We don't lower ourselves to cloak and dagger danger. We do what comes naturally." Her smile broadened, as if she expected him to understand her secrets.

And devil take it, he did. Nick stared at her in awe and fascination. "We lie. We coerce. We do whatever it takes to finish the task."

"That, too," she agreed cheerfully.

"And we look good together?" he added, allowing himself just the very first hint of hope as the preposterous scheme formed in his head.

"I think so," she agreed. "I'll have to resign myself to still another hero, but heroes are apparently necessary these days. Besides, we dance well together. I understand that's important in some courts."

"You'd be very good. Dammit, Nora," he said, before he fell too far into his father's dangerous schemes. "There's a *war* going on over there. I can't take you into war zones!"

"You would take someone else?" she asked, not hiding her disappointment. "I'm sure your father could arrange that."

"Devil and botheration!" He wanted to rip at his hair—or drag Nora into that bed and not come up for days. "I don't want to travel with any other female but you, can't you see that? It's *you* I want, but you deserve London and courtship and pretty clothes and a cottage by the sea and a dozen children. And I've already done London until I can't stand it again. I'm too dastardly a bounder to settle down in polite society. Devil Nick is out, and I just don't think I can or even *want* to tame him again."

It tore his heart out to admit that.

Nora kicked her parasol to one side, rose from the narrow bed, and tugged his hair, enveloping him in rose scent and a woman's generous bosom. Nick inhaled and couldn't move. Even with the parrot screaming curses, his cock pressed urgently against his trousers. So much for that little problem with lust.

"Do you really think I want to go back to teaching grammar in a dull little town after what we've done?" Nora demanded.

She tugged harder, until Nick surrendered the rounded curves covered by little more than gauze and turned his gaze up to hers and tried to listen with his head instead of his cock.

"I taught because I could and because someone needed to, not because I loved teaching," she admonished. "Yes, I adore children, and I daresay we'll have a few. Your father is eager for that. And we'll have to decide how to go on when that happens. But not... right... now."

She leaned over and kissed him.

She might as well have thrown hot coals on dry tinder.

The chair fell sideways as Nick stood and dragged her to him, his heart pounding faster than could possibly be good for either of them. All her soft curves fitted against all the crumbling places he'd thought would never be whole again. She was the glue that held him together. Her hungry kisses fed his starving soul. This bundle of feminine finery and defiant courage satisfied both Nicks in ways in which no other woman had ever succeeded.

And if he stopped to think about what he did next, he wouldn't do it, but Devil Nick won over the Honorable every damned time.

He tipped Nora back to the bed and covered her with his weight before she could think twice and escape. The pain in his shoulder was as nothing compared to the driving ache in his lower parts.

"You can't torment me like that and not expect consequences," he growled. "You, of all people, must know that." He ripped off her bonnet and rooted out her hair pins and smothered her with kisses, drinking her heavenly scent and soft cries with the desperation of a thirsty man.

It wasn't enough. He tore at her gauzy bodice and untied her chemise and thanked the heavens as he finally cupped firm flesh pushed up by a stylish corset. He leaned over and supped there, until she writhed helplessly and moaned beneath him.

Favoring the bad shoulder, he rested his weight on the other, and Nora took unholy advantage by running her hands down his shirt and ripping it from his trousers. She had his trouser placket unfastened in a trice, and seductive hands stripped him bare with caresses.

His brainless cock responded like an eager puppy.

"Of course, I know that," she murmured breathlessly as they ripped and rearranged clothing. "I am here, am I not? Show me your consequences."

"I cannot take you to my family unless you marry me," he warned. "They're not as intrepid as you."

"Oh, I think they may be more intrepid than you know, but the legalities are all yours to define. *This* is what I want." She held his brainless cock and stroked. "I want the man I've come to love."

*Love* squawked the damned parrot. Or maybe it was his own worthless heart. *Love.* He had a name for his affliction.

"I've died and gone to heaven," he said, rolling over on his back to let her have her way. "Angels shouldn't be so beautiful."

"Angels shouldn't do this, either." And she slid over him, onto him, and around him so deftly that Nick thought he might have passed out again.

But his Nora wouldn't accept passivity, and she squeezed him into participation in a manner only a strumpet should know—and his *Nora*, his inventive, sensuous, damnably demanding Nora.

Her cries of release were probably heard across half the island. Not bad for a battered, has-been cripple, Nick thought as he tugged her down harder and drove straight toward her heart. His bellow of pleasure probably kept his crew away for another few hours.

"I love and adore you, my intrepid shrew," he murmured after, and even though he'd thought her sleeping, Nora smiled.

# Chapter Thirty-one

"YOU MEAN, Atherton *married* the princess?"

Overhearing this snippet of conversation, Nora didn't divert from her goal. Georgie's debut ball was a terrible crush, and she meant to grab a few choice foods from the buffet before the dancing began again.

"No, Nora is an archduchess, I think," Georgie was telling her companion. "I think she *could* have been a princess, but she's English, you know. She likes us better."

Nora heard a familiar sigh of exasperation, and she threw a laughing glance over her shoulder. She handed her new husband a plate so he wouldn't intervene in his youngest sister's practice of societal skills.

Nick looked so scrumptious in his black evening attire—without lace or sword or dashing sling—that she almost forgot her food.

"But what happened to the real princess?" the puzzled young voice demanded.

"Oh, it's very romantic." Georgie lowered her voice to a whisper. "She has returned to Mirenze with *two* princes. Nora could have joined them and been a *queen*, but she chose our Nick."

"Sounds better than schoolteacher," Nora whispered, moving down the table.

"It is the intrepid schoolteacher and dashing widow that I married," he corrected. "Anyone can have a plain old princess."

Nora laughed and stole a quick kiss to his newly-shaved jaw. "Whereas, instead of a rake, I married the dangerous pirate who commandeered an entire Navy brig. I love the way people whisper as you walk through the room. Your reputation grows more reckless with each day."

"Just as long as you pull a sword on any of the beauties heaving shoes at my head," he said with unconcern, heaping another delicacy on her plate. "I hear Lady Bell has agreed to take on still another of Quent's nieces or cousins or whatnot for the season. She must have a gaggle by now."

Nora laughed. "That really is the silliest wager. Why don't they just marry and save themselves a great deal of trouble?"

Nick raised his eyebrows. "Marry? Let Quent and his enormous, bankrupt family loose on Lady Bell's fortune? And what does she get in return? A man not allowed into the best homes? I don't think they see each other that way. What put that notion into your head?"

"Us," she said with satisfaction. "Everyone should have what we have. And what the Wyckerlys and Montagues have." She nodded at the other couples experimenting with the scandalous new waltz Nick had insisted on introducing to his mother's ballroom.

"If I take you to the dance floor now, we'll not be seen again for the rest of the evening," he warned. "Eat. Build up your strength. We're still on our honeymoon, and I mean to make the most of it while I can. I've another waltz scheduled for later, after which we can discreetly depart."

"I do love a man who knows what he wants and goes after it," she sighed happily.

"Every man in the ballroom wants you, and they're all furious that a fribble like me has swept you out from under their noses." He heaped a succulent partridge breast on her plate. "It's a good thing we're sailing shortly or they might murder me at my club. I don't want you reconsidering what you could have had if you hadn't been so short-sighted as to attach yourself to the first man you met."

She laughed. "Oh, yes, I'm certain London is filled with gentlemen who would let me wield a sword and wouldn't be astonished if I threatened villains and who would encourage me to keep my dowry for myself. What happens when your pirate gold runs out, and I have to finance our expeditions?"

"You'll be financing grandchildren by then," he pointed out equably. "And my share of my father's estate will be more than enough to send a dozen to Oxford, so I'll not worry overmuch unless you take up gambling."

She leaned against his broad chest while they watched the dancers and nibbled their repast. "Do you think the war will ever end? It would be lovely to ask your sisters and friends to visit if we're in foreign courts."

"There is always a war someplace. We could end up in the Americas." He wrapped an arm around her waist and caressed her middle. "I do hope you travel well."

She admired the shimmering ballroom of beautiful people, elegant candles, rich perfumes, and bowers of flowers. "I am very adaptable, with you by my side. Will we have time to visit my mother before we leave?"

"Of course. You will want to admire the latest improvements on her house. And she will want to tell me all sorts of precautionary tales about royal courts. It is a pity she cannot come with us."

Nora threw a laughing look over her shoulder to her handsome, diplomatic husband. "I love you even when you lie, you know."

With a heated look, he set aside their plates and swept her onto the dance floor she'd been admiring.

They never did finish their supper. And when the next waltz struck, they danced it naked in a private chamber, high above the crowd.

# Author Bio

With several million books in print and *New York Times* and *USA Today's* bestseller lists under her belt, former CPA Patricia Rice is one of romance's hottest authors. Her emotionally-charged contemporary and historical romances have won numerous awards, including the *RT Book Reviews* Reviewers Choice and Career Achievement Awards. Her books have been honored as Romance Writers of America RITA® finalists in the historical, regency and contemporary categories.

A firm believer in happily-ever-after, Patricia Rice is married to her high school sweetheart and has two children. A native of Kentucky and New York, a past resident of North Carolina and Missouri, she currently resides in Southern California, and now does accounting only for herself. She is a member of Romance Writers of America, the Authors Guild, and Novelists, Inc.

For further information, visit Patricia's network:
http://www.patriciarice.com
http://www.facebook.com/OfficialPatriciaRice
https://twitter.com/Patricia_Rice
http://patriciarice.blogspot.com/
http://www.wordwenches.com

Reviews left with on-line booksellers such as Amazon and B&N will encourage advertising promoters to discount this and related books in the future!

CPSIA information can be obtained
at www.ICGtesting.com
Printed in the USA
LVOW12s1019260117
522266LV00002B/173/P